When Your Eyes Close

TANYA FARRELLY

**KILLER
READS**

KillerReads
an imprint of HarperCollins*Publishers* Ltd
1 London Bridge Street
London SE1 9GF

www.harpercollins.co.uk

This paperback edition 2018

First published in Great Britain in ebook format
by HarperCollins*Publishers* 2018

A catalogue record for this book
is available from the British Library

ISBN: 978-0-00-828003-1

Set in Minion by
Palimpsest Book Production Limited, Falkirk, Stirlingshire

Printed and bound by CPI Group (UK) Ltd, Croydon, CR0 4YY

MIX
Paper from
responsible sources
FSC
www.fsc.org   FSC™ C007454

For Dave, an extraordinary writer and husband, without whose laughter I'd be lost.

Chapter One

Nick

Nick Drake pulled up outside the house named The Arches and cut the engine. He was twenty minutes early and there was another car, a dark grey saloon, parked in front of his. He looked at the long white bungalow illuminated by the half dozen lamps that lined the winding drive, and wondered if it were, after all, a good idea to have come.

Shivering, Nick reached into the pocket of his leather jacket and his fingers closed round the pack of cigarettes that he kept there for emergencies. He noted that there were only two left. With trembling fingers, he placed one between his lips and held the lighter to the tip until it burned crimson. He lowered the window and inhaled deeply until the smoke filled his craving lungs, and he felt the rain blow in on the damp night air.

On the passenger seat his mobile phone began to ring. He looked at the screen and saw Michelle's name flash up again. Rain drummed on the windscreen and the phone rang out, and then blipped to inform him that she'd left yet another voice message. It was her fifth call in three days. He knew that he should call her back, but he didn't feel like talking to anyone. Talking meant making things real. And he wasn't ready for that.

A few minutes passed before the bungalow door opened and a security light clicked on. A figure stepped into the rain, pausing to pull up the hood of an anorak before hurriedly descending the driveway. With head down, the woman made a dash for the grey saloon car. The heels of her boots clicked on the tarmac, and the indicator lights flashed amber as she hurriedly unlocked the car and slipped inside.

Illuminated briefly by the interior light, Nick saw the woman pull the hood of her anorak down and run a hand through unruly dark hair. The engine started, and the grey saloon turned and reversed into the driveway, the headlights momentarily blinding Nick as the car turned and disappeared down the lane by which he'd come.

For a few minutes he sat and stared out the windscreen. He drew on his cigarette until there was nothing more between his fingers and the tip, and then he stubbed it in the ashtray, closed the window and stepped out into the rain.

The girl who opened the door was no more than seven years old. She looked at him with big brown eyes. Then a man's voice came from a room within. 'Kirsty, I told you not to answer the door.' The owner of the voice appeared from what Nick imagined was the kitchen. 'Go on in like a good girl.' The man put an arm round the little girl's shoulder to draw her inside. 'Sorry about that,' he said.

Nick shrugged. 'The name's Nick Drake. I've an appointment for nine o'clock.'

'Sure, come on in.' The man stepped back and ushered Nick inside. The child stood behind the man and stared at Nick. He smiled at her, but she didn't smile back.

'Take a seat in here. Tessa will be with you soon.'

Nick was shown into a room not dissimilar to the waiting room in the doctor's surgery. A television played in the corner, the volume muted. He sat in a hard chair by the door and waited. The sound of children's voices came from somewhere within the house.

'Boys, quit messing around down there. Get to bed.'

There was laughter, followed by the sound of running feet and then silence. Nick stared at the television.

'Nick?'

He turned to see a blonde woman in her fifties standing in the doorway.

'I'm Tessa. Do you want to come this way?'

Nick stood and felt the pain in his abdomen as he did so. Tessa put out a hand to shake his, and he followed her across the hallway and into a small, darkened room.

'Please, take a seat,' Tessa told him. Nick sat, and she sat opposite him and picked up a pen. She reached towards a small device on her desk and pressed a button. 'I generally record the sessions, Nick, and send you the file. It can help to do self-hypnosis between sessions. You don't have any objections?'

'No, no, that's okay.' Nick waited, putting his hands between his knees to hide the tremor that had crept into them. He longed desperately for the last cigarette in the pack inside his jacket, knew that that would be the final one. Another bad habit curbed. Outside, the rain continued to thunder down, beating against the window.

'How long have you had a problem with alcohol, Nick?'

'I don't know. I didn't see it as a problem.'

'But now you do?'

He nodded. 'The doctors say if I don't stop drinking I could be dead in a year, eighteen months at the most. And I can't get on the transplant list unless I'm six months clean.'

Tessa scribbled something on her notepad. 'Have you ever tried to give up before?'

'Yeah, but it didn't take.' Nick thought of the AA meetings his ex-wife, Susan, had made him go to – the room of men, most of whom were there only because their wives had insisted. He'd lasted about three months, and then he'd finished up in a bar across from the meeting hall with two of the other recruits drinking whiskey until closing. And he'd thought it was all such a laugh – until Susan had left.

'Any ideas why you drink, Nick?' Tessa's eyes flitted from the page to rest on him, and he fidgeted in his seat.

'Does there have to be a reason?' He knew that he sounded

defensive, but he hadn't come here for counselling. He simply wanted help to detox.

'There usually is. There are various reasons, of course; it can come from pressure at work, or at home … It starts as a means to relax, or to escape … then over time it becomes the problem itself …'

He didn't answer right away; he tried to think back to when his drinking had got heavier. He'd always had a taste for it – had started when he was about sixteen. And as for escape, he'd felt like that for a long time too. He just wasn't sure what it was he was trying to escape from. When things had got bad with Susan … then he had a reason. He guessed that that was when he'd really hit it hard.

'I'm divorced. We fought a lot; I suppose it started then … or at least made it worse.'

Tessa nodded. She didn't say anything, didn't judge him, and he imagined he wasn't the first messed-up alcoholic divorcee she'd dealt with.

'Have you ever been hypnotized before?'

Her voice brought him back from his thoughts, back to the dim room and the sound of the rain outside.

'No, never.'

'Okay.' She put down her pen and smiled. 'If you're ready, let's get started.'

They both stood, and Nick moved towards the chair she gestured to.

'Hypnosis is nothing more than a deepened state of relaxation, Nick. I'm going to ask you to simply lie back, close your eyes and relax. You'll be aware of everything that's going on around you.'

Nick lay back in the reclining leather chair and closed his eyes. Tessa placed a thin blanket over him. He didn't feel relaxed. His body was tense, and he was aware as he lay still of the rapid beating of his heart and the discomfort in the right side of his abdomen. The hypnotist was standing near him. A strong woody fragrance that reminded him of his ex-wife permeated his senses as her soft rhythmic voice cut in on his thoughts.

4

'Now I want you to completely relax your body. The more relaxed you become, the more susceptible your mind will be to suggestion. We're going to start with your feet and work our way up to your head.'

Nick shifted in the chair. He opened his eyes slightly and saw Tessa standing over him, her silhouette dark against the dimmed light behind her. Step by step, she instructed him to relax each part of his body until his limbs felt heavy, the tension gradually subsiding as he sank deeper into the leather seat.

'For a long time, you've been hurting, Nick. And you've been relying more and more on alcohol to deaden these feelings of pain; but it's only by experiencing the negative things in life that you can also appreciate the highs. That's why you've come here today, to reconnect with your emotions, to discover that in order to live again you have to feel.'

The woman's voice was slow and methodical – practised so as not to jolt him out of his physical state of relaxation – but even as he listened to her words, he could feel himself fighting them. Did he really want to get in touch with his feelings about Susan, and the end of their marriage? Since meeting Michelle, he'd put all that behind him. He'd been feeling more positive than he had in years.

'Focus now on an area of your life that gives you happiness. Something that makes you feel confident, that makes you feel proud. Notice how you feel inside, Nick: assured, happy and fulfilled and let these feelings grow.'

Michelle. They're on their second date and he's telling her about the time he got the call to design a house for a well-known rock star in south Dublin. His reputation as an architect is at its peak. A year ago, he landed the big contract to design the house which now stands on a clifftop proudly overlooking Killiney Bay. He's taken Michelle up there to see it, has parked the car on the Vico Road and led her down the steps to the beach, where it's possible to look back up at the house.

'Did you meet him?' she asks. 'What's he like?'

'Sure, he doesn't say much. You know the type.' He reaches out

then, cups her face with his hand and leans in to kiss her. The wind blows her blonde hair in her face, and she clings to him and tells him she's freezing. It's a cold night in February. He feels the spray from the sea blow in on the wind, and he kisses her again and tells her she's beautiful.

'What?' she shouts, and laughs as his words are drowned by the roar of a train passing on the tracks above bound for Bray.

'As you're experiencing these good feelings, Nick, I want you to take a deep breath and squeeze your hand into a fist. Your subconscious mind will memorize these feelings of happiness and whenever you want to feel like this again, you'll simply take a breath and make a fist again.'

They're climbing the steps back up to the Vico Road to where the car is waiting. He tightens his arm around Michelle's shoulders as she stumbles and steadies herself by putting both arms round him. Her laugh rings out in the cold night and he wants to protect her – to keep her safe in his arms. He squeezes his hand into a fist as the woman's voice, coming from some place far away, tells him to do. He's filled with an emotion – something akin to love – although he barely knows this girl. With her he feels elated.

'Okay. Now, I want you to imagine yourself in a situation where you would normally reach for a drink. Take in your surroundings, Nick. Where are you? Who are you with? Try to visualize the scene in as much detail as possible.'

Friday night: the after-work crowd. They're in a pub in Capel Street and the rounds keep appearing before the previous ones have even been drunk. He checks his phone and sees he's got a message from Susan.

Where r u?

He texts back, tells her he'll be home soon – but he doesn't feel like going home. All they do lately is fight. It's easier to stay here with the work crowd, but he knows if he stays too long it'll be worse – that as soon as he walks in the door, the accusations will begin and that'll be it – the whole weekend ruined.

'You're reaching for that drink, Nick. But when you pick it up, you realize that you don't want it. You don't want another drink. I want you to take that drink and pour it down the sink. As you do so, I want you to squeeze your hand into a fist and remember those good feelings, those feelings of fulfilment, those feelings of pride. You're taking control of your life, Nick, free from the burden of addiction, from the need to blot out those painful memories with alcohol.'

Elation. He feels adrenalin course through his body. And he's transported again. This time he's in a house, a strange house – not the house he lives in now, or the one he'd shared with Susan. There's a green suite and green and orange curtains. Everything is brightly coloured, gaudy. He's different too. His hair falls to his shoulders, and he's wearing a T-shirt with Black Sabbath across the front – but he's about the same age as he is now. He goes into the hall. He's got some good news and he can't wait to tell her. He shouts up the stairs: 'Rachel, are you home?' Nobody answers, but he thinks he hears a noise from above. 'Rach? Are you here?' No answer still, but there's a definite bump from one of the rooms upstairs. A feeling of panic rises in his chest. He looks round the room for a weapon, something to protect himself with. In the kitchen he takes a sharp knife from the drawer, and slowly climbs the stairs.

The door to his and Rachel's bedroom is closed. It's never closed, but maybe Rachel is in there after all. Maybe she's sleeping. He glances into the other rooms – empty. He reaches for the handle, grabs it suddenly and pushes the door inwards. Rachel screams and pulls the bed covers up, hiding her naked body from him as though he's a stranger. The man, buttoning up his shirt, jumps from the edge of the bed where he's been sitting, puts his arms out instinctively for protection. Nick sees himself wield the knife. He hears Rachel scream in protest, but it's too late. There's blood on the man's white shirt, on his hands and on the carpet. It's pooling around his fallen body.

Nick squeezed both hands into fists. He tried to summon

Michelle's face, to wake from the nightmare. He heard Tessa's voice and strained towards it like a drowning man.

'I'm going to count from one to five and when I reach five, you're going to wake, Nick. One, two, three ...'

On the count of five Nick opened his eyes. He attempted to sit up. His skin was damp with sweat and his whole body was trembling.

'It's okay. You're okay, Nick. You're in control. Nothing can happen to you now.'

'It wasn't me,' he said.

'What do you mean? What happened?'

'I was in this house, but it wasn't mine. It wasn't my place. I was different – the way I looked. I was there to see Rachel. She ... she was my wife. But I don't know her. I have no idea who she is. It was like I was someone else ... like it was someone else's life. I went upstairs, and she was with someone – a man. Jesus ... it was awful.'

Tessa was quiet. 'What happened, Nick?'

'I had a knife. To protect myself. I heard a noise upstairs, and I thought there was an intruder. And then I saw him in the room with her, and I went crazy. There was blood, so much blood. I know it wasn't real, but, Jesus, what was it ... some kind of nightmare?'

Tessa hesitated. 'Your appearance, Nick. You said you looked different?'

Nick nodded. 'My hair was long. I was wearing a Black Sabbath T-shirt. I've never worn my hair long. I don't understand ... I mean does this normally happen to people under hypnosis?'

Tessa hesitated again. 'Not to any of my clients, no. But there is something called confabulation. It's when the mind creates false memories, and to the individual it can seem extraordinarily real. Some people who experience this believe that they're experiencing remnants of a previous life.'

'A previous life?'

'Yes, but there's no scientific evidence to suggest there's any truth in that theory. It's much more likely – and certainly it's my belief – that the mind distorts memories in the same way as it does in dreams. I hope this hasn't put you off, Nick. It's extremely rare that something like this should happen. And if it happens again, well maybe it's something that needs to be dealt with: a residual fear.'

Nick nodded, but he didn't know what to think. He could still feel the knife in his hand, hear the woman screaming.

Tessa reached for her diary on the desk. 'Do you want to make another appointment?' she asked. 'Perhaps Wednesday?'

He shook his head. 'I'll give you a call,' he said. He took his wallet from inside his jacket and paid. Tessa didn't mention anything about forwarding the recording; maybe she'd decided it was better if he didn't listen back – either way, he didn't ask.

Outside, it was still raining. Nick rushed towards the car. His hands were still shaking as he took the last cigarette from the box, lit it and let the car window down. He put the radio on to try to distract himself from what had just happened. What the hell had that been? Remnants of a previous life ... he didn't believe in any of that mumbo jumbo, and he was glad that the hypnotist didn't either. Michelle was into all that hippy stuff, she'd be intrigued, but not him. It was a nightmare, that's all it was ... it had to be.

On the radio, Black Sabbath were playing 'Paranoid' – Ozzy Osbourne screaming into the night. Fingers trembling, he turned down the volume and inhaled the nicotine deep into his lungs. Then he closed his eyes and squeezed his hand into a fist. Anything to try to distract himself from the nightmare that kept replaying in his head. He thought of Michelle, and how she made him feel, let the emotions wash over him. He couldn't talk to her, not now, not after what he'd just experienced. Instead, he took the phone from his inside pocket and sent a quick text.

Call you tomorrow. N x.

Chapter Two

Caitlin

Caitlin Davis closed the door behind her with a mixture of anxiety and relief. She knew what the evening held, but getting through the day until she'd arrived at this moment had been hard. Several times during the afternoon she'd found herself drifting despite the mayhem of the office and the decisions that needed to be made as to what should appear in the next issue of *New Woman*, the magazine she'd founded almost six years before – the same year she'd met David.

Caitlin threw her handbag down on the bed, sat down and kicked off her shoes. In her stockinged feet she stood on the edge of the bed and removed a box from the top shelf of the wardrobe. Carefully, she climbed down, took the lid off and took out the bundle of photos that lay at the top. David. It was a year today since she'd last seen him. A year since that terrible night when she'd called their friend, Andy, frantic, to tell him he hadn't come home.

Walking through Dublin city centre that afternoon, everything had reminded her of their time together. She'd passed restaurants where they'd eaten, pubs where they'd gone with friends – places that she'd found it impossible to enter since he'd disappeared. In the days, weeks and months of the last year, every man of his height and build had drawn her attention. Every corner she'd turned she'd expected to see him, and each evening when she'd put her key in the lock it was with a sense of dread at the emptiness ahead.

Caitlin picked up a framed photo and allowed herself to feel the ache that his absence had caused – an ache that she tried to quell by keeping busy, but there was nothing that would make her forget. The void that David had left would always be there – and it was only today – on the anniversary of his disappearance, that she would allow herself to be consumed by the total agony of that absence.

She stared at the picture, taking in his smile, the creases at the corners of his grey eyes, the way he had her wrapped tight, both arms around her. God, they'd been so happy together. She'd loved him so much. There was no way she would ever have let something come between them. What happened had been unprecedented. Another person might have collapsed under it. But she'd experienced pain before and had survived. So instead, she'd done the only thing she could do; summoned all her strength and carried on. No matter what it cost her.

She put the picture to her lips, stood it on the bedside locker and lay back on the bed. For the millionth time, she thought of all that had happened that night, of how dismissive the guards had been when she and Andy had gone to the station to report David missing. They'd buzzed the bell at the desk, waited a good ten minutes before the garda on duty appeared. He'd then taken them through to one of the interview rooms, sat there and, disinterestedly, taken notes. He'd told them that nobody was officially a missing person until the mandatory twenty-four-hour period had elapsed. 'You don't understand, David would never do this …' she'd said. She'd broken down in tears then as Andy explained how David was supposed to meet him that evening and had failed to turn up. He tried to impress on the garda how completely out of character that was for his friend.

They'd taken it more seriously in the days that followed. They'd questioned Caitlin in detail, asked her about David's behaviour leading up to his disappearance. Had he been acting in any way strange? Had he ever done this type of thing before? How had his mood been in recent weeks? She'd told them that no, there had been no warning, nothing that would have set off alarm bells. As far as she had been concerned everything was fine.

And how was the marriage, they wanted to know: had they been experiencing any difficulties? Perhaps they'd argued? She'd thought of the years they'd been together; they'd hardly ever argued. And, on the rare occasion when she got annoyed, he'd make some joke to make her come around. David was like that; quick-witted and hard to resist. He was also the most stable person she'd known, a foil to her own sudden moods.

She'd gone through the details with them again and again, told them that he'd left for work that morning as normal. He was a music teacher at a secondary school for boys. The school principal had verified that David had turned up for work at 8.30 a.m. as usual and that he'd left at 4 p.m. that afternoon. CCTV footage showed him putting his violin case in the boot of the car before getting in and exiting the school car park.

The police had carried out door-to-door enquiries, establishing that nobody had seen David return to the house that afternoon. His car had been located clamped in a backstreet in the city centre. A place where, unfortunately, there were no cameras. A ticket in the windscreen showed that he'd paid to park until 5.30 p.m., and an assistant in a music shop in George's Street said that David had been in the store at about 5 p.m. and had bought violin strings. His violin had still been in the boot – one string broken, explaining his purchase. The information given by the music shop assistant had been the last reported sighting.

David's picture had gone up all over the city, on billboards, in DART and bus stations. It had almost destroyed Caitlin to see his smiling face everywhere she went. And still the guards had found no leads. As the months passed and they began to lose interest, Gillian, David's mother, had suggested that they hire a private detective. He'd worked on the case for six months until eventually he told Caitlin he didn't believe he could help her – that sometimes people just didn't want to be found. For Caitlin that was like a slap to the face. David would never have walked out on their life. It was obvious, she'd told him, that something had happened to prevent his return. A few months later, when she'd met the detective in the street, he suggested that it was time she tried to move on, that it didn't look as if David were coming back. He'd asked her out for a drink then, and the only emotion she'd felt was a deep sense of revulsion.

She hadn't got close to anyone since David's disappearance. It was the last thing she wanted. Recently, she'd even found herself the object of a well-meaning matchmaking scheme by a friend who'd been urging her to get on with her life. This endeavour had simply led to her refusing dinner invitations from such friends who clearly had no understanding of how much David meant to her.

Instead she'd sought to fill the void in other ways. She began running, and soon found herself jogging five kilometres each evening in the local park. Recently she'd pushed herself to seven. She'd lost weight, but that wasn't her objective. She'd always been slim. She began running to escape the emptiness of the house in David's absence – and then she found it was the one thing that lessened the stress and helped her to sleep at night. Exhausted, she'd sometimes shower and fall asleep with the TV on, one arm stretched across David's side of the bed. There were mornings still when she opened her eyes expecting to find him next to her.

David had taught her to play the violin. She still practised most evenings and had joined a group of musicians who did a jam session in a wine bar every Wednesday night. Their friend, Andy, was the cellist and he'd invited her to join. Music was a passion that she and David had shared, and when she played she summoned feelings, not of loss, but of the elation she felt when they were together. Often, she'd sit with Andy over a glass of wine and they'd talk of the past. He was one of the only people she felt truly understood her; the only one who felt David's loss as keenly as she did.

The phone rang, and Caitlin put the box of photos to the side. She knew that it would be David's mum. They spoke often, and she knew she'd call on the anniversary of his disappearance. Caitlin had lost her own mother when she was five years old, and Gillian was as warm and compassionate as she imagined a mother should be – unlike the woman who'd brought Caitlin up. During her relationship with David, she'd grown close to his mother and since his disappearance they'd become closer still – each woman seeking a part of him in those he loved.

Caitlin picked up the phone and waited to hear Gillian's soothing voice. Instead the voice that spoke was male.

'David's alive … but don't try to find him. It could be dangerous for both of you.'

Caitlin tightened her grip on the receiver. 'Who is this? What do you—?'

Before she could finish speaking, the caller had hung up, and all she heard was the constant blip of the disconnected line. Trembling, she put down the receiver, then picked it up again. What should she do; call Andy, or Gillian? Surely, they'd advise her to call the guards, but what if it was dangerous as the caller had said? Maybe she ought not to tell anyone. She replaced the receiver and tried to clear her mind. Was it a hoax call? If this man knew something, why had he chosen to call now and not before – and why on the anniversary of David's disappearance?

Caitlin was trying to make sense of the thoughts that collided inside her mind when the phone rang again. After a second's hesitation, she snatched up the receiver. She didn't speak but waited for the man to say something first. If he could play games, then so could she, but this time it was the voice of David's mother that greeted her.

Chapter Three

Michelle

Michelle took a long drink from her water bottle and dabbed the perspiration from her face with a towel as the girls filed past her with smiles and words of thanks for another great Zumba class. She smiled back and said goodnight to each of them by name, but she didn't feel the buzz that she usually got from the workout. Tonight it had been an effort. Unable to concentrate solely on the music, she'd made some mistakes and slipped into the wrong moves at the wrong time. Not that the women had noticed; it was only three weeks into the course and they'd not yet mastered the choreography that accompanied each song.

Michelle shoved the towel into her sports bag and searched in the pocket for her mobile. Three days and still she'd heard nothing from Nick. She looked at the screen in frustration. Every time she received a text message she opened it expecting it to be from him. The last time they'd spoken everything was fine. She was sure that nothing had happened between them that might have led to this. There had been no argument, no cross words, which made his silence simply incomprehensible. She'd tried calling him again before she began the class. The phone had rung out and she'd left a message saying that she hoped that everything was okay.

Throwing on a fleece, Michelle zipped up her sports bag and prepared to go home. She turned off the lights in the sports hall, said goodnight to the security man at the front desk and walked out of the community centre into the dark rain-filled streets. Already damp with perspiration, her hair clung to her forehead. She pushed it out of her eyes and hurried down the street. Outside the car park a homeless man sat, paper cup in hand, the hood of his jumper pulled up ineffectively against the rain. Michelle dug a few coins out of her pocket and dropped them in giving the man a brief smile. He mumbled words of thanks and wished her a good night as she walked inside. She knew his face. She'd talked to him once, some months before when she'd begun volunteering on the soup run with the Simon Community. He'd told her about being made redundant, and about a messy divorce in which his wife had got everything. He swore he didn't touch drugs or alcohol, but most of them said that – it wasn't her job to believe or to judge them. She hadn't seen him in a while, had hoped that maybe his luck had changed, but the same faces always returned to the streets. Some of them she knew by name now – the ones who were glad to chat. This man had stood out because he sounded educated. He'd once, he said, held a senior position in a logistics company, and she wondered again about the circumstances that had led to him being in the street that night.

In the car park, she took the stairs two steps at a time until she'd reached the fifth floor. She hated these places at night – eerily lit by florescent lights – cars packed together, a predator could easily lie undetected waiting on a lone female to return to her car. Keys in hand, she unlocked the car from several metres away, and walked briskly, head held high until hurriedly she pulled open the driver's door and climbed inside. When she turned the key in the ignition the radio came on and the gravellish tones of Tom Waits sang 'Closing Time' into the night.

Nick. She couldn't get him out of her mind. It had been like that from the beginning, but whereas then her thoughts were pleasant and giddy, now they brought fear and uncertainty. She tried to reassure herself. Nick was crazy about her, he'd told her

16

that. Only two weeks before he'd invited her out for dinner to meet his sister and her husband – a step that she believed he hadn't taken with anyone else since divorcing his wife. Afterwards, he'd told her that his sister had been mad about her, and that Rowdy the dog was too, so he reckoned he'd have to keep her. And now a whole weekend had passed without so much as a call.

Michelle spiralled down the ramps and exited the car park. The rain had started to come down heavier, and she turned the wipers on to clear the windscreen. The homeless man had gone – she hoped he'd managed to find shelter for the night. The city streets were almost deserted. A woman struggled with an umbrella blown inside out in the wind and driving rain. Tom Waits's melancholic tones were replaced by the unmistakable sound of Pearl Jam as Michelle found herself turning in the opposite direction of home and driving instead towards Nick's house. She had to find out what had happened to prevent him from calling her. Perhaps he was ill, or worse still had had an accident. Whatever the reason, her fears would not abate until she'd satisfied herself that he was all right – that there was a reasonable explanation for, what felt by now, his interminable silence.

Michelle felt her heart quicken as she turned onto Nick's road. She slowed as she approached the house, terrified that she might see Nick's ex-wife's car in the driveway – or worse. Surrounded by trees, it wasn't possible to see the house until she'd pulled up at the gate. Outside the front door the light was on. It shone onto the wet tarmac revealing the absence of Nick's car. Michelle looked at the clock that showed it was after nine. It was unusual for Nick to be out on a Monday evening. He'd normally have just finished walking Rowdy round the block. She'd learned his routine in the time they'd been together. Though she figured he wouldn't have even ventured out with the dog on a night like this. She was sitting there wondering what to do when her phone blipped. She opened the text, immediately saw Nick's name and read the brief message:

Call you tomorrow. N x.

At least she knew that he was all right. She read the short message several times as though the words might change or give her some clue as to what was going on in his mind. She wondered briefly why he'd signed off with his initial. It wasn't something he normally did. Nor was the single kiss characteristic of his usual effusive messages, punctuated with kisses after almost every sentence. But then the message itself was a mere one line.

Michelle closed the message, put the phone on the seat next to her and started the engine. Wherever Nick was and whatever he was doing he clearly couldn't or didn't want to speak to her. His message had been of little consolation, save the fact that it confirmed he was alive, but that came with its own anxieties – namely that his feelings for her might have changed.

Michelle took a deep breath and tried to still the chaotic thoughts that raced and circled in her mind. She would go home, take a shower and try to concentrate on a book or a movie, anything that might distract her from the negative feelings that Nick's absence had caused her. She knew that to dwell too long on a fear was to fulfil the prophecy – whatever was going on with Nick right now, she told herself it probably had nothing to do with her. He would talk to her when he was ready. The last thing she wanted to do was to push him into anything he wasn't ready for. She had to prove that she was the antithesis of everything his ex-wife had been.

Chapter Four

Nick

Nick woke in the night to the sound of a woman's voice in his ear. He flailed blindly for the lamp and knocked over a glass of water on the bedside locker. When he finally found the switch, the light dispelled the auditory apparition, but failed to slow his racing heart. The voice had been distinct, angry, but what bothered him most was he hadn't caught the words that the woman had said – and yet somehow, he knew her voice: it was Rachel's.

Sweating, he sat up and threw back the covers. Rachel, the woman from his dream; why was it that she seemed so real to him now? He got out of bed and pulled on his jeans. His hands were shaking badly, and a pulse throbbed in his left temple. Had he been dreaming before the voice had woken him? He didn't remember. He just remembered the voice so close to his ear that he'd jumped.

Downstairs, Nick switched the kettle on. He gripped the counter wishing that he'd not poured out the half bottle of whiskey that he'd had in the press two days before. The prescription that the doctor had given him lay on the living room table. He'd been prescribed Valium and Librium, drugs whose names he was familiar with but had never anticipated having to use. The doctor had said there would be withdrawal symptoms, but he hadn't expected to feel this bad. The drugs would have helped to ease the tremors, and now with trembling hands he made a mug of coffee, heaped in four spoons of sugar, and wished that he'd heeded the doctor's advice to have the script filled right away.

Nick took his coffee into the living room, and rummaged in his coat pocket for his cigarettes, but then remembered he'd smoked his last in the car after his appointment – his only immediate means of self-medication gone. He sat back in his armchair, sipped the too-sweet coffee. Bars of light filtered through the venetian blind and bathed the room in the orange hue of the streetlight. It fell on the painting that Michelle had bought him for his birthday the previous month, a print of Van Gogh's *Starry Night*.

Michelle. He was glad she couldn't see him like this. She didn't even know he had a drink problem, or if she suspected it, she'd never said. He was rarely drunk. Over the years his body had developed such a tolerance that he'd had to drink more and more to feel the effects. Michelle drank, too, but one glass of wine and she was more than a little tipsy. She hated the taste of beer and he suspected that she only drank wine to be sociable.

Nick picked up his phone and scrolled through her last few messages. She'd said that she hoped everything was all right. If only she knew how not all right things were. He knew she'd stick by him, he wasn't afraid of that, but why should she have to? They'd only been seeing each other for eight months and he didn't expect her to take on the burden of his illness. He knew it was going to be awful, the abstinence and the unbearable wait for a donor to be found – for someone else's ill fate to determine his continued existence.

He thought about the length of time it might take to find a suitable donor, *if* they found a suitable donor. The doctor had been frank about that. Type O negative was the rarest blood group. He had to face the facts. Apart from that there were the horror stories portrayed in the media: patients who died while on the transplant list, all because there weren't enough people carrying donor cards. He hadn't had one himself, had never even thought about it before he'd found himself in this bind. He hated to admit it, but Susan had been right. He'd screwed up his life.

When he'd met Michelle, he thought that things were turning around, that maybe he had a chance at real happiness, but now he couldn't bear to break the news to her, to drag her into his self-made mess. The thought of letting her go was agonizing, but how could they plan a future when he couldn't be sure that, for him, such a thing even existed? She deserved so much more than that.

Nick gulped the last of his coffee, winced at the accumulation of sugar at the bottom of the mug and thought he might be sick. The caffeine had momentarily eased the thudding in his temple, but his hands were shaking worse than ever and he wondered how he was going to get back to sleep. He remembered an all-night pharmacy that he'd seen a couple of kilometres away and wondered if he was fit to drive. Then he picked up the prescription, stuck it in his jeans pocket and pulled his leather jacket on. He needed those tablets badly.

Outside, the rain was still coming down. Nick ran to the car; he started the engine, set the wipers on full speed and drove out of the housing estate. He was shivering, but his skin felt hot. It was almost 2 a.m. when he pulled into the shopping centre car park, which was empty save for two cars he imagined belonged to the pharmacy staff. Shivering, he cut the engine and stepped into the wet night.

The pharmacist looked at the prescription, asked him to confirm his address and disappeared out the back. One look at him and he was pretty sure the pharmacist could identify a victim of detox. Not only were his hands shaking, he was perspiring too. His hands and face were clammy to the touch. A few minutes later, the pharmacist reappeared. He went through the directions with Nick but didn't refer to his condition. He didn't know what Librium was used for apart from withdrawal, but he knew that his mother had taken Valium after the shock of his father's death, so he supposed these drugs were used to treat a number of conditions. He thanked the man, put the small pharmacy bag in the inside pocket of his jacket and went back out in the rain.

In the car, he fumbled on the floor until he came across a half bottle of water that had rolled under the passenger seat. He swallowed two tablets and hoped that it wouldn't be long before they began to take effect. The rain was still teeming down as he exited the car park; the wipers, set on automatic, raced to clear the windscreen. The coffee hadn't helped; if anything, it had made him feel even more jittery. He thought of the session with the hypnotist – about what she'd said about confabulation. He'd looked it up on the Internet and the definition was just as Tessa had said: a false memory, or pseudo memory, a term that was used in cognitive psychology defined as a recollection of something that had never happened.

He'd considered what she'd said about some people believing that confabulations under hypnosis were memories from their past lives, and he'd changed his search to 'hypnosis and past life regression', laughing at himself even as he did so. If only Michelle could see him now; she loved that kind of thing. He thought of all the times he'd teased her about her interest in the occult. He'd scoffed when she'd told him about her visits to an elderly gypsy lady – even when she'd insisted that the woman had known things, specific things about her family that couldn't simply have been speculation. 'And what does this lady do?' he'd asked. 'Read your palm, your cards?' Michelle had told him that, no, the woman simply held your hand and gently rubbed it, that it was as if by touching you that she could access those private recesses of your mind. 'Of course she can,' he'd argued, 'your hand probably jerks every time she hits on something and she just goes with it.' Michelle had laughed and called him a sceptic. What would she think of him now, making appointments with a hypnotist and reading about regression and past lives?

Nick was preoccupied with such thoughts when a dark shape

suddenly stepped in the road in front of him. He jerked the wheel, thankful there were no cars on the other side of the road. Heart hammering, he pulled into the kerb and checked the rear-view mirror. The man had reached the opposite side of the road and was fumbling with something that Nick imagined to be a sleeping bag. Nick got out of the car, his legs weak, and walked back to the man who seemed ready to bed down in a doorway for the night.

'Jesus, man, are you all right? I could have killed you,' he said.

The man looked at him unfazed and continued setting up his bed for the night, a dirty green sleeping bag that looked as though, like the man, it had been soaked through.

Nick put his hand in his pocket and pulled out a fifty-euro note. 'Look, get yourself into a hostel for the night, man. It's no night to be in the street.'

The stranger looked at him, and at the money in his hand. 'Are you sure? I wasn't asking …' There were tears in the man's eyes.

Nick was surprised at his timbre. He didn't sound like someone who should've been in the street. Embarrassed, he thrust the money into the man's hand.

'God bless you for this,' the man said. 'God bless you.'

Nick dashed back to the car. When he looked in the mirror again, he saw that the man had bundled up his sleeping bag and was walking in a brisk manner in the direction of the city. Only if he were lucky, Nick knew, would he find a shelter for the night.

Shaken by the experience, along with his symptoms, Nick drove home slowly, absorbed still by thoughts of reincarnation. In his search that afternoon, he'd come across an excerpt from a book called *Many Lives, Many Masters*, by a Dr Brian L. Weiss, MD, an American psychotherapist. It told the story of how Weiss, a sceptic, had learned to believe in past lives when a patient of his had been accidentally transported to a past life during standard hypnotherapy. Nick had read the two-page extract and then re-read it. It seemed that Weiss's patient had found herself in a different time and place, just as he had. He'd refreshed his search. The Internet was full of stories of people who claimed to have lived before. Finally, annoyed with himself for even entertaining such a ridiculous idea, he'd closed down his computer. Hocus pocus, that's all it was. What he'd experienced was a confabulation. It had to be.

Chiding himself still for his foolishness, Nick reached the house without further incident. He knew that his jumbled thoughts were most likely a further consequence of the withdrawal from alcohol – something that he hoped the medication would help with when it had had a chance to get into his system. In darkness, he climbed the stairs, longing for the oblivion that sleep might bring and trying to put from his mind what might happen at his next session with Tessa. He would phone her to make another appointment in the morning. Regardless of what might happen, he'd need the woman's help to quit drinking.

Chapter Five

Caitlin

'Cait love, come in.' Gillian stood back, and Caitlin stepped into the hall, shaking the rain from her umbrella before closing the front door. She hadn't told Gillian what had happened, not yet. Instead, she'd broken down on the phone at the sound of her mother-in-law's voice, and Gillian had told her immediately to come over, that she shouldn't be alone, not tonight of all nights. Caitlin had accepted gladly, packed an overnight bag, and driven straight there. All the time the man's words resounded in her head. *David's alive*, he'd said, but who was he, and what did he know? She had to find out.

'I'm sorry, I couldn't talk on the phone, Gillian …' She stood before her mother-in-law and pulled at her gloves, wondering if she had done the right thing in coming.

Gillian put her hand on her arm. 'Has something happened?'

Caitlin nodded, she couldn't keep this to herself. She had to confide in someone. And Gillian was the mother she'd never had. They'd hit it off as soon as David had introduced them.

'I got a call just before you rang. It was a man. He said that David … that he was alive. He said I'm not to try to find him … that if I did, it would be dangerous … I don't know what to make of it. I mean, why now, why today? Whoever he is, he must know something.'

Gillian's hand went to her mouth. 'Did he say who he was? Did he give you any information to go on?'

Caitlin shook her head. 'He hung up before I could ask him anything.'

'Have you called the guards?'

'No, I was going to … but then I thought about what he said. I mean, what if it *is* dangerous? What if David's alive and something happens to him if we get the guards involved? I don't know what to do … that's why I came over … I had to tell someone, do something … I'm not even sure I should be here.'

Caitlin took off her coat and followed Gillian into the living room where a fire burned, and a soap opera played on the television. Gillian picked up the remote control and put the TV on mute. They sat opposite each other, Caitlin on the sofa and Gillian in her armchair by the fire.

'What did this man sound like?' Gillian leaned forward, eager for information.

Caitlin shrugged, trying to remember the voice. 'I don't know. His accent was neutral. Definitely Irish; I think I'd have noticed otherwise. His exact words were "David's alive. But don't try to find him. It could be dangerous for both of you." I wonder who he meant … David and me, I presumed – but he could have meant us, couldn't he? That it would be dangerous for you and me to try to find him. I don't know what to do, whether to call the police or not?'

Gillian hesitated. 'Okay, if what this man says is true, if David's alive, then he's not likely to come to any immediate harm. It's been a year, Cait, and wherever he is, he's been safe.'

'You think we *should* call the Guards then?'

'I don't know. I mean it could be a hoax, someone who read about David in the paper.'

Caitlin thought of the calls the guards had received in the initial stages of the investigation. They'd had numerous reported sightings of David, none of which had led anywhere. 'It would be strange though, no? It's been months since anything's appeared in the paper. Why would someone decide to make a call now and not before?'

26

'I don't know, Cait. We have to look at all the possibilities. I don't want to get my hopes up. Not again.'

Caitlin nodded. 'Oh, Gillian, I'm sorry. I probably shouldn't have even told you, but I couldn't keep it to myself ...'

Gillian stood up and placed another log on the fire. 'What about that detective, the one we hired before? Would it be worth getting in touch with him?'

Caitlin shook her head. 'No, he didn't turn up anything last time. And I didn't get the impression he'd tried very hard either.'

'Okay, I think we should tell the guards then. We can do it discreetly – not call from either of our phones–– but from some-place else. There's every chance that this call is a hoax, Caitlin, you have to be prepared for that, but we won't rest easy if we don't report it. We both know that.'

Caitlin nodded. 'I'll make the call from work tomorrow. No one can overhear me in the office. I'll tell them our concerns about contacting them. I can't see that they'll do very much – we're not providing them with any new information, but at least I'll have told them.'

Gillian sighed. 'Hope is what keeps me going, the thought that we'll see David again. But every time I get my hopes up, it comes to nothing and I suffer the same pain all over again. Sometimes, I think it would be better to accept the fact that David's not coming back. It sounds terrible, doesn't it? But I have to get past the suffering – maybe acceptance is the only way. And you ... you can't put your life on hold. You're a young woman ...'

Caitlin got up, crossed to Gillian and took her hand. 'Don't say that, Gillian. Don't give up ... we can't. Maybe this call will turn out to be something. David's out there somewhere, I'm sure of it.' She squeezed her mother-in-law's fingers, thankful that, terrible as the past year had been, it had brought them closer together. She didn't know what she'd do without Gillian in her life. No matter what happened, she had to preserve that. 'Do you mind if I stay tonight?' she asked. 'I don't feel like going home; I don't think I could face it.'

David's mother put her arm around her. 'You know you're always welcome, Cait. I'd be glad of the company. You don't even have to ask. You've still got a key, don't you? Come over anytime, even if I'm not here, you can let yourself in. This is your home too, same as it was David's.'

Caitlin nodded. With a lump in her throat, she didn't trust herself to answer. Instead, she hugged Gillian, then got up and said she'd put the kettle on. In the kitchen, she stood at the sink and looked out at the rain beating against the window. Gillian had unmuted the television and the homely sound of chatter filled the room. She could feel David here in this house, could imagine him coming up behind her, arms wrapping round her waist as he used to do. She almost expected to see his reflection in the windowpane. Christ, there were times when she couldn't bear it. She took a deep breath to steady herself; this wasn't the time to come undone, not now.

Chapter Six

Michelle

The rain was coming down in sheets as Michelle and Conor made their way from the premises on Capel Street onto the quays, their backpacks loaded with sandwiches and flasks of hot tea and soup. Michelle checked her phone, as she had been doing compulsively all afternoon, while Conor poured soup for the homeless man on the bridge, and then took from his pocket some treats for the Jack Russell who sat obediently by the man's side. No messages. She put the phone away and stooped to fondle the dog's ears.

'How's it going, Tommy?' she asked the man.

He nodded and slurped the soup. She didn't ask if he was hoping to get into a shelter; he'd told her before that he was a loner, that all he needed was the dog, Buddy, for company. 'Have you eaten at all today, Tommy?' she asked. The man stopped to think.

'Had the best steak you can imagine,' he said, 'back in 1993.' He laughed at his own joke as he unwrapped the tuna sandwiches Conor had given him. The dog was crunching on a biscuit as they closed their backpacks and moved on.

Michelle was used to the run. Usually, she even enjoyed it. Nick had asked her if it wasn't too dangerous, but she told him, no, that the volunteers always went out in pairs, and that some of the homeless people were the nicest, gentlest people you could meet. She'd been appalled by some of the stories they'd told her.

They'd been spat on, and worse, by drunken fools who thought themselves superior; their deplorable behaviour proving the exact opposite to their own skewed beliefs.

As they continued along the North Quays, it occurred to Michelle that she hadn't recently seen the homeless couple that usually sat on the Ha'penny Bridge.

'Hey, what's happened to Dolly and Jim? I haven't seen them in a while,' she asked Conor.

Conor sighed and looked at her. 'Jim passed away – pneumonia,' he said.

'Shit.' Michelle felt tears prick her eyes as she thought of the couple always making jokes and sitting close together. She took a deep breath. Conor looked at her and she turned away so that he wouldn't see the tears.

'It sucks, I know,' he said.

Michelle nodded, not trusting herself to speak. It didn't seem right, Dolly without Jim. She wondered where Dolly was, whether she'd been forced to seek refuge in a shelter now that her partner was gone. Michelle took a deep breath, then lowered her head and quickened her step to match Conor's. By the time they were out of sandwiches and had returned to the premises, Nick had still not called.

'I'm off. See you guys on Friday,' Michelle called. She ducked out of the building and ran down the narrow stairs before anyone had a chance to engage her in conversation. Usually sociable, she couldn't face talking to anyone today and as she stepped out into the street she swallowed back more tears. Why hadn't Nick called?

In the car, the tears came again. Something was wrong – and she couldn't bear to be kept in ignorance. She wiped her eyes, breathed deep and turned on the ignition.

It was after ten o'clock when Michelle found herself outside Nick's house again. She turned on the dim overhead light and checked herself in the rear-view mirror, then took her compact from her bag to renew her foundation and coat her lips with pink gloss. She didn't look too bad considering the day she'd had. She took a deep breath, got out of the car and walked up to the front door. Her heart thumped as she rang the bell and waited for him to answer. A few minutes passed and she leaned on the bell again. She heard movement inside, and through the frosted glass of the hall window she saw Nick descend the stairs.

He didn't look pleased to see her. He ran a hand through his already dishevelled hair. She noticed the dark circles beneath his eyes, and his hands were shaking. 'What are you doing here?' he said.

'I was worried. Can I come in for a minute? I won't stay long.'

He stood back, avoiding her eyes as she stepped past him into the hall. He followed her into the kitchen.

'Are you okay?' she said.

'I'm fine. You shouldn't have come, Michelle. I was going to call you …' He still didn't meet her eye.

She put a hand on his arm. 'Nick, what's going on? Why have you been avoiding me?'

'I haven't, I've been busy that's all …' He stepped away from her, crossed the kitchen to the dishwasher and began emptying it.

Michelle stood in the middle of the room, lost. 'Can't we at least talk about it?'

'Sure, but you shouldn't just show up like this. It's not fair.'

'Not fair? Do you think it's fair to just ignore me? I've been worried sick. You haven't called in days. I thought there was something wrong. And obviously there is, but we need to talk about it, Nick. I mean … is it me, am I the problem?'

Nick shook his. 'No, it's not you. Not personally.' He stopped putting away the dishes and turned to look at her. 'I'm sorry, Michelle. Look, I don't know what to tell you. I just don't feel that great right now. Can't we do this another time?'

Another time. Another four days of silence, more maybe? 'No.

I'm sorry, Nick, but I can't go on like this; not knowing what's happening between us. If you want to finish it, then it would be better if you just told me.'

He didn't say anything for a minute. 'Look, Michelle, you know I'm crazy about you. It's just … I don't think I can do this right now. Maybe it was too soon after my divorce, everything happened so quickly.'

She was fighting back the tears. This was the last thing she wanted, and if he was so crazy about her, what the hell was he doing? 'So, what? We just end it – walk away and pretend we never met?'

Nick took a deep breath. He looked like hell, and she wondered if there was something else going on. 'I don't want to string you along … not when I don't know what …'

'Nick, you've been stringing me along for days. I thought we were happy, I thought we were doing great … what happened to change your mind? Is it your ex-wife, is that it?'

'Susan? No, that's got nothing to do with it.'

'What then? I just wish you'd give me a reason …'

'I'm sorry … I guess I'm just not ready. I'm so sorry, Michelle, I really am.'

'Right, well that's it then. There's nothing I can say to change your mind.'

He pinched the sides of his nose, shook his head. For a minute she thought he was crying. It was all she could do to keep back her own tears. 'Right, well, there's a bag of stuff upstairs, clothes … If you don't mind, I'll go up and get it.'

'No. No, go ahead.'

Rowdy sniffed beneath the sitting room door as she passed. She walked on, seeing the dog would surely make her come undone. At the top of the stairs she paused. This might be her last time in this house, and she didn't even know why. She wished he'd change his mind, follow her up the stairs and tell her not to go, but he didn't. In the bedroom, she picked up her slippers from her side of the bed, put them in the bag that she'd left there for convenience. He'd told her there was no need to keep taking it every time she left, and so she'd taken it home once a week to fill it with clean clothes, but this time there'd be no coming back. She stood at the end of the bed, looked round the room, committing everything to memory. When she neared the door, she noticed something on his bedside locker. It was a container of pills and, curious, she picked them up. *Valium* the label read. Surprised, she put them down again. What was he doing taking Valium? He'd never mentioned being on any sort of medication. She'd never seen him take it.

'Did you get everything?' Nick asked as Michelle headed back downstairs.

She nodded. 'Nick, those tablets on your locker … is everything all right?'

He looked taken aback, but then sighed resignedly. 'Yeah, I've just been a bit stressed, you know. Work … the doctor said they'd help.'

'Okay. Look, if there was anything else wrong, you'd tell me, wouldn't you? I'm here for you, Nick, if you need me. I can be a friend if you're not ready for anything more …'

'I know.'

He walked with her to the door. She waited for him to say that he'd call her, anything that might give her hope, but instead he just hugged her awkwardly, and told her to take care of herself.

'You too,' she said, and hurried to the car before he could see just how badly he'd hurt her.

Chapter Seven

Nick

In daylight, Tessa's house was even more impressive. Nick looked out across the lake as he stood on the porch waiting for someone to answer. Round the back, he could hear children playing, their squeals of innocent delight. Tessa answered the door herself this time.

'Hello, Nick. Please, come in.' Her smile was warm as she stepped back to admit him.

The medication had helped, for the shakes at least. He'd felt like hell after Michelle's visit. He'd gone into the sitting room and sat on the sofa crying, the pain so bad that nothing could ease it, and the only one he could blame was himself. The dog had looked at him, puzzled, and he'd buried his face in its fur until the convulsions had eased. But he knew that he'd done the right thing. If he'd been honest, Michelle would have insisted on staying. Better that she think he was a total bastard and get on with her life. She'd get over him; he wasn't that special. Not like her.

'How have you been?' Tessa asked as she led him into the small office.

'Up. Down. The doctor prescribed Librium and Valium. They're helping a bit. How many sessions do you think I'll need before the urges stop?'

Tessa indicated for him to lie back in the chair. 'It's different

34

for everyone,' she said. 'I know it's only been two days, but have you noticed any difference?'

He shook his head, took off his jacket and sat into the chair.

As soon as he did so, the visions came back – the confabulation. He wasn't surprised. His dreams always came back to him as soon as he got into bed at night. He tried not to think about it.

Tessa must have seen his discomfort because she referred to it at once.

'I know you're probably a bit nervous after what happened last time, Nick, but it's not common, so try to put it from your mind. Just lie back and try to relax.'

He took a deep breath, exhaled it shakily.

'That's it,' the woman said.

She began with the same instructions as last time. Her voice was gentle, lulling him towards unconsciousness. This time he didn't fight as much. He allowed his body to slacken limb by limb as she told him to. Sleep deprivation aided his hypnosis. He was aware, but from somewhere far away, of Tessa's voice telling him to make a fist, to think of a time when he felt empowered, when he felt strong. He thought of Michelle again, but then he remembered that Michelle wouldn't be there anymore, and he let himself drift back, and back further still to the time before he married Susan. To his youth and then suddenly to his childhood.

He's in a playground, his father pushing him on a swing. He laughs, asks his father to push him higher. He kicks his legs out, catapults himself into the air, hands gripping the metal chains. Then suddenly, the scene changes. He's the one pushing the swing. He's laughing still, but his laughter is joined by a high-pitched squeal of delight. 'Hold on tight,' he says, as he pushes the swing and the little girl in jeans and a yellow T-shirt flies forward – pigtails sailing behind her as the swing pauses at the crest before making the descent into his waiting hands. 'Okay Caitie, we'd better get going,' he says, as he steadies the swing and helps her down. But she's already running towards the slide.

35

The images shift between his life and the unknown. Sometimes, he's aware of Tessa's voice guiding him. She tells him that he's somewhere quiet, somewhere peaceful and he sees himself in a field by a small stream.

He's gathering firewood, but he's his other self – the one with long hair. He has a moustache. He's just lit the fire when he hears voices, singing. He looks up, smiles. A woman is coming through the trees, it's Rachel. The little girl skips next to her, jumps through the long grass. She runs towards him singing one of their favourite songs – 'Kisses Sweeter than Wine'.

'Nick.' Tessa was calling to him.

Nick? No, John. Johnny, that's what Rachel called him.

'I'm going to count from one to five, Nick. When I get to five, you will open your eyes. You will feel good. You will feel relaxed.'

The images were fading. The woman and the little girl moving beyond reach. He was reluctant to wake. He wanted to stay there in the camp with Rachel and their child. Their little girl, Caitlin. That was her name: Caitie.

His eyes fluttered.

'One. You're coming back now, Nick. Two. You're becoming aware of your body again. Three. You're bringing with you all of those good feelings. Four. You are aware of the sounds around you. Five. You're opening your eyes, Nick. Open them slowly. Keeping hold of those positive feelings.'

He blinked. Closed his eyes again. Caitie.

'Open your eyes, Nick.'

He opened them, saw Tessa hovering next to him. She smiled. 'You did great, Nick. Just take your time now.'

He lay there a few minutes longer trying to hold on to the images of the woman and the girl, but they had faded – nothing left but an all-too-real memory. He opened his eyes, sat up. Tessa had turned the light on, she was poised at her desk waiting for him to speak.

'She was there again.'

36

Tessa eyed him, curious. 'Who?'

'Rachel. The woman from last time. We were camping. I was lighting a fire and they appeared from the trees, Rachel and Caitlin.'

'Who is Caitlin?'

'My daughter.'

Tessa nodded. 'Are you close to your daughter, Nick?'

He shook his head. 'I don't have any children, it was in the dream. In the dream, Caitlin was our daughter – mine and Rachel's.'

Tessa looked perturbed. 'This woman, Rachel, do you know her in real life? Could she be someone from your past?'

'I don't think so. And yet, I feel like I know her; she's so real. And Cait – the little girl ... I'd like to go back,' he said suddenly. 'Maybe I can find out more information, figure out what's going on.'

Tessa shook her head. 'You've done enough for today,' she said. 'I can't explain these images, Nick. Maybe as we go on, it'll become clear. Maybe these people are part of your past, something you've blocked out.'

Nick looked at her, incredulous. 'I couldn't have blocked out something like that. I'd know if I had a wife, a daughter. It's just not possible.'

Tessa picked up her pen, scanned her diary to make their next appointment. 'That's not quite what I meant. Maybe these people take a different form in your confabulations. I'm not sure. We'll just have to see what comes out in subsequent sessions.'

'What about that thing you said before? About past lives?' Even as he said it, the cynic in his head scoffed at the thought. But the images were so real ...

'I'm afraid I don't believe in that. I think we get one chance here, let's try and make sure you get the best one you can. Now, how about Friday?' she said.

Friday. Only two days away – he reckoned he could manage that.

As Nick got in the car, he fought the temptation to phone Michelle. He'd like to talk to someone, to tell them what was happening to him, but he couldn't. Not yet. He had to figure it out himself. Maybe what Tessa said was true. Maybe Rachel was a version of someone he knew, of Susan maybe? Although, even as it occurred to him, he didn't believe it. And Caitlin – his little girl – where had she come from?

Nick got back to the house, took his Valium, and sat at his computer. He typed 'past life regression' into the search engine again, this time ignoring the voice in his head that told him that it was all nonsense. What if it wasn't … if there was the sliver of a chance that it was true? It would explain why the experience he'd had under hypnosis had seemed so real. It would explain why Rachel – her name had even taken on a new significance for him – seemed more than a conjuring of his imagination. It would mean that death was not the end.

Chapter Eight

Caitlin

Caitlin had hung up from the guards feeling frustrated. She'd asked to speak to Walt Gallagher, the sergeant who had been in charge of David's case, only to be told that he'd retired the month before and nobody had deigned to tell her. When she'd asked who had taken over the sergeant's cases, she'd been told in a disinterested tone that the speaker had no idea. His work had most likely been distributed among the force.

Trying to keep her cool, she'd asked if she could speak to someone senior in the office. The man on desk duty had enquired what it was about, making her relay the whole story up until the phone call she'd received the previous night, while interjecting intermittently with the odd 'mmm-hmm' and 'I see.' When Caitlin had reached the end of the story, the man transferred her to someone else, someone who had, apparently, taken over the case from Gallagher. The new sergeant, Trevor Parks, had her retell the story of David's disappearance again. When she'd told him about the anonymous phone call, Parks didn't seem too excited. Instead, he'd told her that more than ninety per cent of the time, this type of call turned out to be a hoax. It was not something to pin her hopes to. Probably, it had been some sicko who'd read about the case in the paper and thought it would be funny to make a crank call.

'But the case hasn't been mentioned in the paper for months,' Caitlin had interjected.

The sergeant had told her then that there had been an article about Ireland's missing in the magazine in the *Sunday World* the previous week. Maybe David was mentioned in that? He didn't have access to the article himself, but maybe Caitlin should contact the paper to find out.

'What will you do?' she'd asked. 'Can you trace the call?'

'We can look at your phone record, see if it's a known number. Apart from that, I'm afraid we have very little to go on.'

Of course. It was as much as she had expected. They'd check the number – if they even bothered with that – but they wouldn't be able to trace it. Was it any wonder so many cases went unsolved?

On Wednesday, she went online and tweeted to find out if anyone happened to have a copy of the missing person's supplement that had been printed with the *Sunday World*. An hour later, she received a message on Twitter. It wasn't anyone she knew, a random follower who had a shared interest in true-life crime. She looked at his profile: @darbryan1. His interests, apart from following true-life crime stories, it said, were film noir and folk music. He looked pretty normal. She read his message.

> *@darbryan1: Hi Caitlin. I have that supplement. Can pass it on if you want it? Dar.*

Caitlin wrote back.

> *@caitlindavis: Thanks. Do you know if there's a link?*

> *@darbryan1: I don't think so. Could post it to you if you give me address?*

Address. Was it a good idea to send some random stranger her address? Maybe there was an easier way to get the supplement. She didn't answer darbryan1's message. Instead, she phoned the *Sunday World*, but they told her they didn't have any spare copies

40

to send out and the supplement wasn't available online.

She sat looking at her computer screen. She could ask darbryan1 if there was any mention of a David Casey in the supplement. She hadn't changed her maiden name when they'd got married, so at least he wouldn't make the connection.

> **@caitlindavis:** *That's okay. Thanks. I don't suppose you recall if there was anything about a guy called David Casey in there?*

> **@darbryan1:** *Hmm, not sure. I can check for you. Hope you didn't think I was some weirdo asking for your address!* J

> **@caitlindavis:** *That'd be great, thanks.*

About a half hour later, she received another message from darbryan1. He'd scanned and attached a page of the supplement. A brief paragraph mentioned David, saying he'd last been seen at a music shop on 16th October 2016, that his car had been found in the city centre but that no leads had suggested where David might have gone. Several sightings had led nowhere. At least now she knew; the hoax call had very likely come about as a result of the article. She'd put her phone number on all of the missing persons posters she'd put up at the time. It was a miracle, she thought, that she hadn't received any calls up until now. The guards had told her it hadn't been a good idea, making her number public like that, but she didn't care. If anything was reported, she wanted to know about it.

> **@caitlindavis:** *Thanks Dar.*

She typed back.

> **@caitlindavis:** *That's exactly what I was looking for.*

@darbryan1: No problem. Happy to help. Too many missing people out there. ☹

She wondered if he had a story of his own, but she didn't ask him.

Gillian wasn't surprised when she told her the response she'd got when she called the guards. She didn't tell her about darbryan1, or the article. What was the point in killing her hope completely? Caitlin was fuming. What sort of person would get amusement from making a call like that? Some sicko. She was glad, suddenly, that David had insisted on their telephone number not going in the directory. At least the man didn't know where she lived. Who knew what a person like that might do? – but God, he'd be choosing the wrong woman to mess with. She only wished that she could track him down. He'd be sorry he'd ever made that call.

Chapter Nine

Michelle

Michelle pulled off the road and parked beside the low wall outside the cottage. A dog barked ferociously, and she strained to see where it was, but among the caravans and general chaos of the garden she couldn't spot it. The lock was not on the gate, which meant the old woman was available. She stepped from the car and hovered outside, looking at the door and the window, checking again to see whether there was any possibility that the dog was loose, but the rest of the garden was fenced off from the footpath, so she took her chance.

As soon as she tapped on the door, a cacophony of barking erupted from the house. The unseen hound started up again in tandem. She heard the old woman telling the dog to stop and a few minutes later the door opened and she was beckoned inside.

Nothing had changed since she'd last been here. The old woman led her into a room filled with old newspapers, religious relics and an array of paraphernalia that must have gathered over decades. In contrast a wide-screen television was mounted above the fireplace, the sound now muted. Michelle sat on the sofa that was covered by an old quilt and tried to ignore the stench of urine and something else, something rotten that she couldn't identify, as the small dog eyed her warily from behind the old woman's legs.

'Life is good?' the woman said.

Michelle attempted a smile. 'Not bad,' she said. She always tried to tell the woman as little as possible: she didn't want to lead her in any way; although, if the woman was still as good as she'd been before, the strain in her voice would be enough to alert her that something was the matter. Nick, in his scepticism, was accurate about that. Michelle knew there were any number of charlatans out there. She remembered the time she and her friend, Anna, had gone to see your man off the television – the one who told horoscopes. They'd gone in one after the other, and afterwards when they'd consulted, they'd realized that he'd been too lazy to even invent different stories. They were both about to meet a man with a tan briefcase. They'd laughed about it after, pockets lighter by forty euros. Anna had sworn never to visit a psychic again. But Michelle knew that the old woman was good. Hadn't she told her about her mother's illness? A sickness of the blood and the bones, she'd said. There was no more accurate description of the cancer that had attacked her mother's bone marrow. Within five years she was gone, leaving Michelle and her sister devastated.

The old woman took Michelle's hand and rubbed it gently, watching her face all the time. 'You work in a place with a lot of people,' she said. Michelle only slightly inclined her head in affirmation. 'A lot of women, dancing.'

Michelle smiled. 'That's right.' The old woman hadn't lost it.

'You're good at your job. You'll have your own business maybe in the next year or so.' Again, the psychic was right. At least that was the plan. She'd already looked into starting her own Zumba and Pilates classes. She'd spoken to a friend to find out what it would entail, setting herself up as a business, taking out personal insurance. She was saving some money before she quit her job to set out on her own. It was her goal, and she knew she'd do it.

'Things haven't been so good in love,' the old woman said.

'No.'

'How long were you together?'

44

'Almost eight months.'

'And everything was going well before. You were thinking of moving in together?'

They hadn't talked about that, but Michelle had thought that it hadn't been too far off. She spent three or four nights a week at Nick's place anyway. He said he hated it when she wasn't there. She did too. She'd loved living alone before. She liked the freedom, the not having to answer to anybody. Before, she'd lived with a man for almost three years, and it had stifled her. Everywhere she went, he'd asked questions. The thing he'd claimed to love most about her, her free spirit, was what tore them apart in the end. And then a year later, Nick had come along.

'Things went bad – just like that.' The old woman clicked her fingers with her free hand, then rested it on top of Michelle's.

Despite herself, she could feel the tears coming. Nick would surely laugh at her for that – a flashing neon sign for the psychic to interpret. Damn him anyway.

'No explanation.'

'No, he just … disappeared.'

'He's torn,' the woman said. 'Wants you in his life and doesn't.' She was silent for a moment. 'Is he well?' she asked then.

'You mean healthy?' Michelle shrugged. 'I think so.'

The woman looked confused. 'A drinker maybe?'

Nick drank a few beers, but he didn't drink too much, did he? She'd never seen him particularly drunk, no more so than a lot of their friends.

The old woman sighed. 'I'm not sure this is a good situation for you, lovey. This man, he has a good heart, but he's not willing to commit. There's a reason, but it's not clear to me. There isn't another woman?'

'No. I mean, he was married before, but that's finished.'

'A child?'

'No.'

'Funny, I see a child. A dark-haired little girl and a woman.'

Strange. There was no child – unless he hadn't told her. He wouldn't have kept something like that a secret – not after eight months, would he?

'How old is this child?'

'Four, maybe five, and Johnny …'

'Johnny?'

The old woman looked sharply at her. 'You said his name was Johnny?'

'No. No, it's Nick.'

'Nick?' The woman looked confused. She let go of Michelle's hand, ran her palm across her forehead. 'I'm sorry, dear. Ignore that. It's … I don't know, I've given you a wrong reading, I think.'

'You think it's someone else?'

'No, not someone else. Sometimes things get confused. I don't know. Maybe you could come back tomorrow, dear. We could try again.'

Michelle took out her purse, but the old woman waved her hand and told her to put it away. 'No money,' she said. 'Not for today.'

Michelle left, disappointed. She thought of the woman's reading. *Johnny.* She didn't know anyone called Johnny. She hoped the old lady hadn't had some premonition about the future. A woman and a dark-haired child. It didn't make any sense, but then the other things did. She'd known that she taught dance to a lot of women. That she planned to start her own business. Maybe she had good days and bad, the old lady. Michelle contemplated how old she might be. She'd first visited her ten years before, and she'd thought she was ancient then. Maybe her powers were going as the years advanced, her visions becoming blurry. Powers. She heard Nick mock her. You don't really believe in all that nonsense, do you? Maybe he was right. Maybe it was all nonsense, and she ought to just get on with her life.

Chapter Ten

Nick

'*Do you know what year it is?*'

Tessa's voice intruded on his vision.

'*It's 1980.*'

'*Where are you?*'

'*At home. It's Cait's birthday. She's five. They've made a cake, her and Rachel.*'

'*Are you Nick or Johnny?*'

'*Johnny. John Davis.*'

A pause on the recording, then he speaks again.

'*She's so happy. We've got her a bicycle. She's starting school soon ... Rachel is planning on going to college.*'

'*What's Rachel going to do?*'

'*Design. She works in a home store, but she wants to be a designer. Interiors.*'

'*And what about you, Nick?*'

He doesn't answer.

'*What do you do?*'

Still no answer.

'*What's going on, Nick?*'

'*Rachel, she says she has to go out this evening. I don't want her to go. It's Caitlin's birthday, but she says she has to. She's meeting Orla.*'

'*Who's Orla?*'

'Her friend. She's trouble, I don't like her.'

'Why not?'

'I don't know. There's something about her. Rachel's annoyed. She says it'll only be for a few hours.'

'Are you jealous? Jealous of Orla?'

'No. I think she's hiding something … she's not being honest.'

'What do you mean?'

'I don't know … I'm not sure yet.'

Tessa leaned forward and stopped the recording. 'That's pretty much it,' she said. 'I bring you out of it then.'

Nick looked at her. 'It's so weird, listening to myself …'

'What do you think is happening, Nick?'

'I don't know. It seems so real and now, I mean the year: I wasn't born then. This sounds ridiculous, but I've been reading about it, you know, the past life stuff. I've always been a cynic, but I'm beginning to wonder … maybe it's the only explanation.'

Tessa wasn't as quick to dismiss it as usual. She doodled on the notepad with her pen. He noticed she'd scribbled the year and the name, his name: *John Davis. Johnny.*

'We'll keep going, Nick. See what happens.'

The craving was strong. Nick pulled into a supermarket car park and went into the off-licence. Just a mouthful. A mouthful would stop the trembling in his hands. He returned to the car with a small bottle of whiskey. He put the paper bag on the passenger seat, breathed deep and made a fist. Michelle. He hadn't heard from her since she'd turned up at the house that night. He'd fought the urge to contact her, had picked up the phone a thousand times, and had to keep reminding himself that it wouldn't be fair. What was done was done. And yet, if he told her, she could help. She could be the only thing between him and that bottle of whiskey.

He took his phone from his pocket, the craving getting worse as the ringing went on. He hung up without leaving a message.

What was she doing? Not sitting by the phone anyway. That was good. He wouldn't expect her to. Maybe she was too angry now to even answer.

At home, he opened the bottle of whiskey and poured a shot. This would be it, his last, something to steady him while he tried to figure out what the hell was going on. He raised the glass to his lips, swallowed it in one and gripped the sink as the liquid burned the back of his throat. He picked up the bottle to pour again, and then, mad at his own weakness, made a fist and tried to overcome it.

Take the drink and pour it down the sink, Nick. Tessa's voice. *You don't want it. Don't need it.*

But he did. He'd begun pouring the second glass when his mobile rang. The jangly sound of it almost made him drop the bottle. Michelle. Her name flashed up on the screen and he answered it before he had time to think.

'Hey. Did you ring?'

'Yeah. Sorry, were you in class?'

'No, soup run. We've just finished.' Her tone was uncertain, but at least she wasn't mad. He couldn't handle that.

'Could you … I mean is there any chance you could you come over?'

A beat before she answered. 'Okay. I'll just go home first, get changed …'

'No. I mean, do you think you could come straight away? There's something I need to tell you.'

She picked up on the urgency in his tone. 'What is it? Is everything all right?'

'I don't want to discuss it over the phone, how soon can you get here?'

'I guess around thirty minutes, all being well …'

Relieved, Nick hung up and paced the room. He looked at the bottle of whiskey, but he didn't pour another drink. He could hold out; Michelle was on her way, she could help him. He

49

screwed the top onto the bottle and put it in the press, Tessa's voice nagging in his head, telling him to pour it down the sink, but he couldn't do that. Not yet. He'd do it later, after he'd told Michelle.

Johnny. What was going on? He turned his laptop on and sat at the table. He had a year now; he had names. He typed the name 'Johnny Davis' into Google. A number of sites came up – nothing that looked familiar. He clicked on Google Images, scrolled through looking at picture after picture – and then he saw it. A grainy black-and-white shot. A long-haired man in a black T-shirt. He peered at it but couldn't make out if it was the same person he'd seen under hypnosis. He went back to the search engine, added the year '1980' and the word 'murder'. Hand shaking, he hit the return key and closed his eyes.

When he opened them again, he found himself reading the words he'd dreaded.

Three Dead in Horror Spree, Child Escapes.

Christ. He clicked the link. It was archived information from the *Independent* newspaper.

The bodies of a man and a woman in their early thirties were found at a house in south Dublin in what appears to have been a domestic killing. The alarm was raised by a neighbour who heard screams coming from the house at around 6 p.m. The woman has been named as Rachel Davis, who lived at the address. Police are still trying to identify the man. In what is believed to be a related incident, a car plunged off Dun Laoghaire pier at approximately 7 p.m. A five-year-old girl was saved in a dramatic rescue by a man who swam out to the car. The driver who drowned at the scene has been identified as John Davis, husband of the deceased woman. He is believed to have handed the child out through a window just before the car was submerged. Police are not currently questioning anyone else in relation to either incident.

The shake in his hand had got worse. This was all so horrifyingly familiar. He clicked on another link, saw himself, or rather Johnny Davis, and the woman, Rachel, smiling at the camera, looking very much in love. *Three dead.* Johnny Davis had killed himself, and attempted to take the little girl with him, but had changed his mind at the last second. The girl, the orphan, Caitlin, was that her name? He searched again, desperate for his assumption to be disproved, for there to be some other explanation for what he'd witnessed under hypnosis.

He scanned the other news stories, but none of them mentioned the child's name. He started again, typed 'Caitlin Davis' into the search engine. It was a long shot; the girl would be what – forty-two now? She could be married, or if not, she could have taken the name of her adoptive parents.

There were a couple of women called Caitlin Davis on LinkedIn. Nick stared at the profile pictures and clicked to enlarge one of them. It had to be her. She bore such a resemblance to the woman, Rachel, that it just couldn't be coincidence. He read her profile. She was the owner and editor of a woman's magazine. He looked at her sites. She had a Twitter account. Her most recent tweet asked if anyone had a copy of a newspaper supplement about missing persons. It was probably a story she was working on, he thought.

Caitlin. Rachel. They'd existed, these women from his confabulation. What would Tessa make of that? But what about him, could he really be Johnny Davis, a jealous husband, a killer? No, there had to be another explanation. Maybe he'd heard about it, read about it somewhere, but even as he considered the possibility, he dismissed it. It was too real. He needed to go back – to be regressed again. If he could piece the whole story together, remember information that wouldn't have been printed in the newspaper, then he would know. It occurred to him that the only person that could corroborate such personal facts was Caitlin. He looked at her Twitter profile again. Caitlin Davis. Whatever happened – he would have to find her.

Chapter Eleven

Caitlin

Caitlin went through the motions of playing at the gig that night. She couldn't shake the memories of David, but then anniversaries and the days surrounding them were the most difficult, everyone knew that. Andy tapped her lightly on the shoulder with the bow from his cello as they were packing away the instruments.

'You okay?'

She shook her head. 'Not really.'

'Want to stay for a glass?'

'I don't think so; I wouldn't be much company.'

'Who says you usually are?' He swatted her. 'Just joshing,' he said. 'Go on; just one. We can talk about it.'

'All right,' she forced a smile and snapped her violin case shut. As much as she wasn't feeling sociable, she didn't feel like returning to the empty house either, not yet.

She was sitting at a table in the corner of the wine bar, a tea light candle flickering on the table, when Andy returned from the bar with a bottle of Merlot and two glasses. 'Don't worry – you're just getting the one. The rest is for me.' He winked and sat next to her. 'Now, what's wrong, Caitie? What has you looking so glum?'

Caitie. Andy was the only one who ever called her that, and it always brought back memories of her father who'd never used her full name. 'The anniversary,' she said. 'Can't believe it's been a year.'

Andy put a hand on her arm and squeezed it. 'I tried calling you on Monday.'

'I know, I got your text. I was with Gillian. God, it was an awful day. I'd just got home, and I got this call … a man telling me that David was alive. I thought it might be something, a real lead, but it turned out to be a hoax after all. Some sick fuck who'd seen David's name in the paper.'

'Oh God. I'm sorry, Cait. Any ideas why now?'

'The *Sunday World* ran a supplement last week about people who've gone missing.'

Andy sighed. 'Have you thought about changing your number?'

'No! What if someone really had information … what if David …?'

'I know, but you should let the guards deal with it, Caitie. What if this person, or someone like him, finds out where you live … have you thought about that?'

'He won't. We're not in the directory. Thank God, David talked me out of that.'

They finished the wine, and then ordered another.

By the time they left the wine bar Caitlin was feeling light-headed. It wasn't an altogether unpleasant feeling. Andy guided her, hand under her arm, out the door and onto the street. It was a quiet night in the city. They walked towards the main street where she waved down a cab. Andy hugged her tight, then pulled back and tucked her hair behind her ears.

'You can be sure of one thing, Davis,' he said. 'David didn't up and leave. He'd have to be mad to do that to someone like you.'

She smiled and extricated herself from his embrace. There were moments when she thought that Andy Quinn wanted to be more than her friend; it was evident in the way he looked at her. He'd been brilliant since David's disappearance; he continued to listen when everybody else had grown tired of it, letting her talk it all out without chiding or judging her. She'd gladly do the same for him, he was a wonderful friend, but she hoped he knew it would never grow into anything more.

It was dark when Caitlin stepped into the hall, but a bluish glow illuminated the living room; she'd left the computer on. She really ought to leave on a light when she was out late; Gillian was always warning her about that. She kicked her shoes off and sat down at the computer. She shouldn't have drunk so much wine; she'd pay for it the next morning. Already there were only six hours until she was due at work. She'd just check her emails and fall into bed.

There was nothing interesting in her mail, except a notification to say that darbryan1 had sent her a message on Twitter. Curious, she opened the website and logged on. There was a short message and a document he'd scanned, a newspaper article about a missing girl, which she skimmed through quickly before reading the message.

@darbryan1: Hi Caitlin. It occurred to me I should have told you my story. Maybe you're not interested or will think I'm odd telling you, a stranger, but I have a feeling that you've been through the same thing. If you want to talk, message me. And if not, best of luck on your own quest. I know I'll never give up mine. Lisa was my girlfriend, she vanished after a night out with her colleagues almost six years ago.

Caitlin clicked on the article again and read it in detail. Lisa Hunt, it said, had last been seen leaving O'Grady's bar at around 1.30 a.m. on the morning of 5th September 2011. There had been an unconfirmed sighting of a woman of Lisa's description getting into a dark-coloured car, possibly a Nissan. After that there was nothing. Lisa, it said, was a twenty-seven-year-old special needs assistant in St Malachy's Secondary School. A picture inset showed a slim dark-haired girl with a beautiful smile. Caitlin sighed. This girl had vanished in the early hours of the morning, more than likely picked up by a predator. Most people would conclude that the girl had been raped then murdered and her body disposed of in the mountains. The least she could do was sympathize with darbryan1.

@caitlindavis: *Hi Dar. I'm so sorry.*

... for what? For your loss? That was as good as saying your girl-friend was murdered. She's not coming back. Okay, she wasn't a man who had disappeared in the middle of the afternoon, but she could still be alive, couldn't she? She thought of that case where the woman had been a prisoner in a basement for fifteen years. She'd fallen in love with her captor, mourned him when he died. For most people it was incomprehensible. For Caitlin it was less so: she continued to love her father even after what he'd done. To begin with, people had told her it was an accident. She was five years old, she wouldn't have understood. When she was older, she'd read the truth – how her father had killed her mother and the man, and then, unable to bear it, had collected Caitlin from a friend's house, where she'd been playing, and had driven them both off the pier. At first when she'd read this, she had been sure it was lies. She had no recollection of the incident. Had no memory of the car plum-meting into the water, or of the stranger who had rescued her. And yet she remembered everything from her life before. She remem-bered how happy they'd been, the three of them together. Those memories were as clear now as they had been back then.

Caitlin shook herself from the past and started to type:

@caitlindavis: *Darren/Daryl? Thank you for sharing your story. You're right, I do understand. A year ago, my husband walked out of the house and never returned. A police inves-tigation and the hiring of a private detective led nowhere.*

Only my instinct tells me that David is still alive. I'm so sorry about Lisa's disappearance. I know the pain you're feeling and hope that someday, we'll both find out what has happened to our loved ones. Best, Caitlin.

She was surprised when a few minutes later, she got a reply.

@darbryan1: Caitlin. I'm so sorry. I figured David must be your husband. It's incredible to think that someone can simply disappear. The pain of wondering if you'll ever see them again never stops, I know … And yeah, it's Darren by the way…

For the next hour Caitlin found herself exchanging details with Dar Bryan. At first, she was cautious, she had no idea who he was after all, but then she thought what harm could it do? Everybody already knew what had happened. And besides, it might help to hear his story. To hear first-hand what other people went through. What they both needed was someone to listen. As Dar pointed out, it wasn't long before people started to avoid you because they couldn't bear to hear you go over the same things time and again. Caitlin had experienced that too, friends who had distanced themselves from her in her agony. One who had bluntly told her that she couldn't do it anymore, that Caitlin would simply have to get over it. The last six months had seen the end of more than one of her fair-weather friendships. Dar Bryan understood; he'd been there. It was the first time she'd spoken to someone else who had.

Chapter Twelve

Michelle

It was less than a half hour later when Michelle stopped the car outside Nick's house. She sat for a moment, looked in the rear-view mirror and attempted to smooth her hair. She looked a mess. If Nick had changed his mind, then he'd surely change it back again. A part of her wondered if she should've told him that she was busy, that she couldn't meet, but his tone had sounded urgent, desperate even, and that wasn't like Nick. She couldn't abandon him, not if there really was something wrong.

He didn't answer the door immediately. She watched the window for movement, saw the hall illuminated briefly as he opened the kitchen door, then heard his step on the wooden floor.

'Hey, thanks for coming.' He stood back for her to pass, and even in the gloom she could see several days' growth on his jaw, his eyes sunken for want of sleep. Whatever was going on, it was serious.

Under the harsh ceiling light, he looked worse than she'd imagined. He indicated for her to sit but didn't sit next to her, opting instead for the armchair where the dog usually sat. There was no sign of the dog, which was strange.

'Where's Rowdy?'

'What? Oh.' Nick got up, opened the back door and the big dog came hurtling through the door. He leaned to ruffle his fur, but the dog made straight for Michelle who welcomed the short reprieve, before whatever it was Nick had to say changed everything. She knew as soon as she saw him that it would.

'I'm sorry, Michelle, for the other night, for not explaining …' So here it was finally, the explanation, it didn't mean that anything had changed.

'The thing is … I'm sick.'

'What?' The surprise was so sudden, it was almost a relief, but for seconds only. 'What do you mean? What's the matter?'

'I'd been feeling a bit off for a while, so I went for some tests, bloods. I didn't want to tell you. The doctor says I need a liver transplant.' He looked at her for the first time since she'd arrived.

'Jesus, Nick. Is it definite? When?'

'They won't put my name on the list for six months, you have to be clean – no alcohol …' Even as he said it, Michelle could smell the whiskey on his breath. She thought of the old woman, her question about whether he was a drinker. 'And even then, there are no guarantees that a donor can be found in time.'

She didn't know what to say. She got up, crossed the room, crouched before him and took his hands. 'I'm so sorry,' she said. 'What can I do?'

Nick shook his head, looked away from her. 'Nothing. You don't have to do anything. That's why I wanted to finish it … it wasn't you, it's because there are no guarantees. A year from now, I mightn't even be here. How can that be fair on you?'

'So, what? You think I'm going to walk away? Don't be stupid, I couldn't, I-I love you, Nick.' The words were out. She'd been biting them back for weeks now, afraid, waiting for him to say it first, but it didn't matter now, did it?

'All I'm saying is, I wouldn't blame you. You don't have to, you know? I wasn't going to tell you at all, I just figured I owed you an explanation.'

'Well, I'm sticking around whether you want it or not.'

The look of relief on his face was heartbreaking. 'Come here,' he said.

As he pulled her to him, she could smell the whiskey again. When they parted she looked round, but there was no sign of the bottle. He must have put it away before she arrived. That wasn't good, not if he was supposed to have given up.

'Nick, have you been drinking?'

'Yeah, but it's the last one, I swear it. I have to get myself straight. I'm seeing someone, a hypnotist.'

'Really? Wow. You're the last person I figured would do that. I can't believe it's that bad … I mean, I've never even seen you drunk. No more than anyone else.'

'That's the thing. It takes more and more to get me drunk. When we were married, Susan insisted that I try to stop, made me sign up for AA meetings, but I didn't really take it seriously. I thought she was exaggerating … but it turns out she was right, about that anyway.'

The old woman's words resounded in her head. *A dark-haired woman and a child.* 'You and Susan, you didn't have any children?'

'What? No … there was a miscarriage. And after that, it didn't happen … we tried.' He leaned back to look at her. 'You hardly thought I'd not have told you about something like that? If I'd had a kid, I mean.'

Michelle shook her head but didn't tell him anything about the old woman. 'Of course not. Look, about the transplant, Nick. What about a live donor, they can do that, can't they?'

'Not in this country … maybe in the States. I don't know much about it.'

'Well if they could … the donor doesn't even have to be a blood relative – just the same blood type. Which are you?'

'Michelle, no – even if it was the same, which I'm sure you're not, I wouldn't let you do it.'

'Why not? The liver rejuvenates – in a matter of weeks it would be like I hadn't even done it. What type are you?'

60

Nick sighed. 'Right now, I need to get on that transplant list – and live donor or not, it's going to be six months.'

'Nick, your blood type?'

'O negative. One of the rarest there is. Try finding someone with that blood type who's willing to donate.'

Michelle sighed. She was B positive. There was no question of her being Nick's donor. They'd have to hope for a miracle. Even on the transplant list, his chances were limited.

She took his trembling hand. 'We'll find a way,' she said. 'We'll beat this.'

'I think I'm going to be sick,' he said and bolted for the bathroom.

Nick shivered through the night as Michelle watched over him. She read the labels on the drugs the doctor had prescribed, and when his stomach had settled to some degree, she gave him the pills and he slept. Even in sleep, he was fitful. He woke relieved, it seemed, to find her there.

'Withdrawal,' he explained. 'It could go on for days.'

'Don't worry, I'm not going anywhere.'

In the kitchen, she looked for and found the bottle of whiskey, which she poured down the sink. She had to make sure he didn't drink, no matter about the angry outbursts her interference might bring on. She was prepared for that. She cancelled her classes for the following day pleading sickness, she would stay with Nick until the withdrawal had passed. She knew she couldn't watch him indefinitely. She'd have to rely on his strength and maybe the help of the hypnotherapist to see it through.

Chapter Thirteen

Nick

Nick had intended to tell Michelle everything, but he couldn't. It was enough that he'd told her about his illness and she hadn't fled. When she'd asked him if he'd like her to go with him to the hypnosis session, he'd said no, that she couldn't be there every step to hold his hand.

The withdrawal had taken days. Days of sweats and shivering and hallucinations. Michelle told him that he had talked in his sleep, and when he'd asked her what he'd said, she told him she didn't know, just mumblings. She made sure that he took his pills every day, and much as he hated taking anything, it helped.

'You look better,' Tessa told him, as he sat at her desk.

'It's true, isn't it, what I've seen?' he said. 'I didn't think it was possible but ...'

Tessa avoided his eye. 'It's too soon to say, Nick ...'

'I did a search,' he told her. 'The name, the year ...' He could tell by her expression that she already knew, that she had searched too – he remembered her scribbling the names and year on her pad.

Tessa leaned forward in her seat. 'Is there any way you could have read about it, Nick? Would you have had any reason ... maybe while you were doing research, something like that?'

He shook his head. 'I'm an architect.'

She nodded. 'And the abstinence, how is that going? Are you over the withdrawal?'

'I think so.'

She made a few notes on the pad. He noticed that she still recorded the sessions, but she never offered to send him the files.

Nick took a breath. 'The article, it didn't mention the girl's name, the little girl that escaped, but I searched, and it's her. It's Caitlin.'

Tessa put down her pen and fixed on him. 'Nick ... I've been thinking, I'm not sure it's going to do you any good to go on with this.'

'What do you mean? I can't stop now. I need to know what's going on ... You will help me?'

There was a beat before she looked up. 'I'm not sure I can help you, Nick.'

'But you searched, didn't you? You know that everything I've said is true.'

She didn't confirm or deny it. 'Even if it is true, even if we have tapped into something, Nick, don't you think it's better left alone? It's a past life, it's done. There's nothing you can do to change it.'

'And what about Caitlin?'

Tessa didn't answer.

'Caitlin is still out there living with the consequences of what I've done.'

Tessa leaned her elbows on the desk, looked directly at him. 'You can't undo it, Nick. It's best to try to forget the whole thing. If this is a past life, and I'm not convinced that it is, then you're not supposed to know any of it. This is not what we set out to do.'

'But what about the hypnosis, we are going to continue with it, aren't we? I need all the help I can get to stay off the drink ... It *is* helping ...'

Tessa sighed and stood up. She indicated for Nick to sit into the chair and covered him with the blanket. 'We'll try today,' she said. 'But if something happens, if you're regressed again, then I'm not sure I can continue with you.' She reached out to turn down the lamp, then paused. 'Nick, you don't intend to look for Caitlin, do you? Think how this would sound. She'd think you were crazy.'

Nick shook his head, and, seeming happier, Tessa began the process, gradually taking him under, taking him back to the days before everything had gone wrong.

He heard Tessa's words, words that by now he knew by heart. He wondered briefly if by summoning them, by conjuring Tessa's voice, he might be able to hypnotize himself.

'Think of a time when you were empowered, Nick …'

His first big job. His employer, Ben Carter, has been watching him closely. He comes upon Nick one evening when he's stayed in the office late, appears at his right shoulder and stares at the plans on the screen. 'What's this?' he asks, and for a moment Nick thinks he's in trouble.

'Just something I've been working on. A dream …' he says.

Ben leans in to the screen, clicks the mouse and begins going through his drawings. It's a house he plans on building – hexagonal, the top floor completely glass. He'll build it overlooking the sea.

'Do you have any more designs?' Ben asks.

'Yes, a few.' He clicks on the folder of designs he's been working on for the past year.

Ben examines each one in detail before instructing him to move to the next. 'These are terrific,' he tells him.

A month later when a big commission comes in from a rich businessman who wants a house built on a plot in Wicklow, Ben gives him the job as well as a substantial increase in salary. It's also the path that leads to Susan.

Nick heard Tessa's voice. 'Make a fist, Nick, and try to hold on to that good feeling.'

He's on the hilltop looking down over the bay.

'How long have you been doing this?' Susan asks him, as they stand on the site looking over his plans. Her father had left the negotiations to her. She's a lawyer, more than capable of negotiating.

'I've been working at the firm for a year,' he tells her.

'And how many jobs have you overseen?'

'This is the first.' She arches one carefully defined eyebrow and smiles.

'I hadn't intended to design it for someone else,' he says. 'Not this one.'

The hexagon he'd been keeping for himself, but when Ben had shown Susan's father, Tom Price, the drawings, he'd insisted that that was the one he wanted, and it was too good an opportunity for Nick to refuse. That one job had made him. When Tom Price's house appeared in the top magazines, he was proud to see his name mentioned in the articles. He had no idea then that he'd end up living in it, if only for a few years.

Nick made a fist, tried to hold on to the feeling he had on that hilltop with Susan. But even as he did so, the picture was changing.

Susan is laughing at something he's said, but her features are morphing into the face of another and he finds himself looking at Rachel.

She stoops to straighten a blanket on the ground, the dome of her belly making it difficult to bend. He tells her to be careful and she laughs and tells him not to be silly, she's fine. They sit and begin to unpack a picnic. The view hasn't changed, it's the same place where Tom Price's house stands now, he's sure of it, but here there is nothing – just hills and fields and the sea below them.

'We should build a house in this very spot,' Rachel tells him. She closes her eyes. 'It's so peaceful.'

He lies back, gently rests a hand on Rachel's belly. He laughs when his touch is met with a kick and Rachel, winded, laughs and lays her own hand on top of his. He wishes he had the money to build her a house in this spot, hopes that someday maybe he will.

He still marvels at the life they're about to bring into the world.

'Okay, Nick. I'm going to count slowly from one to five. When we reach number five, you're going to open your eyes. As I count I want you to make a fist and try to hold on to that positive feeling... two, three ...'

He could hear Tessa's voice getting closer, calling him back, but he clutched at the remnants of the past, unwilling to leave Rachel.

'Nick? Open your eyes, Nick.'

Reluctantly, he opened his eyes.

Tessa looked satisfied. She waited until he was fully conscious before she spoke.

'Any confabulations?'

He didn't answer immediately, but then shook his head. 'No.' He hoped he hadn't said anything to the contrary while he was under, but he was pretty sure he hadn't. He was always conscious; no matter where he was transported to, physically he was still in that room.

Tessa wrote something in the pad. 'Good,' she said, and smiled.

He said nothing. She must have taken his silence for disappointment that he hadn't been regressed. He got up slowly and sat opposite her at the desk.

Tessa looked at him. 'You've done really well today, Nick. I know that you're still bothered by what happened, but you can't chase after it ... This memory, whether it's real or imagined, you've got to let it go, do you hear me? It's not going to help with your current problem. There's a long road ahead and we need you as stable as you can be.'

He nodded, relieved that he'd managed not to reveal what he'd seen. If she was to continue as his therapist, there were things he'd have to try to keep from her. He didn't know if that was possible under hypnosis, but right now Tessa, whether she wanted to be or not, was his portal to the past and he couldn't afford for her to refuse to see him.

She opened her diary. 'Will I put you in for Thursday, same time?' she asked.

Nick nodded and took out his wallet. He was anxious to be alone now, to process what he had seen during the session and try to figure out what it all meant. He knew why he'd seen himself on the hilltop with Susan, that had happened, but to find himself there with Rachel a lifetime before made him wonder if there was a connection.

Chapter Fourteen

Caitlin

Somehow, she'd got through the day. It had been after two in the morning when she'd got to bed and all that wine she'd drunk with Andy hadn't helped. Dar Bryan had told her all about Lisa, about the fact that they'd had a massive argument before she went out the night she'd disappeared, and he couldn't get it out of his head. When she hadn't come home, he'd surmised she'd stayed over at a friend's house, and when she hadn't answered his texts the next day, he'd thought she'd been doing it out of spite. It was only when she'd failed to come home again the following night that he'd contacted the guards. What they called that crucial twenty-four hours had passed, and he'd had to explain too why he was only reporting his girlfriend missing two days after the fact. Caitlin felt sorry for him. It was obvious that he'd been continually tormenting himself since Lisa had disappeared.

Caitlin had sent the last message. She'd sat there waiting for Dar's reply, but it hadn't come. She'd made tea, thinking it might clear her head a bit after the wine, but when he hadn't answered twenty minutes later, she had given up and gone to bed. What was she thinking, it was late, if he had any sense, he'd probably have gone to bed before she'd even sent that final message.

At work, she found herself checking Twitter several times to see if there were any messages from Dar Bryan, but the only message she got was spam from a marketing company wanting her to pay to advertise the magazine. When five o'clock came, she was glad to shut down the computer and leave. The girls looked at her, surprised; it was the first time she'd left the office on time in months.

As soon as she got home, she went upstairs and changed into her running clothes. Her head still wasn't good, she could as easily have pulled back the covers and crawled into bed, but she knew she'd feel better if she pushed herself to do it. Leaving her phone on the locker, she tied her hair back, jogged down the stairs and headed for the park.

As Caitlin jogged, she remembered the nightmares she'd had the previous night. She'd been dreaming about her father. It was one of those crazy dreams where everything was jumbled up. David was there, and then he wasn't. He'd killed Caitlin's father and then run away before the guards could catch him. He'd wanted Caitlin to go with him, but she'd screamed at him to get out. She'd fallen to her knees, taken off her cardigan and tried to stop the blood that was pumping from her father's chest. Then her mother had come in and thought that Caitlin had done it. She'd woken in the early hours of the morning and hadn't wanted to go back to sleep.

She jogged along the pathway that went around the park. There was no one else around. Usually she spotted the same joggers, but then she was earlier than normal. The second time she circled the track, she saw a man sitting on one of the benches near the copse of trees. She passed him, feet thundering on the pavement. He was reading a book and didn't look up.

The bad dreams, Caitlin tried to put from her mind. She'd suffered from nightmares since she was a child, ever since her parents had died. Violet, her adoptive mother, had had to leave the landing light on and her bedroom door ajar, but even that hadn't stopped her from waking screaming. It took years for those nightmares to pass. She still had them periodically, but they'd

69

come back with more fury since David's disappearance. They never made sense these dreams, and now she dismissed them, and ran all the harder to try to forget them.

On her third lap round the park, the man had vanished from the bench, but she caught a movement in the corner of her eye and when she glanced round, she saw him standing at the edge of the copse of trees. He seemed to be looking straight at her. Caitlin increased her speed. She felt uneasy. She didn't normally feel frightened in the park, but then there were normally more people around. She wondered what the man was doing there. She tried to dismiss it, put it down to being jumpy after the phone call, but she couldn't help but feel that he was watching her. She ran on, alert for the sound of feet behind her but she heard nothing. When she came round the circuit for the fourth time, the man had disappeared, but the creepy feeling didn't leave her. Rather than continuing round for a fifth time, as she normally did, she exited the park, watchful for the stranger, but she didn't see him, wasn't even sure if she'd recognize him if she did. It had only been a fleeting glance. She jogged back to the house, chiding herself for her paranoia.

When Caitlin let herself into the house, she paused in the hall and listened. It was as quiet as usual. She went into the kitchen, took out the solitary steak she'd bought and the makings of a salad. She opened the sliding door onto the back garden, went out onto the patio and threw charcoal on the barbecue. She knew it was ridiculous to be barbecuing steak for one, but she loved how it tasted. She hadn't used it until a month ago; it had always been David who'd done the barbecuing. She thought of the time they'd bought it: it had rained for most of that summer, but David had refused to be put off. He'd go outside in a raincoat, cook the steaks and run back inside with them. Caitlin never knew how he managed to keep the thing lit.

She turned on her computer while she was waiting for the barbecue to heat. It pinged to let her know that she had notifications on Twitter. She clicked the icon at the bottom of the screen.

She had two new followers: @darbryan1, and @DavidA. She opened her Twitter account, hovered the mouse over David A's account, stared at the screen in disbelief when she saw that the profile picture was one of a violin. David A: David Anthony Casey. Quickly she scrolled down the page, but all David A's tweets were retweets. His profile gave no information but that he was a music lover and teacher. Christ. She clicked on photos, nothing but the violin.

She sat back, tried to clear her head. What was this? Was someone fucking with her? David had never had a Twitter account. He didn't like to put his personal information out there in the ether, he'd said, didn't like how just anyone could find out about you. Caitlin looked at the dates of David A's retweets. The first was only two days ago. She stared at the screen. Someone was definitely messing with her head. She thought about how the guards might react if she told them; they'd laugh at her, not to her face, but she was pretty sure what they'd say as soon as she left the station.

She was glad that she rarely posted to Twitter, that there was nothing whatsoever to lead whoever was doing this to her. But then she remembered that there was – the wine bar posts that Andy tweeted and she retweeted. They would know where she played, that it was on Wednesday nights. She went into her own profile, deleted last week's tweet and all the previous ones about the music nights. It was probably too late, but it was all she could do.

She shuddered when she thought of the man in the park, of the possibility that she was not being paranoid after all. She clicked on @darbryan1's profile and followed him back. He still hadn't replied to her message. She was relieved when she viewed his profile picture again and was pretty sure it wasn't the man in the park, but that wasn't to say he was innocent. Just because the story about Lisa was true, it didn't mean that she was his girl-friend. He could have done his research, chosen a case that would

71

assure her sympathy. He would have seen her posts about playing in the wine bar too. Now she wished she'd listened to David about social media. If some psycho did have her in his sights, he knew just where to find her.

Chapter Fifteen

Michelle

O negative. When Nick had told her this, she'd felt sick. What were the chances of a donor coming up of this type? She knew it was rare, and if the doctor had said he had a year to live ... It didn't bear thinking about. Her relief that the break-up wasn't about her had been short-lived. She had to admit that despite her protests about staying with him, there was a part of her that wanted to cut and run. Wouldn't it be better for her to end it now and let the healing begin, than to stand by and see Nick deteriorate, knowing she was helpless to do anything about it, forced to watch him die the way her mother had?

Michelle had done everything for her mother. She'd worked part-time to take her to her hospital appointments – followed up all the test results with the doctors, monitored everything they did. When her mother had begun to suffer from confusion, unable to structure simple sentences, it was Michelle who'd identified the drug that was causing the problem. The doctors had denied it, said that confusion was not a side effect of that medication, and yet when her mother had, of her own volition, stopped taking it, her confusion had miraculously subsided and she was herself again.

The whole experience had shaken her faith in the medical system. Michelle knew it was the hospital's fault that her mother was dead. They'd taken their eye off the ball, failed to notice or else failed to tell them that the cancer had returned. They allowed it to run rampant until her mother's bone marrow had deteriorated to the point that there was no way back. Michelle had queried it, asked why they had not been given the results of a biopsy six months previously – surely this along with the blood tests taken monthly had indicated that the disease was not only present but escalating. When Michelle had pointed that out to the consultant, she'd been told that they didn't treat patients on numbers but on symptoms. They were not about to admit culpability, but everybody knew that doctors were run ragged – that long hours and too many patients led to these mistakes.

She'd spent all weekend watching over Nick. She'd wanted to stay again that night, but he told her he'd be fine. Besides, she had the soup run and she wouldn't get back till late. She called Nick before she went out and was worried when he didn't answer, but he called her back immediately.

'Hey, how did the hypnosis session go?' she asked him.

'Yeah, it was fine, good.'

He hadn't told her exactly what happened at the sessions, and for some reason she wasn't sure if she should ask, it seemed something private. 'Do you think it's helping?' she asked.

Nick laughed. 'Believe it or not, I do. She tells me to think of something good, a time when I felt empowered – I have to make a fist as I think about it. The theory is that when I feel the urge to drink, I'm to make a fist and try to get back that feeling.'

'And it works?'

'It seems to. I often think about you.' His voice was soft, and she felt relieved. Things had become so strange between them, it was hard to get back to where they'd been before.

'Will you be okay tonight?' she asked.

'Yeah, I just need to sleep. I'll be fine.'

Michelle was early getting into the centre. Conor was sitting drinking coffee with Barbara and a few of the other volunteers.

Michelle smiled as she took her coat off and hung it on the back of a chair. 'What's up?' she said.

Conor shook his head. 'You haven't heard?'

She looked round at the grim faces. 'No, what's happened?'

'The lad outside the government offices was found this morning.' Conor looked at the mug cradled in his hands.

'Not dead?'

Three nodding heads confirmed it. 'Hypothermia.'

'Christ.' Michelle sat next to Conor. 'We only chatted to him last week. His name was Dan, remember?'

Conor nodded, looked around at the others. 'He'd been sleeping outside the Dáil to give them a wake-up call. Usually he was moved on by security before a politician even got near the place, not that they'd have cared.'

'Maybe they'll pay attention now,' Barbara said. 'Right on their doorstep.'

In the last year, homelessness in the city had reached crisis point. Everybody knew that. You couldn't walk ten paces without coming upon someone in a doorway begging for money. It was the reason Michelle had volunteered. It wasn't enough to give money. She had to do something more, even if it was just soup and sandwiches. The government had vowed a year ago to provide more beds in hostels, but that hadn't happened. Instead, the problem had spiralled.

All the volunteers knew that there was no quick-fix solution to the problem. They weren't that idealistic. There were the usual addicts on the streets, the ones that couldn't be helped, but there were others too, the mentally ill who'd fallen through the cracks in the system, the ones who'd taken oversized loans from the bank to buy houses during the economic boom, only for the prices to come crashing down along with the jobs that had just about enabled them to pay their monthly mortgage.

Michelle often wondered what had happened to the ghost estates, hundreds of houses built around the country with no one to live in them. Some of them half built, abandoned by the builders who'd run out of money halfway through projects. Now everybody talked about the lack of social housing, and the fact that every boarded-up building in the city belonged to the National Asset Management Agency.

Poor Dan. She knew from talking to him that he'd had some kind of problem. She suspected Asperger's. Even when he'd made enough money to pay for a hostel room, he preferred to sleep on the streets. Hostels were lethal, he said, too many people shooting up, drinking, fighting. The streets were bad, but he felt safer out in the open. He'd ranted about the state of the country – everyone ranted about the state of the country.

'You okay?' Conor put his hand on her arm. Barbara was standing, clearing away the coffee mugs. 'Yeah, sorry. It's just … poor Dan. I can't believe it.'

Conor nodded. 'I know. He had to die to get attention. I'm surprised you didn't see it on the news.'

Michelle wrapped her scarf round her neck and started to help Conor load the wrapped sandwiches into the bags. 'I didn't watch it. To be honest, I don't know what's been going on around me the last few days, I've had so much on.'

'Is everything all right?' Conor said. His concern was genuine. She didn't know much about him, except that he had a good heart. All the volunteers had. She could confide in him, she knew, but she didn't want to. She would feel like she was betraying Nick.

'Ah, I'm okay. Come on, we'd better get out there. I can imagine what the mood will be like tonight after Dan.' She put the bag on her back and followed Conor out into the cold night.

Chapter Sixteen

Nick

He saw her as soon as he walked in, slim build, dark hair pulled back from her oval-shaped face. Her resemblance, so close to the woman, Rachel, caused his already-shaking hands to worsen. She was in conversation with one of the other musicians who seemed to be tuning a cello. He thought the music would already have begun when he arrived, but they were only setting up. Nick scouted the room, opting for a small table in a corner where he had a clear view of the band. He tried not to look at the woman – instead he attempted to catch the attention of the waitress, and when he did so he, reluctantly, ordered a pot of tea.

The shake in his hands was still bad despite the medication, but it was anxiety rather than withdrawal this time, caused by seeing the woman, and the fact that this was the first time he'd been in a bar of any kind since he'd started the hypnosis. At the next table, a couple were sharing a bottle of red wine. At another table, a guy was drinking a beer. Nick opened up his newspaper and tried to concentrate. If he had a drink in his hand, he would feel less conspicuous. He reasoned that he could have invited Michelle; he wasn't, after all, going to say anything to Caitlin, he'd come merely to see her. Michelle was observant though, she'd have noticed his discomfort. She would have noted that whatever was wrong was something more than the urge he felt to go to the bar and order himself a whiskey.

The waitress smiled as she set down the tray. 'What time does the music usually start?' Nick asked her, nodding towards the musicians.

The waitress glanced at an old-fashioned clock on the wall. 'About nine. Any minute now I'd say. Can I get you anything else?'

Nick shook his head. 'That's grand,' he said, lifting the lid from the pot, and waiting until she'd gone before picking up the spoon in a shaky hand and stirring.

The musicians were talking among themselves. Nick was close enough to hear some of their banter, and he strained to hear Caitlin speak, but mostly a tall, curly-haired guy held court. The others laughed at his jokes, batted witty responses back and forth. The cello player put his hand on Caitlin's shoulder, leaned in and spoke to her. She nodded and smiled, but she looked tense. He noticed how her eyes flitted round the room, taking in the clientele, and he wondered if she was nervous about the performance, or if she was waiting for someone. Every so often her eyes strayed to the door.

The music started. The tall guy was the lead vocalist and he sang a rendition of 'Georgia on My Mind'. Nick sipped his tea, tapped his foot to the music and divided his time between watching the group and pretending to read his paper. He was careful not to stare at Caitlin who was the only woman among them. It was an interesting outfit, besides the cello and the violin, there was a guitarist, a keyboard player and the singer who sat on a Cajon which he slapped with perfect rhythm.

Nick had played the drums when he was a teenager, something his mother had given in to when his father had built a shed at the end of the garden where they could both practise. He didn't sing, despite the namesake that so many people commented on, but he had been in a band for a few years until the usual differences of opinion arose from too much time spent together. When his father died, and his mother had sold the house in order to downsize, he'd sold his drum kit, but he'd kept his father's Stratocaster, which he kept in pristine condition on a stand in the bedroom. Listening now to the music, he had an urge to play, and thought he must tune it up and begin practising again. He'd never considered himself to be a great guitar player, but he was competent, and in his student days, he could pick up a guitar at parties and play a tune as well as anyone else.

As the band continued to play, Nick began to relax. He tapped along to a mix of swing, rhythm and blues. After about forty minutes, the singer announced that they were taking a ten-minute break. One of the guys took a pack of cigarettes from his pocket and headed for the exit. The cello player leaned into Caitlin and then got up to go to the bar. Nick wondered if he might be her boyfriend. But then he noticed the gold band on her finger, not on his. Friends so, though his body language suggested that he was interested.

Nick was out of tea. He didn't know if he trusted himself to go to the bar, and he knew he hadn't figured on talking to her, but it wouldn't be the worst idea to get talking to the guy, maybe get an introduction to Caitlin that way. Before he could get out of his chair, Caitlin stood up and went to the ladies. Nick went to the bar and stood next to the cellist. The barman was pulling him a beer.

'Great music,' Nick said.

The guy glanced at him and smiled. 'Cheers.'

'Do you have a regular slot here?'

'Yeah, every Wednesday.' The barman asked if the guy wanted anything else and he ordered a red wine. 'Do you play?' he asked Nick.

'I used to, years back. Drums mostly, and a bit of guitar. I'm often sorry I didn't keep it up.' The musician didn't appear to be listening any more. His gaze had strayed to Caitlin who had been waylaid by a man on her way back from the ladies. She looked uncomfortable. Nick imagined that the guy was probably hitting on her.

The cellist took his change from the barman. 'Better get back,' he said to Nick, but instead of returning to his seat, he made his way to where Caitlin was cornered by the man. It was the man who had been sitting alone drinking beer since he'd arrived, and Nick imagined he must have been fairly well on. The last thing any woman needed was a drunk harassing her. Caitlin's friend had wedged himself between her and the stranger. The guy didn't seem to care much who he was talking to, and Caitlin took the opportunity to take her red wine, extricate herself from the situation and return to her seat. The man continued talking; he was now doing pitiable air guitar gestures.

Caitlin was alone now. Nick wondered how he might start a conversation without looking as though he were just another man hitting on her. She was rummaging in her bag, glass of red wine on the floor in front of her. He had an idea, not the best one, but better than trying to start a conversation cold. Passing with his juice in hand, Nick pretended not to look where he was going, his foot caught the glass of wine, and he looked down as Caitlin looked up, startled.

'Oh God, I'm sorry,' he said. 'I wasn't looking what I was …'

Instinctively, Caitlin had stood. 'Don't worry …' she said.

'No, really, so clumsy of me, let me get you another one.' He chanced a look at her face. She seemed to be studying him: she took in the glass and bottle of juice in his hand.

'Really, it's not a problem,' she said.

'Even so,' he said, 'it was my stupidity …'

She signalled to the waitress and pointed out the spilled drink; the glass, at least, was unbroken. Nick stooped to pick it up, and almost dropped his own glass in doing so. Caitlin looked amused as he turned to the waitress who had served his tea earlier.

'I'm sorry, it was my fault. Could I get another, please? What was it?'

'Cab Sauv,' Caitlin told the girl. She looked over at her musician friend, who was still caught by the air guitarist, but he was looking in their direction now.

'You play really well,' Nick said.

On cue Caitlin picked up her violin. The other musicians had come back inside and were making their way towards the stage area.

'Do I know you?' Caitlin asked. She was looking at him hard.

Nick looked at her a moment. 'I don't think so,' he said. He smiled. 'I'd better let you get back to it. Again, I'm really sorry about your drink.'

He turned to walk away, best to keep things brief, he thought. He could speak to her again on another occasion.

'What's your name?' she asked.

'Nick,' he said. 'And you?'

'Caitlin.' Her friend had extricated himself from the drunk. Suddenly, he was standing next to Nick, eyeing him in a far less friendly manner than he had when they'd spoken at the bar.

'All right, Caitie?'

Caitlin nodded. 'This is Nick,' she said.

The musician nodded, curtly, but didn't acknowledge the fact that they'd spoken at the bar.

'This is Andy.' Andy ignored the introduction.

'We'd better get started,' he said, taking his seat beside her.

If he wasn't her husband, Nick thought, he certainly was protective of her, but in that territorial way that he'd seen some men behave with their girlfriends. And that never ended well, friendship or otherwise.

Chapter Seventeen

Caitlin

'Do you know that guy?'

'Sorry?' Caitlin looked up, distracted, as she put away her violin.

Andy was standing next to her. 'The guy who was sitting by himself. You said his name was Nick.'

Caitlin shook her head, looked to where the man, Nick, had been sitting. He'd left without her seeing, and now the waitress was clearing the things from his table. 'No, he spilled my drink ... we talked for a few minutes. Look, Andy, are you rushing off?'

He hesitated. 'I have the van tonight, told Brian I'd take the keyboard. I'm a bit tired, but I could give you a lift home? What's up? Is everything okay?'

'I don't know. A few things have happened in the last few days ... I'll tell you about it on the way home.' Caitlin stopped talking, and smiled as Brian, the keyboard player, came over to talk with Andy.

'You don't mind taking the keyboard, do you? If it's any hassle, I can jump in a cab ...'

'No, no, it's fine. Plenty of room in the van. And you're all right with me dropping it round tomorrow?'

'Sure man. That'd be great.'

Andy helped Brian out to the van with the keyboard. Brian was new to the band. He'd answered an ad that Andy had put on a Facebook group. He didn't talk much, and none of them had got to know him beyond small talk, but they all agreed that he was an accomplished musician. He played with a New Orleans jazz band at weekends. Andy had persuaded Caitlin to go and see them in the Harbour bar a few weeks before to see if Brian would be right for their group. It was one of the rare nights out that Caitlin had enjoyed recently.

Now she stood and waited while Andy opened the back doors of the van and the two men carefully loaded in the instruments. 'Can we drop you anywhere?' Andy asked, but Brian shook his head and told them he was going to walk. He shared a house, Andy told Caitlin, somewhere around Stoneybatter.

Caitlin went around to the passenger side and got into the van. Andy started the engine and turned the heater on. He checked the mirrors before pulling away from the kerb.

'Now, what's up?' he said. 'I could tell you weren't yourself tonight.'

'Someone's set up a Twitter account in David's name.'

Andy turned to look at her, momentarily taking his eyes off the road. 'What? What do you mean?'

'I got this follower on Twitter, goes by the name of David A. The profile picture is a violin. There's nothing else, no personal photo, nothing like that … but all the tweets are retweets to do with music. Someone is screwing with me, Andy.'

'Christ, that's bizarre, Caitie. Did you check – I mean have you got any friends in common, anything like that?'

'I don't know, I don't think so. The account's just been set up. The first tweet was only a few days ago.'

'Is there anything you can do? I mean can you block him?'

'I guess … but …'

'But what?'

Caitlin shrugged. 'I don't know … maybe it's better if I don't. Whoever this person is, he could know something.'

'But what about your information, Caitlin? You don't want

83

this guy to know about you, do you? What you're doing, who your friends are ...'

'But it's too late for that. Whoever he is, he's already seen my profile. He knows about the sessions, for example. That's why I was so uptight tonight. I was afraid he might be there, that he might be sitting there watching me and I wouldn't know. When that guy stopped me, the drunk one, I thought it was him. Then you came along, and I realized I was being stupid. He didn't care who I was, he was just some idiot ...'

Andy was silent for a minute, hands gripping the wheel, looking straight ahead. 'What about the other guy?' he said. 'The one who spilled your drink?'

Caitlin shook her head. 'No, I don't think so.'

'Why not? He seemed keen on talking.'

'I know, I know what you're saying, Andy, and I'm not sure why, but I didn't get that sort of vibe off him. Strange, I suppose, since I've been looking at everyone suspiciously recently.'

'Hmm. I wouldn't be so sure. He was on his own, and I've never seen him there before. He tried to start a conversation with me at the bar. Maybe he thought we were together.'

Caitlin rubbed her forehead. 'God, Andy, I thought you were going to reassure me, not freak me out. I think that guy was okay, really. I just get the feeling. But apart from that, the Twitter account, I mean, there was this guy in the park. I thought he was watching me when I went on my run.'

Andy had just turned the van into Caitlin's road. He slowed down as he approached the house, and Caitlin realized she'd forgotten to leave a light on again, despite her resolutions.

'Jesus, Caitlin. Was there anyone else around?'

'No, I think that's why I got so nervous. There are normally other joggers. It wasn't that this man did anything, he was just sitting there on a bench. I cut my run short he unnerved me that much.'

They'd stopped outside the house. Andy looked at her. 'Do you want me to come in for a minute?' he said.

Usually she'd say she was fine, but this time she accepted Andy's offer. She didn't feel like walking into the dark house alone.

As soon as she opened the door, she felt for the light switch. 'Would you mind putting the kettle on, Andy. I just need to pop upstairs.'

She went upstairs, turned on the landing light and then went into each room, turning on the lights, checking that there was no one there.

Downstairs, she could hear Andy opening and closing cupboards, rattling mugs. He knew where everything was kept. Apart from Gillian, he'd been the only regular visitor to the house since David's disappearance.

'Tea?' he asked when she appeared in the kitchen.

'Thanks.'

Caitlin sat down at the table. Her laptop was there. She was almost afraid to switch it on, but it would be better to do so while Andy was there, rather than allowing something to freak her out later. Besides, she wanted to show him the account for David A, let him know that she wasn't just being paranoid.

Andy moved round the kitchen as she booted up the computer. She logged into Twitter, saw that she had a message notification. She glanced behind her, clicked into her messages. It was from Dar Bryan.

@darbryan1: Hey Caitlin, sorry I didn't reply before...

Caitlin glanced over her shoulder. Andy was coming towards her, mug in hand. She closed the message before he could see.

'Do you want toast?' Andy asked.

She shook her head. 'No, I'm fine, make some for yourself though.'

She remembered nights when they'd all come back to the house together, David, Andy and herself. Andy had stayed on the camp bed in their spare room most weekends. Sometimes, he got out of bed before them, had coffee ready when they finally emerged. It was never an awkward trio. David knew that she liked Andy as well as he did – and he was never jealous either – even when Andy blatantly flirted with her, David knew he had no reason to worry.

Caitlin clicked on the search button – typed in David A's handle. She wasn't prepared for what she saw there; she turned too suddenly, caught the mug with her arm and slopped its contents over the table.

'Andy, quick,' she said, 'look at this.'

A picture had been tweeted earlier in the evening from the wine bar.

@DavidA: Waiting for the music.

It showed Caitlin and Fran, the singer, chatting before the show.

'Christ,' Andy said, putting his mug down and leaning in over Caitlin's shoulder. 'He was there.'

Caitlin scrolled down, nothing else, just that one shot. She looked at the picture again, examined the angle it was taken from.

'That guy, the one who introduced himself, Caitie, it has to be.'

Caitlin shook her head. 'No.'

'What do you mean no? Who else could it have been? He was keen enough to talk, wasn't he?'

'It's the wrong angle,' Caitlin said.

'What do you mean?'

'Whoever took this was sitting to my right. That guy, Nick, if he'd taken it, it would have been from the other side.'

Andy sighed and straightened. 'That's assuming somebody took it from where they were sitting, Caitlin. My guess is, it was taken from the bar.'

He had a point. It could have been taken from the bar, and so any number of people could have taken it.

'What should I do, Andy? Block him?'

Andy stared at the screen. 'No, not yet. He already knows where to find you. Let's just see what he posts next. He might give himself away somehow. Follow him back even – he won't be expecting that.'

'I don't know,' she said. 'I'll leave it for now.' She sat back, picking up the mug of tea that was cooling.

Andy pulled out a chair and sat opposite her. 'Look, do you want me to stay tonight? I'm not comfortable leaving you. I can pull out the camp bed ...'

Caitlin nodded. She hadn't let anyone stay over before, even when she was distraught in the weeks after David's disappearance. She preferred to be alone, but now she was glad of Andy's offer. There was little chance she'd sleep that night, but at least she wouldn't have to worry that the person who'd taken that picture had followed her home.

Chapter Eighteen

Michelle

Michelle pulled up outside Nick's house. She was early, and she wondered if he'd be home. He'd told her that he had a meeting with a potential client and that it might be six o'clock before he got in. Recently, he'd given her a key; in case of emergencies, he'd said, and they both knew what that meant.

She rang the doorbell and waited. Rowdy began to the bark in the back room, but there was no sound of Nick coming to answer. She thought about the key in her bag and wondered if she should use it. Better to text him – tell him she'd arrived. He might be annoyed if she just let herself in. It was starting to rain. She went back to the car and texted him.

Got here early. You on the way?

The phone blipped a minute later:

Caught here for another half hour – let yourself in? xx

She searched in the bag for the key that he'd given her. Things must have been going well with the client if the meeting had run late. She was glad. Nick needed something to occupy his mind. He loved designing houses, she knew that. He'd showed her that house he'd built for that singer. And a photo of the hexagon in

Dalkey; Nick's dream house. She wondered how he could bear now to live in a housing estate, but he'd said that it was temporary – that when he and Susan had separated, he'd wanted somewhere fast. In the future, when he bought land, he'd design another house and rent this property out.

Michelle pushed the door open and stepped into the hall. It was warm. Rowdy started to kick up a fuss; she could hear him scratching against the door, and when she opened it, he put his paws on her chest, almost knocking her over. She put him down and stooped to cuddle him. Nick had got custody of Rowdy when he'd divorced from his wife, who unlike Michelle, didn't care for dogs. She wouldn't have the dog in the house, Nick had told her, and had made him put a kennel in the garden. Michelle was the opposite. She'd have had Rowdy sleeping in the bed with them, but even Nick drew the line at that.

Michelle went upstairs. She'd begun leaving a bag of her stuff in the bedroom again, and she pulled out her slippers, kicked off her shoes and left them neatly by the bed. Everything was neat in Nick's house. It was something they joked about. Towels went into the washing machine after every shower; the bedclothes were changed at least twice a week. She sometimes thought he had a touch of OCD he was so particular about things. But at least he could laugh at himself. He'd told her he'd been thinking of letting a room to a friend who was having trouble finding a place, but when he'd mentioned it, his friend had turned him down, saying that he couldn't even eat in Nick's house without the plate being whipped from under him the minute he'd finished and Nick appearing with a cloth to wipe up the crumbs.

Michelle looked round the room. She'd stayed over so often now that she could visualize every aspect of it when she wasn't there. There were the bundles of loose change that Nick kept on the windowsill, the branch of pussy willow in a glass jar, so out of keeping with everything else. She wondered why he kept it. His desk had a pen holder and a calculator, no papers or books strewn across its top as there were on her small desk in the apartment. All of Nick's papers and drawings were filed neatly in the cabinet beneath the desk. He'd shown her some of the designs he kept there.

Michelle noticed that the blue light of Nick's computer was on: he hadn't shut it down completely. She figured he wouldn't mind if she checked her mail, so she clicked the mouse to rouse it. The computer whirred, and the screen came on. At the top of the screen, several windows were open. Michelle clicked on one of them and suddenly she was looking at a photo of a dark-haired woman. She wasn't looking at the camera; it looked like the picture had been taken when she was unaware. There was something on the woman's lap. Michelle looked closer and discovered that it was a case of some sort, maybe for a musical instrument. She began to feel queasy. She clicked on the next photo; it was a house, the hexagon that Nick had told her about: the house that he'd designed for his father-in-law and that he'd shared for a number of years with his wife. There was nothing else that would cause her to question anything, only the picture of the woman.

She went back to it, right clicked on the file to access its details. When she saw that it had been taken only two days before, her worries amplified. She thought back to yesterday's phone call. When she'd asked Nick what he'd done the night before, he'd said he'd gone to bed early. Michelle sat back and chewed on her thumbnail. She didn't want to snoop. She should just ask Nick who the woman was, tell him that she'd opened the computer to check her mail. It wasn't as if she was hiding anything. If she didn't look properly though, who knew when she'd get another chance? Checking her watch, and listening for any noise downstairs, Michelle accessed Nick's browsing history. He hadn't erased his cookies, why would he? Nobody looked at the computer but him. Michelle trawled through the recent sites, her confusion growing. She scanned an archived newspaper article about a murder-suicide from 1980, skimming through the details. She was about to click on another link, Nick's Twitter account, when she heard the front door open. Rapidly, she returned the computer to sleep mode, and appeared at the top of the stairs just as Nick called her name.

'Hey. Sorry, I got delayed,' he said.

Michelle forced a smile. 'How did it go?'

'Really well. I got the contract, just a few details to be worked out.' He grinned and pulled her into a hug.

Who was the woman in the picture? She looped her arms round his neck, trying to put it out of her mind for the moment, and pulled him close. It was good to see him smiling again. When they met, he'd smiled all the time. She'd told him he was one of the most cheerful people she'd ever met. It was one of the things that had attracted her to him, his positive attitude. But what was he hiding from her?

'That's great,' she said. 'Really great.'

They walked into the living room, his arm still around her. Rowdy ran in circles round him. He stooped to fondle the dog's ears. 'Now, I didn't get a chance to get any food in, so we can either order in and watch a movie, or I can get cleaned up and we can head out for a bite?' Nick playacted with the dog, rolling him over and scratching his belly. Michelle wondered how she could ask him about the woman without spoiling his mood. He'd given her no reason to mistrust him. She decided to ignore the picture and ask about the article instead. That way he'd know that there was every chance she'd seen the picture too.

'Nick, I booted up your computer to check my mail. I hope you don't mind – there was an article about a murder – I wasn't snooping …' she added quickly.

Nick's smile was gone. He stood up, and without looking at her, crossed to the window. 'Did you read it?' he said.

'I scanned through it,' she said. 'The headline caught my attention. I was just wondering about it …'

Nick turned to face her. 'I think we'd better sit down,' he said.

Chapter Nineteen

Nick

Nick sat at the table and Michelle sat opposite him. 'This is going to sound really bizarre,' he said. 'Although maybe not to you because you believe in this sort of thing.' His intonation rose on the word believe, unable to keep his old scepticism out of his voice, even though now he absolutely believed what he was about to say. And she would too, that was what worried him.

'You know how I've been having hypnosis?'

Michelle nodded.

'Something strange happens every time I go under. I become someone else.'

'What do you mean?'

'The hypnotist told me that it could be something called confabulations – false memories. But I know it's not, that these events I'm seeing really happened.'

'What events?'

Michelle was leaning in towards him, keen to understand. Most people would think he was mad if he told them this story, they'd probably think he'd been having hallucinations related to his illness or his withdrawal. Michelle wouldn't, she'd believe the truth, that he'd slaughtered two people and then taken his own life. She'd believe that he had been Johnny Davis. Even if he still had doubts himself, this was the type of thing that fascinated Michelle.

'The first time I was hypnotized, I found myself in this house ... it wasn't anywhere I knew. It was like watching a film. I looked different, but I knew that it was me ...' He paused and looked at her. 'Michelle, I did something terrible.'

He could see Michelle's mind working, putting it all together, and in a way he was glad that she'd seen that article, that he didn't have to put into words what he'd done.

'You think you're the guy in the article. The murder-suicide ...' Michelle reached out and took his hand. It was unexpected and a relief.

'I know I am,' he said. 'I've had memories of my wife, my daughter ... Her name is Caitlin; she's still out there, Michelle. I tried to kill her, to take her with me ... She was five years old.'

'Is she the woman, the woman in the photo?' Michelle was hesitant.

He'd forgotten that he'd left that file open too. Now he nodded. 'I've seen her. It wasn't hard once I knew her name. I searched the net, found her on Facebook and Twitter. She plays music in a wine bar on Eden Quay. I went there last night. I'm sorry I didn't tell you. It was something I needed to do on my own.'

'Of course.'

Michelle was quiet for a minute. He wondered what she was thinking. 'You'll probably want to go,' he said. 'Get away from me. I wouldn't blame you.'

Michelle shook her head. 'I'm amazed that you believe it, that you don't just take the hypnotist's word ...'

'At the start, I didn't want to believe, but then there were names, dates ... I can't *not* believe it. It feels too real.'

Michelle looked up suddenly. 'What was his name, your name, then?'

'Johnny Davis.'

Michelle nodded. 'Now it makes sense,' she said.

'What does?'

'When you disappeared, when I thought it was over and

couldn't figure out why, I went to see that psychic, the old woman I told you about before. We thought it was a wrong reading, the woman apologized. She'd referred to you as Johnny, said that you were connected to a dark-haired woman and a child. Jesus. I'll bet she was dark, the woman, wasn't she?'

'Yes.'

'That's so strange, isn't it? She'd tapped into that, Nick, she'd tapped into your previous life.'

Nick looked at Michelle, she was excited that the woman's words were true, but he wasn't sure that she fully understood the gravity of what it meant, for both of them.

'Michelle, I killed my wife. Slaughtered her lover and killed her, and then …'

'I know. I know, Nick, but it was a previous incarnation; it's not now, not this life.'

'I left my daughter to deal with that. Five years old and orphaned. I have no idea what her life was like …'

'But she's okay, isn't she? I mean you saw her. She's a musician.'

'It depends what you mean by okay. She's alive, she's out there. I don't know what happened to her after, if there was family that took her in, if she was adopted … I need to know, Michelle. I need to find a way into Caitlin's life, to make up for what I did somehow.'

Michelle took a breath. 'How do you propose to do that? I mean you can't tell her who you are, who you were. She'd think you were crazy.'

'Of course I can't tell her who I am. But if I could find some way to meet her, to talk to her.'

Michelle frowned. 'That won't be easy. Unless a man is in a woman's circle, a colleague, something like that, she'll think he's hitting on her. You said that you saw her profile, did you find out anything about her, any idea what she does apart from playing music?'

'She's a magazine editor. I viewed her profile on LinkedIn.'

Michelle was nodding. 'Okay, that's better. What if I were to write to her, propose writing an article on health and fitness, something like that? A woman's magazine should go for that kind of thing.'

Nick considered this. It certainly wasn't a bad idea as a way of making contact. 'And then what?' he asked.

Michelle shrugged. 'I could try to arrange a meeting with her to discuss the article, try to find some common ground when we meet, befriend her. I'm not saying it would be easy, but it's probably better if I try to make the connection rather than you. If you try and it goes wrong, then it's unlikely you'll get a second chance.'

'I already spoke to her,' he said.

'Oh.' He registered Michelle's look of surprise. 'What did you say?'

'Nothing much. It was at the gig. I sort of accidentally knocked her drink over. It might sound weird, but there was a moment when there was a spark of something, like maybe she knew. She couldn't, of course, it would be ridiculous to think so, but I think she felt something, some kind of recognition. She asked me my name.'

Michelle didn't look happy.

'You think I shouldn't have done it?' he said.

'No ... not necessarily. She could have felt something – some connection, but be careful, Nick. I still think the best thing is if you leave this to me. The last thing you need is her thinking you're some kind of creep.'

Nick winced as he felt a dull pain in his abdomen. He needed this to happen. He knew that he would never be able to give Caitlin back what he'd taken away, but if there was something, anything, he could do to make her life easier, he would.

'I'm sorry, I didn't mean ...'

'No, it's not that. Pain,' he said. 'Some days it's worse than others.'

Michelle reached out to him. 'Are you okay? You-you haven't drunk anything?'

'No, ten days and counting ... only another twenty-three weeks to go, give or take ...' He smiled, trying to lighten the mood again, as the pain subsided.

Michelle got up and put her arms around him. She didn't tell him that it would be okay. She'd never be that flippant. He'd told her the worst and she was still here. He knew that she'd do everything she could to help him. He just hoped that it wouldn't all be in vain, that she wouldn't be the one to suffer in the end.

Michelle pulled back and kissed him. 'Okay, show me this LinkedIn profile,' she said. 'Maybe I can find an email address on it. If not, at least we can find out the name of the magazine and I can call the office tomorrow.'

'Okay, we'll try it your way. God forbid she'd think me a creep.'

'Oh God, Nick, I didn't mean it that way ... it's just, you know how it is – strange man starts talking to a pretty girl in a bar ...'

'Who said she was pretty?'

'No one, I just assumed. Is she?'

Nick laughed. 'She's my daughter, Michelle. Not in this life, but she's still my daughter. Now you really are making me sound creepy. Come on, I'll show you any info I was able to find about her.' He took her hand and led her to the stairs, amazed that she was still here, and she was willing to help him.

Chapter Twenty

Caitlin

When Caitlin woke, it was to the sound of rattling delft and cupboards being closed below in the kitchen. She lay on her back and for those first few seconds she thought that it was David, her brain in its sleep-filled fug cancelling out the last year. Then she remembered the previous night, and that it was Andy who was moving about in the room downstairs.

She grabbed her phone from the bedside table, saw that it was just five minutes before her alarm usually went off. Now she disabled it, pulled on a cardigan and went downstairs.

'Hey, how are you doing?' Andy was sitting at the table. Before him, a rack of toast and an almost-full pot of coffee. Her place was set with a cereal bowl, a spoon and her mug, the one David had bought her with a cartoon cat on it.

'Figured you wouldn't have much time before work,' Andy said, seeing her eye the setup.

'I don't usually take breakfast,' she said. Rather than being grateful, his act, of what she would later reason was kindness, made her angry instead. It wasn't his fault he wasn't David. She just wished so much that he was. 'I'm going to take a shower,' she said. 'I assume you need to get going, so you can let yourself out when you're done.' She turned and walked out of the kitchen before Andy had a chance to say anything in return.

When she came out of the shower, she listened for any sound

downstairs. Hearing none, she figured Andy must have left, but minutes later as she dressed for work she heard the surge of the tap, the sound of Andy washing up his breakfast things. She wished that he would just leave, surprised by her resentment – but all his presence did was remind her of all the things she missed since David had gone.

'Caitlin?' He called her name twice before she answered. She could picture him standing at the bottom of the stairs. It wasn't his fault, she thought. He didn't deserve this.

'Yes?' she said, walking to the bedroom door.

'I'm heading off. If you need anything, just call me.'

'Thanks, I will.' Relief, as she heard the front door bang behind him.

When Andy had gone, she went downstairs. He'd cleaned up his breakfast things, but left her place set as it had been. She poured a mug of coffee, it was still hot. She sat at the table, booted up her computer and shook cornflakes into her bowl. On Twitter, she searched for and found the picture that had been taken in the wine bar the previous night. David A had not uploaded anything since, and she sat there staring at the image of herself, looking to one side, her violin case on her knee. Who had taken it?

She scrolled back, once again, through the few tweets on David A's profile, tried to think logically about what someone might have to gain by impersonating her husband. She could think of nothing except that they wished to confuse her, to set her on edge. Last night, they'd certainly achieved that goal. She'd been glad of Andy's offer to stay over, had slept all night knowing that she wasn't alone, that she was safe from whoever it was that was playing games with her. With that thought came regret about the way she had responded this morning to Andy's being there.

She remembered the message she'd received from Dar Bryan. She opened it now. It was short, a simple apology for not having replied ... and a few lines to say that he'd appreciated her listening.

Nothing to suggest that he was the creep who was impersonating David, but then how could she know for sure?

Caitlin looked at the clock, gulped down the last of her coffee and put her mug in the sink. She thought of the man who had been at the gig the night before, the one Andy had been suspicious of. Nick, he'd said his name was. She'd had a strange sensation that she knew him, felt the oddest pull towards him. She could understand why Andy was suspicious, but she'd felt no discomfort, had detected no malice in his presence. Instead, she'd wanted him to speak to her, had felt disappointed when he'd returned to his table after exchanging just a few words. Her gut response to him had surprised her. It wasn't that she felt attracted to him, she hadn't felt like that about any man since she'd met David, and even less so since he'd been gone. She'd felt something though, an urge to talk to this stranger, who could, she reasoned, be anybody, could, as Andy suspected, be the man who was watching her. And yet, incomprehensibly, she was sure he wasn't.

Caitlin arrived late at the office. She sat at her desk and opened her email. There were several articles that had been forwarded to her that needed approval. She'd be stuck there late no doubt, but she didn't mind. It was better to cram her head with work, leave no space for other things. First, she'd check just one more time. She logged into Twitter, clicked again on David A's account. Nothing new. She thought about what Andy had said, to follow his profile and see what happened. She hovered the cursor over the button, thought of the message that would appear in the man's notifications: *@CaitlinDavis is following you.*

Click. Now she'd wait and see what he did next.

'Caitlin?' She looked up to see her assistant, Jenny, standing in the doorway. 'Noelle Travors has withdrawn that article she sent us on near-death experiences. Apparently, she got a better offer.'

Caitlin shook her head. 'Right. Next time she sends something, reject it. She's a pain to deal with, and frankly, I think we can do better. There was an interesting one about obesity in children, run that instead.'

'Right-o. Everything else is on track.'

Caitlin turned back to the screen as Jenny returned to her desk. New tweets scrolled before her. Her attention was caught by one from Dar Bryan – a retweet of an appeal for a missing man. Caitlin clicked on the link.

Chris Hoey was last seen leaving his staff Christmas party in the Russell Court Hotel in Harcourt Street in 2012. New CCTV footage had placed Chris talking with a man outside a twenty-four-hour garage in Ranelagh. Gardaí hoped that this new information would jog someone's memory. They said that they were anxious to talk to the man who'd spoken to Chris on the forecourt that night.

Caitlin retweeted @darbryan1's tweet and logged out of her account. What chance was there that anyone would come forward with information? Slim, she guessed. People didn't want to become involved, didn't want to be embroiled in someone else's problem. She knew that only too well.

For the next few hours, Caitlin worked steadily. She read through articles, approved them or returned proofs to Jenny. She was entirely absorbed when the receptionist, Maeve, appeared at the door, smiling, carrying a bouquet of pink and white flowers.

'Special occasion?' Maeve said, coming into the office and holding the bouquet out to Caitlin.

'No. Are you sure they're for me?'

'Yep, the envelope says so.' Caitlin stood up to take the flowers.

'Will I get you something to put them in? I think there's a vase in the canteen ...'

'Yes, if you wouldn't mind,' Caitlin smiled. Anything to get Maeve out of the office. As soon as she was gone, she looked at the envelope. Her name was there in black ink written in a cursive hand, the florist's probably. She opened it and withdrew the small card with gold-embossed edges.

For Caitlin – in admiration always … x.

Seeing Maeve return, she shoved the card back into the envelope, forcing a smile as Maeve fussed with the flowers, positioning them in the vase.

'Beautiful, aren't they?' she said. Caitlin agreed, knowing that Maeve was hoping she'd expand on that and tell her who they were from. At least she had the tact not to ask. Maeve had only worked for the magazine for six months, but she figured the girls would have filled her in about her circumstances. Everyone loved a good tragedy. As soon as Maeve had exited the office, Caitlin took the card from its envelope again, closed the office door and phoned the number of the florist.

Chapter Twenty-One

Michelle

Michelle couldn't sleep that night after all that Nick had told her. And in the early hours of the morning she rose, sat down at her laptop and typed in the names of John and Rachel Davis. After some scrolling, she found the newspaper story that she'd seen on Nick's computer and read it again. She had told Nick that it didn't matter, that it was a different life, that he was a different person, but she wasn't sure if she really believed that herself. Curious about Caitlin, and whether Johnny might have any other living relatives, she searched for and found a copy of his obituary. 'Survived', it said, 'by his father, Dr Maurice Davis, his mother Celine, sister Lydia, and daughter, Caitlin. John Davis had been waked at his family home and had been removed to Saint Brigid's Church in Castleknock.

Caitlin paused. If Johnny's father had been a doctor, there was the possibility that he had worked at home. A lot of doctors had in those days. She opened a new search engine and typed in the doctor's name and *Castleknock*. Instantly, the surgery's address appeared. Michelle grabbed a pen and scribbled down the details. She then looked at the other sites that the search engine had brought up: Dr Maurice Davis had died in 2010, aged 86. He was survived by his daughter, Lydia. It was a long shot, but there was every possibility that Lydia Davis still lived in the family home.

Michelle went back to bed after her search, managed to catch some broken sleep, and then rose early with two things on her mind. First, she would call Caitlin Davis's magazine and propose writing an article, and then she would make her way out to Castleknock to see if she could find Lydia. If anyone could tell her what Johnny Davis had been like before the murder-suicide, it was his sister.

At ten o'clock, Michelle tapped in the number of *New Woman* and asked to speak to Caitlin. She was asked to hold the line, followed by the drone of elevator music. The previous evening, as she and Nick had browsed Caitlin's profiles on social media, she'd changed her plan of writing an article about health and fitness: it was too run-of-the-mill. They probably ran articles about it every other week. Caitlin's tweets were about missing persons and human rights, so it was far more likely that an article about homelessness would appeal to her. And given recent events, Michelle had a strong urge to write one.

'Hello. Can I help you?' the voice was bright, upbeat.

'Hi, am I speaking with Caitlin Davis?'

'No, this is Jenny. I'm the assistant editor. What can I do for you?'

Disappointment. The assistant editor: of course it was too much to think that she'd have got directly through to Caitlin. She probably received hundreds of calls every day, most of them fielded by her assistant. Never mind, it was a starting point. She could only hope that the subject would interest Caitlin enough to enable her to speak to her directly later on. She launched into her proposal with Jenny, who made encouraging sounds and asked if she could put her proposal in writing and send it directly to her. Michelle did more than that. As soon as she started writing, she discovered that it was easier for her to write the article than to sum it up in a few sentences.

She began by explaining her reasons for volunteering with the Simon Community. She talked about the people she'd met in her years of working with those who'd fallen through society's cracks, wound up by lamenting the loss of the man who had died outside the government offices, hoped that his tragic death would bring to light the seriousness of the homelessness crisis to a seemingly blind Establishment. She read over her work, satisfied that the article said everything she felt was necessary, that the language was as concise as she could make it. She felt a frisson of excitement as she attached it to the email, which she hoped would satisfy the assistant editor and make its way onto Caitlin Davis's desk.

Rather than sit around and wait for a response, she decided to tackle the second thing on her list: she grabbed her car keys and drove out to Castleknock, where she hoped she would find Lydia Davis.

An hour or so later, as Caitlin turned into the estate, she slowed down to check the address again. A left brought her onto the avenue, and she drove slowly past the row of identical houses, scanning the numbers on the doors for number ten. A middle-aged woman out sweeping leaves from her driveway stopped to lean on the brush and watch her go past. Michelle slowed to a stop. Number ten was two doors down from the sweeper, whose eyes followed her in curiosity.

Without looking at the woman, Michelle got out of the car and walked up to the front door. The house was well-kept, the owner had made an attempt to make it look different from their neighbours' by changing what seemed to be the standard front door. They'd had the windows replaced too with brown double glazing adorned with a stained-glass rose in each of the small opening sashes. The person who lived here had aspirations above this old estate.

Michelle rang the bell and waited for an answer. She'd rehearsed what she'd wanted to say, but still she had no idea how the woman might react to her. Didn't most people shun journalists, close doors in their faces with a no comment? She braced herself as she heard a noise within, tried to arrange her face into not quite a smile, but a friendly demeanour.

'Yes?' She knew immediately that the woman who opened the door was not Lydia Davis. She was too young, not much older than she was. Her daughter perhaps?

'Hi, I'm looking to speak to a Mrs Davis … Lydia?'

'I'm afraid you won't find her here. I've been living here for almost ten years. I did get bills in the beginning addressed to someone by the name of Davis, but I've no idea where she moved to.'

Disappointed, Michelle thanked the woman, and walked back down the driveway. Lydia could be anywhere. She could be dead for all she knew.

'Miss?'

Michelle looked up, startled, to see the woman with the sweeping brush beckon her.

'I couldn't help but hear … you said you were looking for Lydia?'

Michelle nodded. 'That's right. Do you know how I might get in touch with her?'

The woman looked at her keenly. 'Are you a relative?' she asked.

'It's related to a family matter,' Michelle answered.

The woman nodded. 'You'll find Lydia living out on the old Ashbourne Road. She has a mobile home out there. Doesn't mix with no one. It's Bill Thornton's land, but he doesn't mind, let's her stay there. She's been there near on a decade now.'

Michelle tried not to look surprised. 'Can you tell me where it is exactly?' she asked.

She listened, attempted to make a mental record as the woman gave her some convoluted directions out to Thornton's field. She got the general gist, but knew she'd have to stop for directions on the way.

The young one working in the service station didn't know anything about Thornton's field.

'Never heard of him,' she said, chewing gum disinterestedly as she took the coins for a bottle of Coke that Michelle didn't want and counted out her change. A man came out from the back of the shop just as she was about to turn away from the counter, and she tried her luck again.

'Bill Thornton?' the man said. 'About two miles out the road there. Keep on till you pass the Bell Tower; the house is away over the field, but it's the first one you'll come to.'

Michelle thanked him, took a long swallow of the Coke seeing as she had it, and got back behind the wheel. Before long, she came upon the pub the man had told her about, and shortly after she spotted Lydia Davis's mobile home in the field. Beyond it, a long way off the road, stood Bill Thornton's white house.

Michelle pulled in as close to the farm gate as she could and checked her mirror before stepping out. The place, which she imagined was once all fields, now ran parallel to a dangerously busy road. She pulled back the bolt on the gate and followed a track worn in the grass to the door of the mobile home. As she drew nearer she heard a radio playing inside, but she could see nothing through the net curtains that shaded the small windows. She tapped on the door, stood back and waited. A shuffle of steps and the door was pulled open. The woman who stood before her looked older than she'd expected. She squinted at Michelle with suspicion.

'Yes?'

'I'm looking to speak to Lydia Davis?'

'What do you want?' There was no hint of anything akin to friendliness in the brusque voice.

Michelle pushed on. 'I was hoping to talk to you about your brother, Johnny ... about what happened in the eighties. I'm writing an article about domestic crimes ... what might lead to such terrible events ...'

'I've nothing to say about it,' the woman told her. 'Thought I'd seen the last of you lot. You just can't leave it alone, can you?'

Before Michelle had a chance to say anything more, the woman had slammed the door and gone back inside.

'I'm sorry, I didn't come to upset you,' Michelle called through the door. 'I simply wanted to find out what Johnny was like … I'm not here to judge anyone.'

Suddenly, the radio was turned up, drowning out her words. Lydia had made her point. There was nothing more to do but leave.

Michelle hadn't driven a quarter of a mile when a jangling started up from her pocket. With a glance in the mirror, she swerved onto the hard shoulder and grabbed it before it could stop.

'Hi Michelle. This is Caitlin Davis of *New Woman*. I'm just ringing to tell you that we really like your article, and we'd like to run it next week.'

Caitlin. Nick's daughter. This was her chance. 'Hi Caitlin. I'm delighted to hear that. That's great.' Her mind raced, thinking through what she could say to keep Caitlin Davis on the phone, to persuade her to meet.

'I've got some other ideas that I'd like to discuss with you,' she said.

'Oh yes?' There was interest in Caitlin's voice. 'That's good. I'd like to run a series of articles in the coming weeks. Clearly, you've written this from an insider's perspective and it rings true. It tells people what it's really like out there on the streets. I wondered if we could do some follow-ups, maybe you could interview people, tell their stories. They wouldn't have to be named, of course, but to heighten awareness …'

'I'd love to,' Michelle said. 'I'd appreciate the chance … I wonder if it would be possible to meet to discuss it? I'm sure you're very busy, but …'

'No. That would be good. Let me check my calendar, we'll run with this one next Friday, but we could meet before that … maybe this Wednesday, would twelve o'clock suit?'

'Wednesday.' Michelle tried to think that far ahead. If she had anything on, she'd cancel it. This was too important. 'Yes, Wednesday would be great,' she said. 'I look forward to meeting you.'

She was trembling with a mix of adrenalin and excitement when she hung up. She may not have got far with Lydia Davis, but she would have plenty to tell Nick when they met that night.

Chapter Twenty-Two

Nick

'How are you feeling, Nick?' Tessa sat forward in her seat and opened her notepad.

'Better,' he said. 'At least with the cravings.'

'Good. That's great.' She scribbled something on the pad. 'Last time you took alcohol?'

Nick thought for a moment. 'Eleven days ago.' He thought it best not to mention his little slip-up.

'And are you using the techniques, are they helping?'

Nick nodded. 'Yes. I'd say so. I'm back working.'

'That's wonderful, Nick. And how about sleep? Are you sleeping okay? Any nightmares?'

'Not so bad.' He wondered if she noticed his evasiveness.

She didn't say anything, put down her pen and came around to his side of the desk. She smiled. 'You're doing really well, Nick. Now, whenever you're ready, you can take a seat.'

Nick sat back into the recliner. His feelings about being regressed, since he'd met Caitlin, were contradictory. He wanted to go back there, to find out more about his wife, Rachel, and his little girl. At the same time, he was afraid of what the sessions might uncover. He wasn't sure if he could deal with what he might find.

'Relax your limbs, Nick. Let that calm feeling wash over you, taking with it all the tension, all the anxiety …' Tessa's voice, soothing, lulled him backwards in time.

109

His body grew slack as he followed Tessa into the past.

'Okay, I'm going to bring you back slowly, Nick. Bit by bit, we're going to revisit those moments when you felt good – when you didn't rely on alcohol to bring about a false sense of fulfilment.'

His life begins to unravel – moments glimpsed and then swept away again as his memory is set to rewind.

He's back in the house in Dalkey again, sitting outside on the terrace that looks over the sea. It's one of those rare warm days when there isn't a gale blowing across the bay. He's relaxing, earbuds in, listening to music, the sun warm on his face. He doesn't hear Susan come in, jumps when she lays a hand on his arm, and then laughs at his reaction.

'Hey you,' she says.

'Jesus, you gave me a fright,' he says.

'Clearly.' She grins, pulls out the other chair, sits next to him. 'It's not a bad life, is it?' she says.

He smiles. 'Could be worse.'

'Or better,' she says.

He looks at her. She seems in an oddly happy mood. 'Come on,' he says, 'I know you have something to tell me?'

'Well …' She leans in towards him. 'We're going to be parents.'

He sits up, at first, he doesn't know how he feels, then the realization hits him. 'Seriously? My God … when did …?'

'I've suspected for a few weeks, but I didn't want to say anything. I've just been to Doctor Breen and she confirmed it. Roughly eight weeks, she said.'

Susan is looking at him, clearly delighted. She's had more time to get over the shock, of course. He's happy too, at least he thinks he is, but he also feels an overwhelming sense of responsibility.

'You are happy?' she says, frowning.

'Yeah, of course, I mean … wow.' He starts to laugh; his feelings are still ambivalent, but he doesn't want to spoil it for Susan. It's not like they hadn't intended to have a family, they just hadn't intended to start it this soon. They'd always been careful.

'I've got a scan next Thursday. They won't be able to tell the sex yet ... not for another month or two, but ... would you like to know?'

He nods. 'Why not? That way it's easier to prepare, isn't it?' He doesn't know why, but he already feels that it's a girl. With that instinct comes worry, a sense of guilt, and he has no idea why. He would love a girl, would probably be one of those overprotective fathers that wouldn't let any boy so much as look at her. He tries to shake his inexplicable feeling of guilt, of burden. He's going to be a father. This is the glue they need, him and Susan, to really make a life.

'Where are you, Nick?' Tessa's voice intrudes on the scene.

'At home. Susan's come in. She's told me we're going to have a baby.'

'Does that make you happy?'

'Yes.' He's aware even as he says it that it's not entirely true, but it's what people expect him to say. He can't say that he doesn't know. That he needs time to figure out if he's truly happy. And he can't explain this feeling; this sense of foreboding. He tries to reason with himself, thinks that maybe every new parent feels this ... He's still trying to work it out when the scene flashes forward ...

He gets the call at work. It's Susan's friend, Anna, telling him to get to the hospital – that something's happened. He asks her if Susan's okay. 'Just get here,' she says. He checks his mobile: five missed calls from Susan over an hour ago; two more from a number he doesn't recognize. He gets a text from Anna on the way to the hospital giving him the name of the ward and the number of the room Susan is in.

Susan looks terrible. She's not crying when he gets there, but it's clear that she has been. Her face is swollen and red.

'What happened?' he says.

Susan looks at him, stonily. 'This is your fault,' she says.

He is shocked by the venom with which she spews the words. 'What ... the baby?'

111

'Dead,' she says. 'The baby's dead.'

He collapses into the chair that Anna has vacated. She's standing, awkwardly. 'I'll leave you ...' she says.

'Don't.' The word is an order.

'What happened?' he tries again. Susan turns on her side away from him. Anna puts a hand on his arm, mouths something sympathetic, but he shakes her off. 'Where's the doctor?' he says.

He accosts a young Filipino nurse who comes into the ward. 'I want to speak to a doctor.'

'I'm afraid they're on the wards,' she tells him.

'Well, this is a ward, isn't it?' he barks. 'I want to know what happened here.'

'I'll try and call a doctor now,' the nurse tells him, and is immediately called away by another woman buzzing for assistance. He storms out to the nurse's station looking for answers since his wife refuses to even look at him.

'Nick? Are you okay?' Tessa's voice again. He reached towards it, wanted her to take him from that place, from that memory. She hadn't taken him back far enough. She needed to take him back further, to before the bad stuff, before his marriage caved in. Before the blame began.

'Nick ...' Tessa was calling his name, bringing him out of it.

He began to surface as she counted from one to five, her voice soothing. When he opened his eyes, they stung, and he realized that he'd been crying. Embarrassed, he rubbed at his eyes with the sleeve of his sweater. Tessa told him to take his time, asked him if he'd like a glass of water, but he shook his head and told her he was all right.

At the desk, she sat back and looked at him. 'Unfortunately, we can't avoid the bad things, Nick. We need to access them to get to the core of the problem, find out what it is that's making you want to escape through alcohol.'

'She blamed me. The baby died, and Susan blamed me. She said I didn't want it and that the baby knew.'

Tessa nodded. 'I'm sorry, Nick.'

'It seemed irrational, but the doctors said it was normal, that she was taking the trauma out on me. But I knew it was more than that, that she was right. It wasn't that I didn't want the baby, I wanted it more than anything. But I couldn't be that baby's father and I couldn't figure why … now I think I do. It's to do with the past. I must have known, in my subconscious, what had happened … what I'd done to Rachel and Caitlin.'

Tessa leaned her elbows on the desk, looked at him from over the steeple of her fingers. She didn't say anything, forced him to go on.

'I didn't know,' he said again. 'But what happened before, it's part of what tore my marriage apart. I was afraid that if I had another child …'

She waited until he had trailed off. 'What happened after the miscarriage, Nick?'

'Susan came home from the hospital. She barely spoke to me for weeks. We skirted round one another. Then she said that we should try again, that she wanted a baby. I didn't know if it was a good idea – I thought she was trying to replace the dead child. I told her maybe we ought to wait, give it time. She accused me again of not wanting a child, and I gave in, thought it might be the only thing that would fix us. I needn't have worried. Nothing happened after that. We tried for months, and nothing.'

'Did either of you talk to anyone at the time – a counsellor?'

'No.'

'And Susan … do you talk now? Did your marriage end amicably?'

Nick looked at his hands. 'Not exactly. Things got worse. I started staying out, avoided going home. We don't really keep in touch. She texts sometimes, sends a card at Christmas. I think she's met someone. I hope she has.'

Tessa tapped the pen on the pad. She hadn't written anything while he was talking. 'You could be right, Nick,' she said.

He looked at her. 'What about?'

'The past – what happened before affecting your decisions in this life.'

'You do believe that it's true then – that it's not just confabulation?'

'It's a possibility, Nick. And if that's the case, we must let the memories come. I checked the dates, the circumstances. It's not something I'm comfortable with ... not something that should have happened, but it has and there doesn't seem to be another explanation for it. I don't want you to repress it – or to try to keep it from me if something further happens in these sessions. I'm not encouraging you to actively pursue it either, I want you to understand that. But hypnosis is about uncovering the suppressed, and if the problems in your previous life are the underlying cause of your alcoholism, then they need to be acknowledged – and I'm willing to do that.'

Tessa sat back after this long speech, asking Nick if he understood.

'Thank you,' he said. 'Don't think I'm comfortable with it either, but I need to find out everything.'

'What's your schedule like next week?' she asked. 'Does Monday work for you?'

'Monday? Sure,' he said. That was only three days away. Clearly, Tessa thought the quicker they dealt with the past, the sooner he could be healed.

Chapter Twenty-Three

Caitlin

The florist hadn't been able to tell Caitlin anything. An order had been placed over the phone; the message delivered as it had been dictated by the caller. 'Well, how did he pay for them?' Caitlin had asked. 'He must have given you the name on his debit or credit card?'

'I'm sorry, we can't give out that kind of information,' the woman had told her.

Damn her to hell, Caitlin thought as she hung up. It was there on file, of course, if anyone ever decided to take her seriously. She couldn't phone the guards and tell them that someone had anonymously sent her flowers though, they'd laugh at her.

She'd kept the flowers, not because she wanted them, but because she was afraid that in discarding them, she might get rid of a clue – something that would lead her to the person that had sent them. It was impossible, she knew. What would she find among the bouquet apart from the card? Regardless, they stood now in a vase in the hall and were the first thing she saw when she came through the door. If only they were from David, but she knew that they couldn't be.

And then there was Andy. She felt bad about the way she'd spoken to him. He'd stayed over to make sure she was okay, and she'd repaid him with cold indifference, no, not even that, what she'd shown that morning was contempt. She took out her phone to text him, then changed her mind. A text was too impersonal, a cop out from having to talk to him. She'd call him as soon as she could, much as she didn't feel like talking.

She had never been one to have a large circle of friends, instead getting fixed on one person. David had been that person from the moment they'd started going out. She hadn't pursued him, hadn't needed to. She'd stayed distant enough to lure him and it wasn't long until she'd had him hooked. She hadn't been good at keeping in touch with the few friends she had and so it had been natural that Andy was the one she'd turned to – their mutual friend. Someone who cared for David almost as much as she did. Others had of course been concerned about David's disappearance, at least in the beginning. Weren't people always interested in tragedy, in the novelty of it?

She remembered when the other kids had found out that she was adopted. She'd been five years old and had gone to live in a new neighbourhood where she knew no one. Her parents had been dead only a few months and she'd been trying hard to get used to her new home and to the woman who had adopted her – she always felt it was the woman who had adopted her, the man gave her no reason to believe that he'd ever wanted her. When he left just a year after she'd gone to live with them, she wasn't sorry, but then the woman began to act differently too. She was cold, withdrawn, and Caitlin felt that she blamed her for the man leaving. When she thought about it now, she wondered that they had ever passed the stringent tests that couples were put through before they were finally allowed to adopt. The process itself took a minimum of two years, which had given them plenty of time to think about it.

The kids at school had been interested, wanted to know who she was and where she came from, and what had happened to her parents. She told them that her parents had died in an accident – that was what the adults had told her – and she was too little to understand anything else. She'd only discovered the truth

116

by accident, searching one day through a box of papers in Violet's room, she'd found them – newspaper cuttings that told the real story. She was twelve years old at the time, old enough to understand, but with too many years of ingrained love for her parents to change her mind about them. For years, she'd comforted herself with memories of the three of them – herself and her mother and father – a happy family. The violence of their deaths stunned her, didn't tally at all with the people she'd known as her parents.

The couple who adopted her had lost a little girl. Caitlin had seen the photos the first time she'd gone to the house, and she'd thought that she was going to have a new sister. She wasn't sure how she felt about that, but there was no other child. She had died, been taken from them suddenly with a fever. She was the replacement, the same age as the little girl, Becky, had been when she'd died. They looked quite alike – both dark-haired, blue-eyed girls. It was the reason she'd been chosen. The woman had chosen her to continue where Becky had stopped, but she was different from Becky, and the man despised her for it.

Life continued with the woman. She wasn't unkind to her, but she was distant. And maybe she was right in blaming Caitlin for the man's leaving – though she couldn't think what she might have done to make him dislike her. As an adult, she'd decided that she wasn't to blame, that the man would have left anyway, that whatever had existed between the man and the woman had been torn asunder by the grief they'd suffered.

She didn't refer to the woman as 'mother' even though she'd told her to. Caitlin already had a mother and no stranger was ever going to take her place. She didn't address her as anything until she was twelve when she began to call her Violet.

Violet didn't object to this. She'd long given up hope of replacing Becky. She did her duties mechanically, fed and clothed Caitlin, gave her a good education. They got on well enough, but at a distance. They were neither family nor friends. Nowadays, Caitlin kept in touch with Violet, but infrequently. They didn't have much to talk about, and she phoned her only as a duty. There were far worse fates that could have befallen her if Violet had not adopted her. What she felt for her most was a sense of pity that nothing she wanted had come to her. When the man left, no one else had come along, so it was just the two of them. She supposed that Violet was glad of her for company, but she never particularly showed it. They were two strangers thrown together by their equally ill circumstances, but no feelings of warmth grew between them as they might have done.

Over time, the children at school teased her about being adopted. Whereas in the beginning they were curious, sympathetic even, their knowledge turned to ammunition whenever a childish disagreement broke out. She remembered the chants of 'Go home and tell your mammy' and then 'she can't, her mammy's dead'. Those were tough times, but she never told Violet. Instead, she ignored the jibes and stayed with her one friend – a girl called Linda Doherty who'd sat next to her on her first day. They'd remained friends until they'd parted ways to go to different secondary schools, and in time their friendship, too, had fizzled out.

Caitlin opened the door to see the flowers on the hall table. She sighed and went upstairs to change into her jogging clothes. She thought of the friends she and David had spent time with, those who'd disappeared not even six months after he had – a gradual withdrawal, unreturned calls. When she realized that she was the one making all the effort, that it was she who initiated every meeting, she stopped, and the phone, for the most part, remained silent. Only Andy and Gillian called consistently to make sure that she was okay.

Andy. She flopped down cross-legged on the bed and picked up the phone. It'd be best to get it over with. She wanted to apologize before Wednesday came around again and she had to face him. Wednesdays had been the best day of the week for her over the past six months – the social element was good for her, as much as she felt like locking herself away. But now there was the person masquerading as David on Twitter to worry about. Would he be there again this week? And what could she do about it? She wasn't going to change her habits because of some creep who thought he'd scare her. She wasn't going to be intimidated like that.

Andy's phone rang out. She sat on the edge of the bed and pulled her runners on. She'd just reached the bottom of the stairs when the phone rang. She sat down on the steps and answered.

'How are you doing?' Andy sounded chirpy, typical of him to ignore the fact that she'd insulted him. Sometimes he was too nice; she'd prefer if he stood up for himself, told her she had no right to talk to him like that, no matter what she was going through. She tried to focus on that rather than allow his passivity to irk her. Otherwise, she'd end up lashing out at him again before she'd even had a chance to say she was sorry.

'Look Andy, I want to apologize. I was awful to you yesterday.'

He made some dismissive sound but didn't deny it.

'No one's stayed over since David's been gone. When I heard you downstairs, there were a few seconds when I thought it was him, and then … ugh, look, it's no excuse, you were there for me, you didn't deserve that …'

'Forget it, Caitie. It's fine. I figured I'd crossed the line.'

'No … look, you've listened to me go on and on … don't think I don't appreciate that. You're the only one who has, apart from Gillian.'

'Did you get the flowers?'

She didn't answer straight away. 'That was you?' she asked.

'Sure, didn't you get the card?'

'No, I mean, yeah, but there was no name on it. I rang the florist's. They wouldn't give me any information. But why were you sending me flowers anyway?'

'It was your birthday, wasn't it? But hang on, what did it say on the card?'

119

'It said, "with admiration always …" No name on it.'

'That's not what I put, they must have mixed up the cards. I just told them to put: *Happy birthday, your friend, Andy*."

She took a breath, aware that he could probably hear her irritation on the other end. 'My birthday's not till next week. Anyway, there was no need to send me flowers. I thought they were from him; whoever that creep is pretending to be David.'

'Oh Jesus, I'm sorry, Caitie. I can imagine … bloody florist. I'll call them tomorrow …'

Caitlin sighed. 'There's no need, it's just a stupid mistake. But Andy, please … don't send me flowers. I'm-I'm not comfortable with that.'

'What? Can't a friend send flowers? What's wrong with that?' He sounded annoyed. 'I thought it was your birthday.'

'It's not that, it's …'

'I'm not trying to take David's place, Caitie, if that's what you think. I'm just being a friend.'

Caitlin closed her eyes. 'That's fine,' she said. 'As long as you know that's all it can ever be. I'm not saying you want anything else, it's just it's better to say it now rather than risk any misunderstandings …'

'Oh, don't worry. It's loud and clear, Caitlin. No flowers – nothing that might be misinterpreted …'

'For God's sake, Andy. I'm trying to be straight here. I'm sorry if I've bruised your ego.'

He laughed but it was a harsh sound. 'I think you might be the one that's got the wrong end of the stick … I care about you, Caitie. I cared about David and that's why I look out for you. I'm not making any moves here … I've never thought of you like that. To be frank, you're not my type.'

His words, so unexpected, stung. She didn't believe him – there had been signs, particularly in the last few months – but if she wanted to keep him as a friend, she'd have to take him at his word.

'Well, that's good then. I didn't mean to insult you, Andy, but it's a relief to get things out in the open. Now we both know where we stand.'

He didn't answer, and she figured the best thing would be to wrap up the call. She tried to sound less curt, get back to the reason she'd called. 'Anyway, I just wanted to tell you I felt bad about the other morning. I was grateful you stayed. I'd better let you go, I'm just on my way out for a run. I'll see you Wednesday?'

'Sure, yeah, Wednesday.'

She hung up, knowing that she'd angered him, but glad she'd set things straight.

Chapter Twenty-Four

Michelle

Michelle and Nick had stayed up late talking about all that had happened. She'd begun by telling him about finding the address for Dr Maurice Davis, and then about going out to the old Davis house, which had led her to Lydia's mobile home out in Thornton's field.

He was quiet when she told him that she'd gone out there.

'What were you hoping to find out?' he'd asked.

And she knew that he'd sensed her doubts, but she managed to persuade him that it was for his sake, not hers. 'I wanted to find out what Johnny was really like before any of it happened,' she told him. 'Find out what drove him to do what he did.'

Nick had taken her hand, told her that she didn't have to stay with him.

She'd told him then about Caitlin, and about the meeting she'd managed to set up, and he was too surprised and impressed by the fact that she'd pulled it off to dwell on her visit to Lydia. It was the first step, she told him. Her intention was to get to know everything about Caitlin Davis, and that way allay some of his guilt about the past.

On Friday, Michelle's article would be published in *New Woman*, and she decided to impress Caitlin by getting a head start on the article she'd mentioned about interviewing the homeless in the streets. She showed the article to the leaders at the

Simon Community and told them about Caitlin's request for the follow-up with more personal stories. The woman in charge, Clare, had agreed at once, telling her that as long as she didn't mention any names, and she explained to the people she interviewed exactly what she was doing, she could go ahead – it was the kind of exposure the crisis needed, especially after the death of poor Dan.

Clare sent another volunteer out to work with Conor that evening. Michelle would go with them too, but if she found someone willing to talk to her about their situation, she'd stay behind and catch up with the other volunteers at a later point.

The first person she spoke to told her he'd been on the streets for almost a year. His mother had died and without him knowing had made a will leaving the house he lived in to his brother. The brother had forced him to move out, sold the house and gave him nothing. He'd told him he could stay with him and his wife for a few months until he'd sorted something out, but the man refused. He had his pride, he told her, and the underhand way his brother had convinced his mother to sign the house over to him sickened him so much that he couldn't even look at him anymore.

Michelle sat down next to the man, listened to him speak. 'But why did your mother put the house in his name only?' she asked, gently.

'Trickery,' the man said. 'I used to have my own place – well, my wife's place. We'd moved into her parents' house after her mother had passed. Kevin and his girlfriend were renting – throwing away more than a thousand a month on a one-bed flat in Rathmines. He convinced the mother that I was doing well, that I had a roof over my head, no mortgage 'cause Angie's parents had bought the house. And I *was* doing well for a while, but sure no one can tell what way the future will go. Angie got sick of me – found a new fella – wanted me out of the house, and so I moved in with the ma. Of course, I had no idea what the brother had done – that he'd screwed me over.'

'And what about your wife? Does she know you're living like this?'

'Agh, we haven't spoken in two years. She probably thinks I'm still in the mother's –probably thinks the house came to me – nothing to do with her anyway.'

'But wouldn't you be entitled to something from the house you shared with your wife, the house you were both living in?'

The man shook his head. 'It was her parents, I'd take nothing off her. It's her inheritance, not mine. And besides, the only thing we could do would be to sell it, and neither one of us could buy anything with half the money. Your man is up there now, instated as if it were his. No shame.'

'And what about the government? Couldn't you apply for social housing?'

'Ha! Do you know how long that list is?' he said. 'I wouldn't even be entitled to the dole because I don't have a permanent address.'

Michelle nodded sympathetically. She knew all this, knew too that most people would rather be in the street than stay in a hostel. It was safer outdoors, at least safer than being in a room full of junkies.

'Would you mind me telling your story? I wouldn't mention your name, of course. Show people that there are plenty of genuine cases, people who shouldn't be in a predicament like yours.'

'Sure,' he said. 'Doubt it'll have much effect, no one gives a damn. But you're good for trying, for doing this. If it weren't for people like you, like the Simon, we'd be a lot worse off.'

Not everyone Michelle met wanted to talk. There were the ones covered in their sleeping bags that she let be, others were drunk or stoned, and then there were people who just wanted to be left in peace, who had no intention of talking to anyone who wanted to print something about them.

The numbers by which homelessness had increased in the last few years were staggering. The queues that formed outside

124

the GPO every night at the soup kitchen were getting longer.

Michelle looked at her watch. She'd spent a long time talking to the man who'd been tricked in the will. She'd need to talk to at least three others with diverse stories if she were to show the reality of homelessness. She wouldn't gloss over it. If there was someone with an addiction who was willing to speak, she'd talk to them too. She wouldn't discount anyone.

The next girl she spoke to was in her twenties. She told her she'd only been on the streets a few weeks. 'Me whole family are addicts,' she said. 'I'm not. I'm not into any of that shite. Me sister's on heroin – me Da's an alco – fucked me out 'cause I was getting on to the rest of them. Ah yeah – didn't want to hear me preaching. Fucks your head up, that stuff, so it does. Now look at me.'

'Did you go to anyone for help? Your local councillor maybe?'

'Yeah. Dead nice, he was. Said he'd try to help me get a gaff. Suppose something'll turn up anyways.'

'Does your family know you're sleeping rough?'

The girl shrugged. 'They couldn't give a—' Suddenly, a figure nearby caught her attention. 'Here Deco, any skins, have ya?' The tracksuited man turned, raised a hand and started in their direction, but was waylaid by another slouched figure propped up on crutches in a shop doorway.

Michelle straightened and thanked the girl for talking to her. She didn't like to judge people, but Deco, now coming towards them, didn't look like someone to mess with. She took a couple of sandwiches from her knapsack, gave them to the girl and moved on.

Leaving the city centre, she walked towards the river where she knew Conor and the other volunteer would be by now. The Liffey boardwalk was a camping ground for the homeless at night. She stepped onto the boardwalk; the river was black under the mock gaslights that lined the bridges. It wasn't a place she'd usually walk alone. In the river, something bobbed in the water;

125

she saw that there were several objects, glinting silver. Curious, she walked to the railing and looked down. Beer cans floated on the surface, more than a dozen of them. Soon they'd fill with water and sink to the riverbed. Another one whizzed through the air and landed softly. A group of men were congregated on benches further along. One of them was standing smoking. He kept stepping back and forth on the balls of his feet as if in time to music.

'Hey, could you stop for a sec,' the man said, as he saw Michelle coming towards him.

'Sorry,' she muttered, walking quickly past him, head up. She wasn't usually afraid in the streets at night, but here by the river the threat was palpable.

Up ahead, she spotted Conor and the other volunteer, a girl whose name she didn't know, and she hurried to catch up with them.

Chapter Twenty-Five

Nick

Michelle. Susan. Rachel. Everything rewound at speed. Tessa hadn't changed her technique; she hadn't needed to. Within minutes, he was catapulted back to the past.

'Where are you, Nick?'

'*The house. There are lots of people. They've come to pay their respects.*'

'To who?'

'*To Rachel. And to me too, I suppose. They shake my hand, but they're embarrassed … And Rachel won't look at me.*'

Tessa's voice was gentle. 'Who's died, Nick?'

A pain in his chest, like he was experiencing it now. He breathed deep to quell it. '*Daniel. He's just a child, a toddler … it's so small – the coffin. He's laid out, but I can't bear to look at him. Caitlin's come into the room. I don't think she should see him like that, but Rachel says she should, that it's better that she understands what's happened. I don't think she does though. She's too young. The adults waylay her, making a fuss, and she giggles. She pays no attention to the coffin. The guests avoid me. They've come for Rachel, not for me, and that makes me feel even more out of place. I have this awful feeling, like whatever's happened to put Daniel in that box is my fault. But I don't know why … I don't know how I've come to this place.*'

'What's happening now, Nick?'

'*More mourners. A hand on my arm, a woman … I shrug her off. I don't want to speak to her. I don't want to speak to anyone. I break away from her and she calls after me, but I need to get away, get out of this room.*'

When Tessa brought him to, his heart was beating fast. He was glad to be out of the room, away from that little coffin and the accusing eyes of the mourners. What had happened to that child – his son? Tessa was looking at him, waiting for him to speak.

'The way they looked at me,' he said. 'It wasn't pity, it was contempt.'

'Why do you think that is, Nick?'

'I don't know, but I have this terrible feeling, like maybe it had something to do with me.' He looked at Tessa. 'What if I did something? I mean … I don't know anything about Johnny Davis. Look, what he … *I* … did to Rachel … what if I? … I wish I knew what was happening. When I'm under, I get one small piece of the jigsaw, never enough to put a proper picture together. And then there are things I haven't seen under hypnosis, but that I suspect … For example, that day, the day that I walked in on Rachel and that man … he was someone I knew. I could feel it. I think I'd suspected that Rachel was having an affair, but not with him. He was a friend. I think that's why I lost it. Johnny and Rachel were happy before. Something must have gone really wrong for it to end the way it did. And the boy, our son, I don't know but maybe that was the catalyst. His death, particularly if it was my fault, maybe that's what drove them, us, apart.'

Tessa didn't say anything immediately. Then she put her pen down and looked up. 'Remember, not everything you're seeing is necessarily true. From what you've told me, the visions may be a manifestation of the guilt you've been harbouring since your wife's miscarriage.'

'A confabulation?'

'Exactly.'

'So, how can we know what's real and what's not?'

'It might be that we never will. But in terms of your treatment, that doesn't matter. What you see under hypnosis, whether from a previous life or not, will still be an expression of your feelings, of the things that you've repressed. Don't forget our aim here, Nick. The only reason we're doing this is to uncover the reasons for your alcohol abuse to help you stay sober in the future.'

He nodded, imagining what the hypnotist would say if she knew he and Michelle were planning on meeting Caitlin. She would discharge him, of that he was sure. And so he had to make sure that no matter what happened over the coming weeks in terms of Johnny Davis's daughter, he didn't reveal anything under hypnosis.

Nick called Michelle as soon as he was in the car, relieved to hear her cheery voice. For a moment, it was like it had been a month ago – before the doctor had delivered her grim prognosis, and Michelle's voice alone was enough to make him smile like he hadn't done in a long time, not since his divorce. Now she asked him how the session had gone, and he took a breath and told her the whole story. He'd have preferred to do it face-to-face, but she was on the soup run that evening, and he wouldn't see her.

'What did Tessa say about it?' she asked.

'The usual, that it mightn't have happened, that whole thing about false memory.' Suddenly, he had a thought. 'You mentioned that Johnny's father, the doctor, had died, right?'

'Yes, in 2010. He's buried in Castleknock.'

'Okay. So if there was a child, maybe he's buried out there, in the family plot...'

There was a pause on the line. 'Nick, are you sure you want to know?'

'I have to. At least if there's no evidence of this child, I can forget about it, accept Tessa's theory...'

'And if there is?'

'Then I've got to find out what happened to him.'

'I don't know, Nick. Are you sure it's a good idea? You've got enough to deal with ...'

'If it were you, you'd want to know, wouldn't you?'

Another pause, before Michelle breathed 'yes' down the line.

'I know you're worried – but never knowing, that would be just as bad ... now that I've come this far, I have to know the rest. I have to know just what kind of man I was and do whatever I can to make up for it now.'

He rang off, promising Michelle that he'd text her if he discovered anything. He knew she was worried that the whole thing would send him back on the drink again, but it was like he said, not knowing would be no better.

He tapped the search engine on his phone, typed in the obituary details for Maurice Davis, and checked the name and location of the small cemetery in Castleknock. When he closed the app, he sat staring at the photo on the screen, a snap of himself and Michelle, windswept and grinning crazily on a weekend away in Galway. It made him wish for the millionth time that he could press rewind and erase the last few weeks. He sighed and started the car, the sooner he got to that cemetery, the sooner he would know.

Chapter Twenty-Six

Caitlin

Caitlin had stayed late in the office the previous night so she wouldn't have to go in so early today. She had a meeting with the girl who'd written the article on homelessness at twelve o'clock in a coffee shop, but rather than staying in bed late, she'd got up at eight and had gone for a run. As she ran, she went through all the things that had happened since the phone call. There was the man in the park, which may just be paranoia, then the messages from Dar Bryan, which may be simply a coincidence. The Twitter page set up in David's name had been done to freak her out, that was something that couldn't be dismissed, but whoever was doing it, she wasn't about to let them control her life. She'd get on with things but remember to be vigilant.

The girl hadn't yet arrived when she got to the coffee shop, but she was early, so she sat by the window and ordered a cappuccino. She was glad to be out of the office for once – wondered if she should maybe take a holiday. She hadn't gone anywhere since her trip to Romania with David. They'd spent ten days travelling by train around the region of Transylvania – they'd gone bear watching and trekking in the hills as well as visiting old medieval towns and castles. It had been one of the best holidays they'd been on. That had been almost three years ago. And apart from a few days she'd taken off after David's disappearance, she'd worked right through, making sure she hadn't had too much time to think, because she knew if she had, she'd have been completely useless.

'Caitlin?'

She started and looked up to see a pretty blonde girl with a notebook standing by her table.

'Yes.' She stood up, and the girl extended her hand and smiled, though she looked nervous.

'I'm Michelle, thanks for agreeing to meet me.'

'Not at all, happy to. Do you want to get yourself a coffee before we get down to it?'

'Sure. Can I get you something?' Michelle put her stuff down on one of the chairs, unwrapped her scarf, shrugged out of her jacket and hung both on the back of the chair.

'No, I'm good, thanks,' Caitlin said and watched as Michelle made her way up to the counter.

Michelle's article had really struck a chord with her, particularly the part that touched on why people ended up on the streets. It wasn't that the reasons she'd cited were new, it was that people often dismissed them. She'd begun to wonder how many people there were out there whose families knew nothing about their whereabouts. Mental illness was a factor that was often over-looked. She admitted that she herself had often walked by a homeless person who looked able-bodied and hadn't given them money because she couldn't see a reason why that person couldn't find some kind of work. But mental illness wasn't always visible.

These were the people who Michelle talked about falling through the cracks. When Caitlin had read the article, she'd wondered again about all the cases of the missing. She'd said it to Andy at the start: what if something had happened to David, what if he'd had an accident and couldn't remember who he was? What if he'd ended up just another one of the hundreds of anonymous people sleeping in doorways in the city? Andy had said that would never happen. That if David had had an accident, he'd have been brought to a hospital – and they'd phoned around everywhere, hadn't they? Caitlin had said she wasn't convinced, and there was no guarantee they'd ever come across David if he was sleeping rough. No matter how small the city was, it was vast when it came to its homeless.

Michelle returned with her cappuccino and sat opposite her. 'I'd really like to thank you for agreeing to print my piece,' she said.

'Of course. It's fantastic. Have you published many articles?'

Michelle blushed. 'No, that's the first.'

Caitlin smiled. 'In that case, I'm glad you sent it to us. How long have you been working with the Simon Community?'

'Just going on two years. In that time, I've seen things go from bad to worse. I'm sure you know yourself, you can't walk ten paces without coming across a homeless person in Dublin. The government isn't doing anything about it. They talk all right; do you remember two years ago, the Taoiseach swore he'd have every homeless person off the streets in the next few years? Instead, twenty families presented themselves to police stations in the city last Tuesday night. I had to write about it. If we don't keep bombarding people with the facts, the government is never going to take it seriously. Although, they can't turn a blind eye now, not with Dan dying right under their noses.'

'Dan?'

'You must have heard about it? He's the homeless man who died outside the government offices recently.'

Caitlin nodded. Michelle was passionate when she talked; what she'd written had come from the heart. 'Did you know him?' she asked.

'Yes. He was lovely. To look at him, you wouldn't think anything was wrong, but I think he had Asperger's, and was bipolar, I think, too. He didn't have any family; his parents had died a couple of years ago. The council wanted him out of the house. He'd been sharing a flat before, but it hadn't worked out and he'd moved back in with the parents – this was before they got sick.

133

They hadn't got around to putting his name back on the rent, then his mother got cancer, and nobody thought of it. There were more important things to worry about. She died four months after she was diagnosed, and a year later the father died – massive heart attack. Now they're all gone; the whole family wiped out.'

'Jesus, that's awful. Do a lot of the people you meet tell you their stories?' Caitlin asked.

Michelle nodded. 'You get to know them. Some people are so glad to talk – all day people walk by them. It's like they're invisible. All they want sometimes is to tell someone their story, who they are. They're people – people whose luck turned for one reason or another. What we need is for more people to care.'

Caitlin nodded. 'A year ago, my husband went missing. He went out to work and never came back. People don't want to hear about it. I've got friends who just stopped calling, who couldn't bear listening to me crying and talking about David all the time.' She had no idea why she'd said that. It wasn't that she wanted Michelle's pity. Sometimes, she just had a macabre need to talk about it. She couldn't help it.

Michelle looked startled. 'My God, I'm so sorry,' she said.

Caitlin nodded, reaching for her bag, taking her phone out and showing Michelle the picture she still kept there. Michelle took the phone from her, and Caitlin watched as she looked at David's face and handed it back to her. 'I can't begin to imagine what that must be like,' she said. 'And the police turned nothing up? No leads?' Michelle asked.

Caitlin shook her head. 'It's like he just vanished off the face of the earth. Reading your article, it got me thinking, I wondered how many people are out there and no one knows where they are.'

'Quite a few, I'd say.'

Caitlin liked this girl, she was concerned about others – wanted to help. She wasn't the type who would walk out on someone with a hard-luck story. 'So, you'd be on for doing another article then – to tell some of the personal stories of the people you meet?'

Michelle nodded. 'I've already started, in fact. I talked to a few people the other evening, heard some diverse stories. I want to show that these people are not just statistics, they're human beings.'

'Great. Just make sure you don't name the people involved, obviously.' Caitlin reached into her pocket and gave Michelle her card. 'Do you think you could have it written for next week's edition?'

'Absolutely.'

'Great. You can send it to me directly; my email address is there. Now, I don't know if you're in a hurry, but you said you had some other ideas, could you tell me about those?'

Chapter Twenty-Seven

Michelle

Michelle couldn't believe how well her meeting with Caitlin had gone, and not in a forced way either. They had clicked as soon as they'd begun talking. When she'd told Caitlin about her idea to write an article about health and fitness, she'd shown enthusiasm, asking her about her day job, and by the end of the conversation Michelle had talked her into trying a couple of Zumba classes gratis. She didn't know if Caitlin would show up, but either way she had her next article on the homelessness crisis to submit to her in the next few days.

Caitlin's story about her husband's disappearance was shocking. She wondered how Nick would take it and hoped that it didn't add to his guilt. The woman had lost first her parents and then her husband; her path until now had been far from an easy one.

She'd been bursting to call Nick when the meeting had ended, but he'd already told her that he had a session with the hypnotist in the afternoon, and so she texted him instead:

Went well. Call me when you get a chance xx.

She went home and practised choreography for her classes for the rest of the afternoon.

Nick called just after six o'clock. She began telling him about her meeting with Caitlin, but he interrupted, saying that he wanted to hear everything in person, that he had things to tell her too, and that he'd like to take her out for dinner.

They met in Toscana, her favourite Italian restaurant in Dublin. She arrived first and perused the menu. When Nick arrived he looked tired – there were purple crescents beneath his eyes – but Michelle didn't comment. The sickness had started to show more and more. If she thought about it, she'd begun to notice it a few months back. He'd lost weight without explanation, and when she'd mentioned it, he'd laughed about it. Said it wouldn't do him any harm, that he'd been forming a gut as he got closer to forty. He seemed edgy today, too, and she wondered if he was craving a drink. His hands shook as he hung his jacket on the back of the chair.

'So, it went well?' he asked. He'd sat down, forgetting to kiss her first. She put it down to his eagerness to hear about Caitlin.

She nodded. 'She's really nice. We talked non-stop for more than an hour. And she's given me a deadline for another article, so I'll definitely get to meet her again.'

'That's great,' he said. He picked up the menu, distractedly, and began to scan it before the waiter arrived. Michelle had already decided what she would have. She thought she'd better get the worst out before she got any further. There was no point in making small talk about how nice Caitlin was and then landing the punch.

'Nick, Caitlin told me something terrible. A year ago, her husband went missing. Went to work and never came home.'

'What?' Nick put the menu down, focused at last.

'I know, I couldn't believe it. Imagine what she's going through.'

'Jesus. Poor Caitie.'

Michelle looked at him. Caitie. Was that what he'd called his little girl?

'Maybe we can help her,' he said.

'Help her? How?'

He shook his head. 'I don't know … if we could find out more about her, about her husband … The Garda won't do anything on a cold case like that. The number of people missing in Ireland runs into the thousands. Every day there's a new poster up. Most of these people, and not just women but men too, they're never found.'

The waiter came and took their order. Michelle leaned forward, took Nick's hand. His fingers trembled under hers. 'Come on, Nick. What can we do? We're not private investigators.'

'No. But we'd probably make a better fist at it than some. You can bet half the families of missing people have gone down that route, and to no avail. There are some who must have spent everything they had and have nothing to show for it.'

'What about the people who don't want to be found though,' she said.

He nodded. 'There is that. The ones that just walk out on their lives. But if I could do something … I owe it to her, Michelle. I need to find some way of … not undoing it, I can never do that, but making up somehow for what I did.'

Michelle nodded. She knew he was in earnest. More than that, he was determined. He would try everything he could to find his daughter's husband. 'Nick, did you find out anything … about the boy?'

He nodded. 'I went out to the cemetery, it's a tiny place at the back of a church. You should have seen me wandering around in the dark like a ghoul … but it was there alright, Luckily, I had a flashlight in the car. On the headstone it said: Maurice, his wife: Celine and at the very top: Daniel – two years old, he died in 1980.

Michelle leaned forward. 'I'm so sorry, Nick, but you don't how the child died; it might have been natural causes … At least you know that whatever happened to him, it isn't related to the incident with Rachel. It would have said in the news articles if there was another child involved.'

'You'd hope so … anyway, I'll know soon enough. I got in touch with my friend Gary, you know how he works in the office of Births, Deaths and Marriages? He couldn't give me a copy of the certificate, it would be more than his job was worth, but he did say he'd access the file and check the cause of death.'

Michelle glanced at him, worried. She was about to ask him whether he thought it was a good idea, and whether he'd told Gary why he wanted this information, when the waiter arrived with their meal. As soon as the waiter had left, Nick took her hand again.

'Listen, there was something else I wanted to talk to you about … don't worry, it's nothing bad. In fact, the opposite I hope … What would you think about moving in with me? You stay over most nights anyway and you're spending a fortune on that flat …'

Michelle looked away so that he wouldn't see the tears that sprung to her eyes. She'd been hoping for this for the past few months, before he'd told her anything about his diagnosis. 'Are you sure?' she asked softly.

He leaned in and touched her face. 'I don't ask these things lightly, you know that.'

She nodded and squeezed his hand, not trusting herself to speak.

Chapter Twenty-Eight

Nick

That night, Nick lay in bed turning everything over in his head. During the hypnosis sessions, he often slipped between lives. Susan, his ex-wife, would become Rachel, a metamorphosis so smooth he didn't even notice the jump cut between scenes. In some ways, it felt as though his two lives were linked, that Susan, the miscarriage, and the demise of their marriage all happened as a result of the violent killing of Rachel, and now possibly, Daniel.

He lay on his back sleepless, thoughts tumbling round his head. Michelle was snoring lightly. He felt a pang as he watched her sleep. He wished that he'd met her sooner. Maybe he wouldn't be in the predicament he was in now – maybe he'd have been happy and wouldn't have destroyed his body with alcohol. He was glad he'd asked her to move in. She could leave that one-bedroom apartment she spent half her salary renting. He'd worried about whether it was fair – to ask her to do that when he might not be around in a year's time? If it was asking too much of her? He knew he preferred it when she was there, though. He'd already been thinking of asking her to move in before he'd got the diagnosis. He'd begun to hate it when she wasn't there, when it was just him and Rowdy.

For the first time, he thought about whether he should make a will. He could leave the house to Michelle; that way, at least if something happened to him, she would be comfortable. He could give her that at least.

The next morning, Nick was up early. Michelle was still sleeping by the time he finished his coffee. He eased open the bedroom door, leaned over and kissed her lightly. 'I'm off to work,' he said. 'Stay as long as you like.' Michelle stretched and pulled the covers up, looking at him sleepily. 'Will you be here when I get back?' Nick asked.

Michelle smiled. 'Depends what time you get in. I've got the soup run later.'

'Well, come back here after. It doesn't matter what time, okay? Let yourself in.'

'Okay.'

For the rest of the morning, Nick lost himself in the new design he was working on, drawing out the plans that he and the client had discussed. After lunch he went out to view the site again. It was a plot of land out in Greystones in Wicklow, and he enjoyed the spin out of the city and along the south Dublin coast.

On the way back, he took a detour, turning off the N11 for Shankill and following the coast road to Dalkey. He intended just to see the house, to pull in on the road at the bottom of the hill and think, but he found himself taking the small fork in the road that climbed steeply up to the hexagon. He stopped the car on the gravel driveway and got out. The house was just as it had been when he'd left it two years before. If he walked round the first of the five walls, he'd see directly into the bedroom that he had shared with Susan – he'd built it so they'd have a clear view of the sea from all the rooms at the front of the house without compromising their privacy. The house was at such a height, though, that anyone who wanted to see through the windows would have to drive up there. That was one of the advantages of such elevation; that, and the view of the coast.

As Nick stood in front of the house, the scene between Johnny and Rachel instantly came back to him. It was in that exact spot where they'd picnicked and he'd said they'd live here some day when they had the money. It was strange to think that his soul had returned there and done just that, that as Nick he had carried out the wish of his former life.

'Nick?'

Nick turned to see Susan coming around the side of the house, a cloth in her hand. 'I thought I heard a car.' She was looking at him curiously.

'Sorry,' he said. 'I didn't think you were at home ... the car isn't in the drive.'

'It's being serviced.'

'Ah.' They stood there, awkward. 'You look well,' he said.

Self-consciously, she raised a hand to her hair. 'You lie as well as ever,' she said. But there was humour in the barb. 'Do you want to come in? Or are you just going to stand around admiring the view?'

Nick followed her round the back to the where the double glass doors opened onto the small garden, more relaxed now that she didn't seem to mind his being there.

'Coffee?' she asked, opening the press.

'Please,' he said.

'The usual way?'

'Yeah, but with four sugars.' Susan arched an eyebrow. 'I'm off the drink,' he said.

She nodded. 'Good. Good for you, Nick,' she said, but this time she wasn't mocking him.

Nick watched as she prepared their coffee. She did look well. She was as slim as she'd always been, her face was bare of make-up. She put the mugs of coffee on the breakfast bar and sat opposite him.

'How've you been?' he asked.

She shrugged. 'Good. Just getting on with it ... you know how

142

it is.' She smiled. 'And you? How long have you been off the drink?'

'Nearly three weeks ...'

'Aagh.'

'It's for good this time, doctor's orders,' he said.

She nodded, but she looked concerned. 'Is everything all right?'

'Yeah, I'm fine,' he said. 'Just haven't been doing the old liver any good.' He considered whether to tell her the whole story, about how he'd be dead in a year if he didn't get a transplant, but he didn't want her to think that was the reason he'd come. And besides, it was nice to chat to someone who didn't know his predicament. He wondered if they could salvage a friendship from what had been. He didn't know, though, if she still held the past against him.

'It's been a while since I saw you. Are you doing okay?' he asked.

Susan smiled. 'I keep busy, you know, justice never sleeps and all that.'

'Well, you always did thrive on it.' He took a sip of the too-sweet coffee, winced at the amount of sugar it took to reduce his cravings. 'No time for a social life, I suppose?'

'I'm seeing someone, if that's what you're asking me.'

'Ah.' Susan always could cut through the small talk.

'A lawyer,' she added.

He groaned. 'God, that should make for interesting arguments.' He glanced at her, wondering if the joke was in bad taste, but she laughed.

'Maybe, it's early days ... but we seem to get along. And you, is there anyone in your life?'

'Yeah, I'm seeing someone too – Michelle. She's ... she's great.' For some reason, he didn't feel like elaborating. To describe Michelle would be to divulge, and once you began to divulge, it was difficult to stop. He looked at his ex-wife. She looked happy, relaxed. He hadn't seen her look this relaxed in a very long time

– maybe never. Not even before – 'Suse, we might have been all right, if it hadn't happened, mightn't we? If we hadn't …'

'Nick, let's not … It's-it's taken a long time for me to get to this point. To stop blaming, you … blaming myself. What happened to Noah wasn't our fault.'

'Noah? It was a boy. You knew?'

She nodded. 'They told me in the hospital after it happened. I'd had that scan a couple of weeks before. At the time we said we'd wait, remember? That it'd be a nice if it were a surprise. But after … I asked if they could tell me. I didn't name him, not straight away. It was later on I thought he had no grave, wasn't even a proper person – not for them. But I could name him – in my head I could think of him as Noah.'

'Noah.' Nick said it out loud. As he did so, he had a flashback – of himself as Johnny in that room again, lifting the boy.

Susan's words summoned him back to the present. 'It wasn't our fault, Nick.' She repeated. 'I thought it was, I blamed you. But it didn't happen because of you, us or the way things were in our marriage. It took over a year of counselling for me to see that, to get through it.' She put a hand on his arm. 'It was an accident, that's all. There was nothing we could have done any differently, the outcome was always going to be the same. It was just bad luck.'

Nick was nodding. Bad luck – but had he brought that bad luck on them? 'I don't know,' he said, getting up. 'Maybe, I …' He wanted to tell Susan that it was his fault – he felt like it was – but he could see how much she'd moved on, how much the therapy had helped her. 'I'm sorry, you're right, of course. I'm so glad to see you doing so well.' He drained his coffee, swallowing the sticky mass of sugar at the bottom of the mug.

Susan was looking at him, concerned.

'I should have told you that before,' she said. 'You should think about it too, Nick, about seeing someone. I know you've never believed in that kind of thing, but it does help.' She stood up.

'It's good to see you – and to hear you've met someone. I hope she keeps you on the right track.'

She walked with him to the car. It was hard to lighten the mood again after they'd gone down that dark path, but it was a conversation they'd needed to have. Even so, her words would have made him feel so much better if he'd heard them before he'd started hypnosis, if he'd heard them when he believed that he was innocent. Now he felt like his past was the reason for everything, that every misdeed he'd committed as Johnny Davis was reaping repercussions in this life.

When he opened the car door and turned to say goodbye, Susan reached out and hugged him. They held each other tight, and all he could think was that when they separated, he might just fall apart.

Chapter Twenty-Nine

Caitlin

Caitlin drained the last of the water in the bottle and threw it into her backpack. Michelle was towelling herself off, saying a cheerful goodbye to the other women as they filed out of the hall. Caitlin had been surprised by the intensity of the workout, twenty minutes in and she was fighting for breath. But she'd got into it, moved forward to stand in the second line of women so she could see and imitate the correct moves rather than be blocked by the woman with two left feet in front of her. She'd heard that Zumba was fun, and found that it was true – she loved the music too, a hip-swinging Latin beat. Now she hung back, waiting until the other women had left, to have a word with Michelle.

'Hey, I'm delighted you made it,' Michelle smiled at her as she stuffed the towel into her bag. 'Did you enjoy it?'

Caitlin nodded enthusiastically. 'Loved it. I don't know why I haven't tried it before. Lack of time, I suppose, I'd normally be running circles in the park now. But I have to say, this was a lot more fun.'

Michelle nodded. 'I always hated exercising. Running on a treadmill in the gym just didn't appeal to me. But when I started this ... I've always loved dancing so, despite the intensity, it doesn't really feel like an exercise class to me.'

Michelle picked up her bag, and Caitlin walked with her. The café in the fitness centre was still open; it would be for another hour until the next class ended.

'Do you want to get a cold drink or something?' Michelle asked.

'Sure.' Why not, Caitlin thought. She wasn't rushing home to anything. And since her run-in with Andy, she'd decided that maybe she ought to distance herself from him a bit, not rely on him so much. She needed to get out and meet new people, make new friends – she needed, to some degree, to try to get her life back.

'How's the article coming along? Did you get a chance to talk to anyone?' Caitlin asked.

Michelle nodded. 'I think I have enough material. I'm not working tomorrow, so I'll start typing it up. I should get it to you by tomorrow evening.'

They got their drinks and sat at a table by the window.

'We got a good response from the first one,' Caitlin told her. 'A lot of people commented on our Facebook and Twitter pages. You should take a look.'

'Really?' Michelle looked delighted. 'Wow, that's great. Anything that gets the word out. Look, last night when I was out on the soup run, I was thinking about what you told me … about your husband. If you'd like, I could circulate a photo – show it around – you never know who might have seen him. Somebody might remember something.'

Caitlin hesitated. 'We did that,' she said. 'At the time. Posters went up everywhere. They were distributed to organizations like Simon and the Salvation Army, all the shelters … It's really nice of you, but … it's been a year now, I doubt it would turn up anything new. And most of the people who are in the streets now, they probably weren't back then.' Caitlin took a long drink of orange juice.

Michelle shook her head. 'Unfortunately, some of them probably were. You see the same faces time and again. They disappear for a while and next thing they're back … those are the ones it's hardest to help. But look, if you change your mind, just let me know. I'm happy to help out in any way I can.'

Caitlin put a hand on Michelle's arm. 'Thanks, Michelle. I really appreciate it.' She sat back in her chair; she didn't want to talk about David tonight. She was feeling elated after the class and she wanted to hold onto that feeling for as long as she could. 'And what about you?' she asked. 'Is there a man in your life?'

Michelle's face coloured and she smiled. 'Yeah. We've been together about eight months. I'm moving in with him this weekend.'

'Ooh, big step. Are you nervous?'

'No. Well, not really. A bit, I suppose, if I'm honest.' She looked as if she were going to say something more, but stopped.

'You'll know if it's right,' Caitlin said. 'And if you think it is and it's not, nothing's irreversible.' That wasn't strictly true, as she knew only too well, but she tried to focus on the present, on the woman before her who was now draining her drink and standing up to go.

They left the centre and walked out into the night together. 'Listen, do you have any plans this weekend?' Michelle asked her. 'No, why?'

'We were thinking of having a barbecue on Saturday, a kind of celebration of me moving in. Would you like to come? It's nothing major, just a few friends coming round.'

'Well, I'd love to. I don't think I've got anything on.' Caitlin thought of the weekend looming before her. Ever since David's disappearance, she dreaded weekends. She tried to think of ways to fill them and often went for work drinks with her colleagues on Fridays even though she never particularly felt at ease. The girls were nice enough, but she liked to keep her distance, didn't allow any of them to cross the boundary into her personal life. She often went to the cinema with Andy on Saturdays if he wasn't out with the lads. They shared an interest in art house movies

148

and the Irish Film Institute did good food, so between dinner and a film, it killed a few hours.

'Great. Here, I'll give you my number,' Michelle told her.

Caitlin took out her phone and unlocked it. As she did so, she saw that she had a missed call from Andy along with a new voice message. She cleared the icons. 'Great, shout it out to me and I'll call you, that way you'll have mine too.'

They parted, Michelle promising that she would text her the address, saying that she really hoped she'd come.

Caitlin felt happy as she walked back to the car. Michelle was the first friend she'd made in a long time. She seemed genuine, and was surely a nice person given that she was a volunteer. She rang into her voicemail as she walked down the street, listening to Andy apologizing for his off-handedness the other day. She knew he wouldn't be able to stay away for more than twenty-four hours, he never could. Still, she'd take her time in calling him back. It would be good to go to the barbecue at the weekend and meet new people. Andy had been good to her, maybe too good; it had got intense without her even realizing it. It would do them both good to pull back a bit. No matter what protestations he made, she knew that he had feelings for her and there was nowhere that could go. Not ever.

She pulled into her driveway, one of the Latin rhythms still going round in her head as she tapped her fingertips on the steering wheel. A wind had picked up, and the bin which she'd put out for collection when she'd left that morning had blown several feet to stop outside her neighbour's house. The lid was lifting and slapping back down as she got out of the car, gripping the door to prevent it being wrenched from her hand. She leaned in, took her backpack from the passenger seat and slung it over her shoulder. As she wheeled the bin back up the street and in the driveway, she got the horrible feeling that someone was watching her. She hurried towards the door, key poised. Rather than bring the bin round to the side gate where she normally put it, she tucked it in against the wall, and put a brick on top to stop the lid from banging.

She'd just got in the door and turned on the lights when her phone started ringing, the sound of it jangling her nerves. She pulled it from the pocket of her hoodie, saw Andy's name flash on the screen and knocked it onto silent. It continued to ring mutely on the table. He was far too anxious to speak to her. It was starting to make her feel smothered.

She checked the doors and windows, took the chilli she'd cooked the day before from the fridge. She popped it in the microwave, went into the front room, pulled down the blind and zapped the television to life. It was only half past eight, but it felt later. She tried to shake the creepy feeling she'd got, thinking about Michelle's invitation as she sat down to eat the chilli and poured herself a glass of red wine.

She didn't check her computer that night, didn't see the latest photo that David A had uploaded.

Chapter Thirty

Michelle

'You'll never guess what!' Michelle said, as she threw her sports bag down on the living room floor.

'Probably not,' said Nick, lowering the volume on the TV and standing to kiss her.

'Caitlin turned up at my Zumba class. And that's not all, she's agreed to come round here on Saturday for a barbecue.'

'A barbecue?'

'Yep, I told her we were having a barbecue to celebrate my moving in with you. We'll have to invite a few others so it doesn't look strange. So – did I do good?' She stood back to survey his expression.

'Good? Astonishing, more like. I can't believe you've managed to pull this off. You only just met her last week.'

'What can I say? We clicked. She likes me. And to be honest, I'd say she's making a big effort to try to get herself out there.'

'Wow.' He wandered into the kitchen, and she walked after him, watched him fill the kettle and take two mugs from the press. 'Tea?'

'Sure.' He hadn't been a fan of tea, but since he'd stopped drinking alcohol, he'd been drinking it by the pot. She'd bought several varieties in the health food shop, but she hadn't yet convinced him to try any of her fruit fusions. He said they smelt like cheap perfume and he'd rather stick to the original. She

151

cringed as she watched him add spoon after spoon of sugar.

'I wish I hadn't gone to see her playing in the wine bar now,' Nick said. 'She might suspect something, think I'm some kind of oddball.'

'Don't be ridiculous! Why on earth would she think that? You know how small Dublin is, you run into the same people all the time. There was a girl who turned up in my Zumba class a few weeks ago that I used to pass every evening when I was working on Aungier Street.'

'Hmm, I suppose. You don't think it'll look a bit too coincidental though? It's only two weeks since I was there. I wouldn't want her thinking I was some kind of crazy fan!'

Michelle laughed. 'Hardly. You've only seen her once, it's not like you're there every Wednesday … you're not, are you?' It had just occurred to her that she hadn't seen him the previous Wednesday.

'God, no,' he said. 'I'm not that stupid. Now, who should we invite? Saturday's just a few days away.'

Michelle could see how nervous Nick was about meeting Caitlin. She hoped he really hadn't been to the wine bar more than once. He'd been quick to change the subject, but she'd have to take his word for it. 'I could invite Siobhan,' she said. 'And maybe Clare and Keith, but not too many couples. A few single people would be good – we don't want her to feel the odd one out, especially since I'm the only person she'll know.'

Nick handed her the mug of tea, took a sip of his own. 'When are you going to phone your landlady to give notice?'

She shrugged. 'Soon, I guess. She's not going to be happy. I already told her I was going to renew the lease. Just as well she's been so blasé about sending it on. The old one expired three weeks ago. I hope she doesn't use it as an excuse to keep my deposit though.'

'She can't, the place is spotless. And besides, you haven't signed anything. She hasn't a leg, as they say.'

152

'Yeah, I guess.' She smiled, not wanting him to know she had her reservations. What she'd told Caitlin was true: it wasn't that she didn't want to move in with Nick – but she worried that the anxiety of looking after and then potentially losing another person she loved would be too much for her.

She tried to think positively, but she had to be realistic too. Neither of them knew what the outcome of Nick's predicament would be.

'What are you thinking about? You look like you're about to go to the guillotine.'

'Hmm? Nothing. Just the landlady.'

'You do want to move in, don't you?' he asked, concerned.

'Of course I do. Why else would we be having a barbecue to celebrate?' She hoped that her flippancy covered any of the lingering reservations in her mind.

He smiled, but she could see he was anxious. 'About Caitlin. Have you talked to her about me at all? You haven't told her anything about me being sick, have you?'

'Of course not, I wouldn't do that. I haven't told anyone, and I certainly wouldn't tell her.'

'Good. I'd rather she didn't know. I don't want her looking at me like someone who's dying.'

Dying. Nick was dying. His body was slowly going into decline, but she didn't want to think about that, couldn't think about it or she'd break down. And she didn't want to think of him that way either. He was more than his failing body, the same as her mother had been. In fact, Nick's experience under hypnosis had proved that when this body failed, he would return in another – a step further in the evolution of his soul.

'Michelle.' She looked up when he said her name. 'We have to keep fighting this thing. If I give in to it, become a sick person, have people look at me like that, then it will beat me. I intend to live as fully as I can for whatever time I have left. And I don't want to have to think about it all the time.'

153

'I know, Nick. Don't talk like that … I know you won't give up, and I'll never give up on you either. I hope you know that?'

He nodded, pulled her close. 'I love you,' he murmured. She closed her eyes and squeezed him tight. It was the first time he'd said those words.

Chapter Thirty-One

Nick

Nick was lighting the barbecue when the first knock came to the door. He looked at Michelle and exhaled. The shake in his hands was bad despite having taken his medication. Michelle rubbed his arm and disappeared inside the house. He looked up at the sky – overcast – what did they expect, having a barbecue in early November? Earlier, he'd swept up the leaves and dusted off the garden furniture, which hadn't had much use that summer. As long as it didn't rain, he thought; out here in the air, it was better. He wasn't sure how he would be if he were trapped in the house with their visitors – with Caitlin.

There was silence for what couldn't have been more than two minutes after Michelle had gone inside the house. Nick took seven deep breaths, standing by the barbecue, eyes closed. He'd just reached six on his outward breath when he heard voices: Michelle's, slightly high-pitched, laughing, and then, to his momentary relief, Siobhan's.

He was standing there making small talk with Siobhan as Michelle got her a drink when the doorbell rang again. He waited, hoping that Michelle would go to answer it, that she hadn't strayed from the kitchen. A moment later, Keith and Claire, and his own friend, Gary, appeared at the glass doors that led to the garden. He fixed a smile on his face and waved them over. At least now there were other people, he could always immerse himself in conversation with Gary if he needed to withdraw.

Michelle appeared with a tray of drinks and eased it onto the table. She'd asked him the day before if he was okay with there being alcohol, if it would be too much of a temptation for him. He'd made a face and told her that her white wine spritzers certainly wouldn't tempt him. Apart from that there'd be nothing stronger than a few cans of lager. It was okay, he said, he could handle it. Wouldn't he have to handle it wherever he went from now on? He may as well try to get used to it.

But now as he slugged a glass of cranberry juice he'd have given anything for a real drink. He watched Gary open a can of Carlsberg, felt his shakes worsen and excused himself to check the barbecue, which had begun to smoke.

Half an hour passed. He'd already done the first round of burgers and Michelle was dishing them out, but Caitlin still hadn't arrived.

'Maybe she won't turn up,' Michelle said, appearing at his shoulder. Nick nodded and arranged chicken wings on the barbecue. The smell of the food was making him queasy, but he was glad to be occupied.

'You pacing yourself, or what?' Gary asked him, his plate piled high with Michelle's Greek salad, licking sticky fingers as he eyed the glass next to Nick.

'Ah, I'm off it,' Nick told him. He picked up the tongs and turned the wings.

Gary's guffaw was expected, as was his chuckle and predictable comment of 'how long will that last?'

Nick turned away from his beery breath, the craving so strong that he almost wanted to kiss him, just to inhale it. Michelle was standing across the lawn, laughing at something that Claire had just said when the bell went again. Their eyes met across the grass, and she gave him what was meant to be a reassuring smile, but the smell of the food coupled with anxiety was threatening to make him heave.

'Gaz, do you think you could look after this for a few minutes?'
he said, bolting not into the house but around to the side gate
where he could escape out the front and into the house as soon
as Michelle had brought Caitlin through.

He reached the gate, eased it open and crept round the side
of the house. He heard the front door close and gave it a few
more minutes before letting himself in and hurrying up the stairs.

In the bedroom, he went to the window. Careful to stay close
to the curtain, he stretched his neck and peered down. Gary was,
dutifully, by the barbecue. The other three turned as Michelle came
out, a woman in a black dress and leather jacket by her side. Hands
were shaken, smiles exchanged. She looked different from when
Nick had seen her playing at the wine bar. Her hair, which had
been tied up that night, now hung in waves to her shoulders. He
stood back as Michelle glanced at the house, first at the door and
then at the upstairs windows. Christ, he'd have to go down there.
Wasn't this what he'd wanted, a chance to meet Caitlin, to see what
kind of woman Johnny Davis's daughter had grown up to be?

He went into the bathroom, popped another anti-sickness
tablet from its blister and swallowed it with water from the tap.
He took another Xanax for good measure – he wasn't due one,
but what he'd taken clearly hadn't worked and he had to get
through the afternoon. He owed it to Michelle, at least, for all
her efforts.

Gary nabbed him as soon as he walked into the garden. He
was where Nick had left him, tongs in one hand, turning rather
crisp-looking chicken wings.

'All yours', he said. 'Hope they're not overdone.' Nick managed
a smile, grabbed a large bowl and instructed Gary to toss the
wings into it. Gary nudged him and asked who the woman was
who had just arrived.

'Don't know, she must be some friend of Michelle,' Nick said,
shrugging. When he looked up Caitlin was looking at him curiously
– he smiled briefly and turned back to what he was doing.

'How's everything coming along?' Michelle came over and asked. She'd left Caitlin with the others. Chirpily, she asked Gary if he wouldn't mind bringing out a few plates from where she'd stacked them on the kitchen table. 'Aren't you coming over to say hello?' she whispered to Nick. Nick nodded.

'More grub's up!' he shouted across to the group, but Caitlin had already detached herself from them and was walking towards him. Nick could feel his panic rise.

Michelle turned to follow his gaze. 'Ah Caitlin, this is my other half, Nick!'

Caitlin peered at him hard. 'Nick? But we've met before, at the Ormond, a couple of weeks back.'

'Have we?' He clicked his fingers. 'That's right – you're the violinist.' He forced a smile and shook her hand. Her grip was surprisingly firm. He turned to Michelle. 'I stupidly knocked her drink over in the wine bar – small world.'

'How do you two know each other?' He hoped his effort at acting wasn't as bad as he felt it was.

Michelle played along. 'The article I did about homelessness, it was Caitlin who published it. *New Woman* is her magazine.'

Caitlin nodded. 'Terrific piece,' she said. 'We're running the follow-up next week.'

Gary appeared with the plates just as Nick was about to answer, and the rest of the group descended on the scene. Nick was relieved, his nonchalant attitude seemed to have worked. Caitlin hadn't reacted to him like he was some kind of weirdo, now all he had to do was act normal for the rest of the afternoon. He told himself his paranoia was unfounded. Caitlin had no idea who he was or about his past.

He watched Michelle and Caitlin talk, easy with one another, and slowly his anxiety ebbed away. He was filling the dishwasher, the chatter of the others and the sound of Tom Waits's 'Closing Time' drifting in through the open window, when he felt someone behind him.

'Sorry, I didn't mean to startle you,' Caitlin said, as he turned.

'No, you didn't, it's fine,' he said, waving her apology away.

She was staring at him and her eyes, he noticed, were a deep shade of blue, almost navy. 'Have we met someplace before?' she asked.

'The wine bar ...'

She shook her head. 'No, not the wine bar, I mean before that?'

'I don't think so.' His heart rate had picked up again.

She leaned against the edge of the table, head cocked to the side, assessing him. 'I'm sure we have, or maybe not met, but I've definitely seen you before ... You weren't in the park, were you? Last week?'

'Which park?'

'There's a little park near my house where I go running. You don't run, do you?'

Nick shook his head and laughed. 'No. God, the way I feel right now, I don't think I'd get as far as the garden gate.'

'Hmm. Well, I've definitely seen you somewhere before.' She straightened, pulled out one of the kitchen chairs and sat down.

'It's possible,' he said. 'I'm sure it'll come to you ... do you live around here?'

'No. I live on the northside, between Marino and Clontarf.'

'And you run a magazine. Michelle's really chuffed that you published her piece. She's so passionate about her volunteer work.' He glanced out the window to where Michelle was laughing with Gary and Siobhan.

'She sure is. It's admirable ... so many people out there know what's going on, but do nothing about it. Michelle cares, that was obvious from the minute we met. How long have you been together?' she asked.

'Oh, about eight months.'

She smiled. 'And so you decided to take the next step. Any nerves?'

'No. Michelle is great. There's nothing to be nervous about.'

He suddenly felt uncomfortable discussing Michelle. He was surprised at Caitlin's forthrightness and wondered if she was testing him, but he wasn't sure why she would. They had only just met. And it wasn't like she knew Michelle so well either. He decided, since she was being so direct, to bat the ball back at her.

'Michelle told me about your husband. I'm sorry, that must be really tough.'

She nodded and looked away. 'It's more terrible than anyone can imagine. People keep telling me I have to move on, and even though it feels impossible, I know they're right. That's why I came today, to meet new people – to try to move forward inch by inch. Michelle seems lovely – the first genuine person I've met in a while.'

Nick looked out the window again. Michelle had just extricated herself from the others and was approaching the house. 'She certainly is that,' he said. 'I know we've just met, but if there's anything we do for you, Caitlin – anything at all …'

'Thanks Nick, I really appreciate that.'

Michelle appeared in the doorway and looked from one to the other, curious. 'We're all out of food out here, chef,' she said. Nick wasn't sure if he was imagining it, but her smile seemed a little forced as they followed her outside.

160

Chapter Thirty-Two

Caitlin

Caitlin had seen the photo posted on David A's Twitter feed a few hours before going to the barbecue. It was a photo of the park where she ran, she was sure of it. She recognized the laneway where the trees met overhead, how the light dappled through the pale green leaves. There was no caption, no words, just the picture. Whoever had set up this account wanted her to know that he was watching her, that he knew where to find her if he wanted to. It wasn't David, of that she was sure, but she was determined to find out who it was and why they'd begun toying with her.

She had been shocked when she'd seen Nick at the barbecue, more so when she discovered that he was Michelle's boyfriend, the host of the event, but she figured she'd hid it well. She'd had years of practice hiding her emotions: she'd been doing it ever since her parents had died. It didn't take much effort anymore.

She thought of Andy's words, of the fact that Nick had shown up in the wine bar, and of how the photo of her had appeared on David A's account just hours later. She'd probably have thought nothing of it, wouldn't even have noticed him, if it hadn't been for that clumsy act of spilling her drink. And yet, there was nothing threatening about him.

He was awkward around her, sure, but nothing about him gave off an air of menace. When she'd mentioned having seen

161

him before, when she'd deliberately asked him if he ran in the park, there hadn't been a flicker. And besides, he was a stranger. He knew nothing about her, save what she'd told Michelle, and the fact that Michelle had submitted to the magazine could hardly have been a ploy, could it? What could they possibly want with her, this couple? Nothing, she hoped, because she genuinely liked Michelle, but she'd have to watch her step. Until she found out who was behind that hoax call and the fake Twitter account, she couldn't trust anyone.

On the desk, her phone buzzed. 'Michelle Carlin's here to see you.'

She'd been expecting Michelle, had invited her to the office to submit her article rather than having her email it over. She wanted to see her again, but without Nick. That way she might find out more about him and, if he was the person behind this hoax about David, Michelle might let something slip.

Caitlin rose from her desk and took the lift down to reception. 'Michelle, lovely to see you again,' she smiled. 'How are you doing?' They walked down the hallway, away from the receptionist's curious ears. 'How was the rest of your evening?' she asked, as soon as they'd stepped into the lift.

'It was good, the others left soon after you did so it didn't wind up very late. I hope you had a good time?'

The lift stopped, and they stepped out on the third floor. Caitlin led Michelle to the canteen where they could get a coffee. It was a quiet time; the morning breaks had finished and it was too early yet for lunch. All the same, they met Julie Morrison, one of the editors, who looked at Caitlin rather guiltily as she slipped past with a coffee.

'It was lovely. Your friends were very nice. And Nick.' She cast a glance at Michelle, who smiled, but looked, Caitlin thought, momentarily anxious. Maybe she was being paranoid though, because a second later the expression, if it had ever been there, was gone.

'He enjoyed meeting you. We should do it again,' Michelle said.

Caitlin nodded, took two cups and headed for the coffee machine. 'What does he do –Nick?'

'He's an architect.'

'Really? What type? Commercial? Anything I'd know?'

'Both commercial and private. He's designed houses for some pretty well-known people, celebrities even.'

'Yeah – like who?' Caitlin asked, raising her voice over the hissing of the coffee machine. She took her mug and asked Michelle what she wanted as Michelle told her about the house Nick had designed for a rock star in Killiney Bay.

'He took me there on our second date, trying to impress me, don't you know.'

'And did it work?'

Michelle laughed. 'Looks like it, doesn't it?'

They took their drinks and went to sit in a corner of the canteen which had a large window overlooking the River Liffey and Dublin's Ha'penny Bridge.

'How did you guys meet?' Caitlin asked.

Michelle laughed. 'This is slightly embarrassing, but on *Plenty of Fish*. I say it's embarrassing because I was totally against Internet dating. I'd had a break-up almost a year before and I wasn't having much luck on the pub scene … if anything it was just depressing to see what was out there. So, one of my friends was thinking of trying it and she persuaded me to as well. I had a few chats, got a few messages from creeps looking for one-nighters, and then Nick was the first person I agreed to meet.'

'Wow.' Caitlin was genuinely intrigued. 'How does it work? I mean … I presume you have to upload a picture, but can just anyone see it? Weren't you afraid you'd be spotted by someone you know?'

'Yeah, I was really nervous about that. To be honest, I was delighted to shut the account down. I'd spotted a couple of guys

I knew on it.' Michelle laughed. 'And wait for this, I got a message from an old university lecturer.'

'Ugh no, you didn't answer him?'

'Of course not. I don't think he knew who I was or anything. There were about seventy students in the class; we never really had any direct communication with him. But luckily I closed my account soon after that. I'd been on a few dates with Nick and one evening he told me that his sister had asked him if it was serious … fishing, he was, to see what I'd say. I told him that I was if he was and that's pretty much our story so far.'

Caitlin sipped her coffee, considering what Michelle had told her. She was very open; she didn't seem like someone who had something to hide. 'How about writing an article about it?' she asked.

'No way! Jesus, I'm not going on record about that.' Michelle was quiet for a minute, and then, her voice gentle, she asked, 'How did you meet David?'

David. Caitlin stopped smiling. Had she told Michelle his name was David? Of course she had. She'd said it when, in a moment of weakness that first time they'd met, she'd shown her his picture. 'I don't really want to talk about it, it's hard …'

Michelle put her hand on Caitlin's arm for a moment. 'I'm sorry, I shouldn't have asked. I've been thinking about what you told me, and this might sound ridiculous, but there's this woman – I've visited her a few times – an old itinerant woman who tells fortunes. Maybe she could tell you something. I don't know if you believe in anything like that, but she's really good. When my mother was sick, she told me exactly what the problem was … a sickness of the blood and the bones, she said. And that's what it was.'

'Is your mother still alive?'

Michelle shook her head. 'She died two years ago – Multiple Myeloma – it's a cancer inside the bone marrow.'

'I'm sorry. What about your father?'

'My parents split up years ago. He lives in the north. We don't really keep in touch.'

Caitlin looked at Michelle and wondered if the reason she liked her so well was because they had so much in common. 'I know how it is. Both my parents are dead. They died when I was little … an accident.'

Michelle nodded. Caitlin didn't think she looked very surprised, although she was probably just being diplomatic.

'Do you have any siblings?' Michelle asked.

Caitlin shook her head. She thought of the boy, it was a hazy memory now, so much so that she wasn't even sure it had happened. 'No, just me,' she said. 'I was adopted by a couple, but they broke up about a year after they took me in. He didn't want me, and she blamed me for his leaving. We're not close. Actually, David's mum is more like a mother to me now. She's the only family I've got.'

'How old were you when your parents died?'

'Five. But I remember them as though it was yesterday. My mother loved to sing, my dad too. They were always making recordings. I've got a cassette, one that was in my tape recorder, that my mother used to play sometimes to get me to go to sleep. I don't know where everything else went … I was only allowed to keep a couple of toys. One of the social workers took me to my house and told me I could pick out just two things. The rest I suppose got packed up to go to some charity or other, but I've still got that cassette with them singing and joking.'

'Wow. That's incredible. It must be hard, though, listening to it. What happened to them?'

Caitlin shrugged. 'Car accident … some crazy driver ran a red light.'

It was a story she'd grown used to telling. It didn't even feel like a lie anymore. And even if it was, it wasn't her lie. She'd believed it, visualized it for years until she'd found those clippings – so to repeat it came naturally. She wondered how Michelle would react if she told her the truth. She'd never told anyone the truth. Not even David.

'About the fortune teller though,' she said, shaking herself from the past, 'it wouldn't really be my thing. It's not that I don't believe in it, I'm open to most things, it's more that it would creep me out. I'm a coward like that.' She smiled, made a point of looking at her watch. 'Now we'd better get to looking at this article – I hadn't meant to keep you all day.'

Chapter Thirty-Three

Michelle

Michelle didn't know what to make of Caitlin's account of how her parents had died. It wasn't that she might have been lying that bothered her, not really. In her place, Michelle would have attempted to evade the question altogether. It was the fact that Caitlin didn't *look* as though she were lying, so either she was very adept at it, or she believed what she'd said to be the truth. She hadn't had a chance to tell Nick yet. She'd rather wait until they were face-to-face.

'What's up? You seem miles away,' Conor said as they made their way away from the North Quays and towards Abbey Street.

'Oh, nothing.' Michelle knew she'd been quiet. She'd been thinking about what Caitlin had told her that morning, about her adoptive parents being cold. She didn't know how much of it, if anything, she should tell Nick. He'd blame himself, she knew that. If Johnny Davis hadn't lost it, Caitlin wouldn't have been adopted. End of.

It was beginning to drizzle with rain. Michelle pulled up the hood of her blue raincoat and quickened her step to match Conor's. It had been one of the tough parts of volunteering at first, being out in all weathers, but she'd grown used to it and now she didn't mind so much. Strangely, she seldom seemed to get sick even when she got soaked through.

It was strange too, she thought, how little she knew about

Conor. They'd been doing the rounds together for more than six months, but their talk never moved beyond the superficial. She liked him. He struck her as unflappable, someone who would remain calm no matter what way the tide turned. 'Do you think there should be an onus on adoptive parents to tell a child about their past?' she asked him now.

He didn't answer straight away. 'I suppose it depends on the circumstances and on the child – whether they could handle it.'

'And what if it was something bad – say the parents had been murdered, for example?'

'Hmm … I don't know. I mean, thinking about it, my instinct would be to tell the child the truth, but there are so many reasons why kids end up in care and all of them are bad. It's like … what if your parents were junkies? Would it be better to know that or just to think they gave you up and you never knew why? You could argue that the kids should know – for medical reasons if nothing else – because there might be a chance that they've inherited some genetic illness. I guess for that reason alone I think it's important for everyone to know who their biological parents are. Murder though, that's pretty rough …'

'Yeah, it might be easier to tell them that their parents had been killed in an accident.'

'Could be. I mean, you wouldn't be hiding anything like medical facts – but then you couldn't tell the kid their real identity either. They'd be bound to find out the truth; all they'd have to do is type the names into Google these days. A headline story like that, it'd come up straight away. Interesting dilemma. What made you bring it up? Is it something you came across when you were doing those interviews?' He looked at her sideways, blinking against the rain.

Their next stop was huddled a few hundred metres away in a doorway, sleeping bag disguising the human form – not an inch of anything visible.

'It was just something I saw in a documentary,' she said.

When they stopped by the man in the sleeping bag, she took out the photo of David. She'd mentioned to Conor what she was planning before they'd left, told him how the woman she'd written the article for had her own story. She hadn't mentioned Nick.

The man, sitting on sheets of cardboard, was one of their regular stops. He had been on the streets for as long as Michelle had been with the Simon Community.

'Hey, Stevie, how are you doing today?' Conor leant down and handed the man his usual sandwich: tuna and cheese. If you gave him anything else, he'd make a face. That was the thing about volunteering, you got to know the people, their likes and dislikes.

Michelle held the picture of David out to him. 'Stevie, have you ever seen this man?' Stevie stopped unwrapping the sandwich to look up. He sat forward and peered at the picture.

'Might have …' he said. 'What's he done?'

Michelle shook her head. 'He's missing. I thought I'd show the picture around, see if anyone recognized him.'

'Hard to know, but … there's a fella like him I've seen up at the Capuchin … has a beard, but he looks like him round the eyes.' Stevie traced around David's eyes without touching the print. 'Yeah, could be …' he said.

Michelle felt a bubble of excitement. She knew she shouldn't. There was every chance that Stevie was wrong, but still. They exchanged a few more words with the man, and Conor passed him a ten-pack of cigarettes before they moved on. Seeing Michelle arch an eyebrow he gave a rueful smile. 'I know, but what else has he got?' he said, and Michelle smiled. Conor often gave something to the regular faces, if not cigarettes, then a second-hand book.

At every stop she showed the picture of David. The next few people shook their heads, saying they didn't know him. Then she handed the photo to a woman who stared at it for a few minutes before slowly nodding. She jabbed at the picture with her index finger. 'Yeah, I think I've seen him … down at the day centre.'

'The Capuchin?' Michelle asked.

'Yeah. In the mornings. I go down there, have a shower, you know.'

'And you've seen this man?'

The woman pulled back from the picture, began picking at the wrapper of the sandwich. 'Ah well, I couldn't swear on it or nothing, but it looks like him ...'

Two possible sightings. She knew it shouldn't, but it raised Michelle's hopes. 'Do you think there's anything in it?' she asked Conor.

He shrugged. 'I wouldn't pin my hopes on it, but you never know.'

She nodded. Conor was right. It would be some fluke if she found Caitlin's husband that easily, but still ... She wondered if she ought to say anything to Nick. There was no point unless it could be substantiated. She'd go to the centre and show David's picture to some of the volunteers there. She knew they must see a lot of faces, but if he was someone who went there regularly, they might just recognize him.

Chapter Thirty-Four

Nick

Nick was sitting at the table with his laptop in front of him, Bruce Springsteen's 'Dancing in the Dark' at low volume in the background, when he heard Michelle's key in the door. Rowdy, lying in his bed in the corner of the room, lifted his head to look up, then jumped out, tail wagging, and went to the closed living room door.

'Hey, what are you up to?' Michelle dropped her backpack, stooped to pet the dog, and then put her arms round Nick's neck.

He gestured towards the screen. 'Trying to find out as much as I can about Caitlin's husband. I found his name easily enough; he's still a Facebook friend of hers. Naturally, there haven't been any posts for over a year. His surname's Casey and he worked at Gabriel's boys' school. He'd been there for several years before he disappeared, according to the dates. I wrote down a few names, people who seemed to like everything he posted, had a bit of banter going on. Of course, that doesn't mean those people were close to him. We all know what Facebook is like; people you haven't seen in twenty years might look like your best friends. I did come across a familiar face though – a guy called Andy Quinn who was playing in the band at the wine bar with Caitlin. There are a lot of photos of the three of them. I imagine he'd be worth talking to. Although he wasn't too friendly the night I met him, he seemed really possessive of Caitlin and not necessarily in a healthy way.'

'Nick?'

'Hmmm?' He was still looking at the screen, scanning through different sites. He looked up when Michelle pulled out a seat and sat next to him.

'I'm not sure Caitlin knows what happened to her parents.'

'What do you mean?' he said.

'We talked about it earlier when I went around to her office. She said that her parents died in a car accident.'

Nick nodded, his mind working. 'Okay …'

'I was thinking about it, and maybe she said it because she didn't want to say they'd been murdered, I probably wouldn't, but … I don't think she was lying … it was too smooth.'

'But her name is Davis, right? If the adoptive parents had really wanted to make sure she didn't find out, surely they'd have changed her surname. They'd realize that all she'd have to do is search, the same as I did, and bingo, she'd find out the truth.'

'Not necessarily, I mean it would've taken a lot more effort back then, things weren't at the click of a button. And besides if they didn't tell her her parents' Christian names…'

'True.' He paused, digesting this, thinking that maybe it wouldn't be such a bad thing if Caitlin didn't know. At least she'd have been saved the pain of that. 'Did she say anything else? Anything more about her husband?'

'Not particularly. She's close to his mother. Her adoptive parents split up, the man wasn't in the picture at all, and the woman … they're not really close.'

Nick shook his head. 'I've got to find this guy. At least find out what happened to him. It's the only thing I can think to do …'

'What if Caitlin finds it strange? I mean, if you talk to this guy Andy, he's surely going to tell her, and what would she make of that?'

'That's true. But I don't have a choice. I have to talk to the people who knew David. The Internet will only get me so far.'

'What if you talk to her? You could tell her you've got a friend who's a detective or something, that you could ask him to look into it as a favour … I know if my husband was missing, I'd be willing to accept all the help I could get.'

Nick squeezed her hand. 'It's not a bad idea. Better than looking like a pair of do-gooders she's just met.' He got up and paced the room. 'What exactly did she say about her adoptive parents, was it bad?'

Michelle shrugged. 'Like I said, the guy left. She seems to think the woman blamed her. The woman wasn't cruel or anything, just cold I think. The way Caitlin put it, it sounded like she just went through the motions of caring for a child. She's already been through so much in her life – do you think maybe if she doesn't know what happened with Johnny and Rachel, it might be better to keep it that way?'

'Yeah, I suppose it's partly cowardice, but I was thinking the same. Of course, we don't know that she doesn't. Maybe she's just repeated it so many times it's easy for her to say.'

Michelle nodded. 'I was thinking about it all afternoon, whether children have the right to know where they come from. I don't know what I'd do in that situation, if I were the parent I mean. I think I'd probably lie too. How could you expect a young child to understand? Maybe when they were older, but then too much time would have passed … I'd probably never get around to telling them.' Michelle yawned.

He guessed it had been a long day for her. He was feeling shattered himself. But then he'd felt like that most of the time since his diagnosis. 'Why don't you head up to bed? I'll be there shortly, as soon as I tidy up down here.'

He saw Michelle hesitate, then she spoke. 'There's something else. I wasn't even going to mention it because it might be nothing. I'll know tomorrow …'

'What?'

'I thought it might be a good idea to show David's picture

when I was doing the soup run, see if it jogged anyone's memory, if anyone had seen him. Two of the people I showed it to said they might have seen him at the Capuchin day centre. Neither of them could be sure, and it might come to nothing, but I'm going to go over there to talk with some of the volunteers.' She stifled another yawn. 'Like I said, I wasn't going to say anything until I'd spoken to them ...'

Nick nodded. He couldn't believe all that Michelle was doing to try to help him, first by making contact with Caitlin, then by finding out about Lydia, even if that had come to nothing. Now this, a lead – no matter how tenuous – in the search for Caitlin's husband. He stood to hug her, then winced as a stabbing pain stopped him in his tracks. Michelle moved towards him swiftly, putting a hand on his arm. 'You okay?'

He exhaled, afraid to move too suddenly again. 'I haven't been great. I keep getting these pains.' He took her hand. 'Michelle, I just want to say thank you ... what you've done so far, it's incredible. You're incredible, but then I already knew that. Even if nothing comes of tomorrow, don't think I don't appreciate you trying. Go on now, you head up to bed, I'll be there in a few minutes. Oh, by the way, how would feel about going to the wine bar on Wednesday evening? Caitlin did say we should come, and maybe we'd get a chance to talk to that guy Andy. He might be more amiable if you're there. Wouldn't think I was hitting on Caitlin at least.'

Michelle turned at the door and smiled. 'It's a date,' she said. And he smiled back through another searing pain.

Chapter Thirty-Five

Caitlin

Caitlin arrived late so she wouldn't have to speak to Andy before they began playing. He was already seated along with the rest of the group and they were clearly waiting for her to arrive. Andy looked up as soon as she pushed the door open; she could feel his eyes on her as she entered the bar. She was relieved to see Michelle and Nick were sitting at a table in the corner near the door. Good, let Andy see that she had more friends, that she didn't have to rely on him.

'Hey, we thought you weren't coming. Is everything okay?'

'Yeah, fine,' she said. She smiled briefly to take the chill from her response, then set her case on the floor and snapped the locks open. Andy didn't have time to say anything more as she took the violin in her arms and nodded to the group to show that she was ready.

She didn't know if it was her irritation with Andy, or if the paranoia of recent events had coloured everything, but the proximity of the other musicians made her feel claustrophobic. She felt their eyes on her as she played and any prolonged look, any awkward glance, was a cause for suspicion.

At the interval she stood, ready for escape.

'Caitie,' Andy called, and she had to stop. 'Would you like a drink?'

She shook her head. 'I'm good, thanks,' she told him, laying her violin in the case and crossing the room to where Michelle and Nick sat.

'Wow, you play so well,' Michelle said, rising from her seat to embrace her warmly. Nick stood too and shook her hand, which struck her as endearingly formal. He asked her if she'd like a drink, and she glanced towards the bar and saw Andy pay the barman. He turned quickly, catching her eye before she could look away, and she turned back to Michelle, hoping that would discourage him from joining them. Much to her annoyance, he did anyway.

'We met a couple of weeks ago,' he told Nick. 'Didn't know that you had already met each other?'

'We didn't,' Caitlin said stiffly. 'I didn't know that Nick was Michelle's boyfriend.'

'Ah,' Andy smiled. He looked pleased that her two new friends were a couple, that Nick was suddenly no threat – as a man at least. He held his hand out to Michelle. 'Andy. Lovely to meet you. Can I get you anything, a top-up?' he asked, eyeing their glasses of juice.

Michelle shook her head. 'No, we're good, thanks.' She smiled and took a sip of her drink. 'I love the music; how long have you guys been doing this?'

Andy looked at Michelle. 'Oh, I don't know, two years maybe? Caitie joined us about six months ago, didn't you? I finally managed to convince her she was ready.'

'Oh? How long have you been playing, Caitlin?'

'About two years. David, my husband, taught me. He was an incredible musician.' She felt the need to mention David, to break the illusion that this was a double date. She was still seething at the fact that Andy had insinuated himself upon them.

She asked Michelle about her Zumba class, and heard Andy ask Nick something about the band he used to be in. As the conversation broke into two pairs she struggled to concentrate on what Michelle said; she was half-listening to the two men, surprised by Andy's sudden friendliness towards Nick. She wondered if he was trying to lure Nick, if he was following up on his suspicion that Nick had been the one to take that photo – the one he claimed had been taken from the bar. Caitlin looked round the room now. She couldn't see the other musicians; they were probably outside smoking. She didn't like that new guy, Brian, there was something about him that gave her the creeps. It was the fact that he didn't say anything, and she'd caught him looking at her a few times. She thought she might mention it to Andy, try to find out something more about him. And it would be no harm, she supposed, if Andy did talk with Nick. Just because she liked Nick and Michelle, didn't necessarily mean they didn't have their own agenda. She'd have to try to get over her annoyance with Andy. He had, she reminded herself, been her only confidante for the past year. She couldn't forget that. She just wished he'd back off a little. How could she tell him that without making the situation worse? He'd surely accuse her of narcissism.

She looked at her watch now and tapped Andy lightly on the arm as she saw Brian reappear at his keyboard. 'Andy, we'd best get back.'

'Yeah, sure.' He stood. 'Lovely to meet you guys. Talk later yeah?' Nick shook his hand. Michelle smiled, said that if they left before the end, she'd give Caitlin a call. She'd love to meet for a coffee.

Nick had barely looked at her throughout the conversation – instead talking to Andy the whole time. He looked up now and smiled. 'It was lovely to meet you again, Caitlin.' Something in the way he said her name was oddly familiar. She smiled at them both and returned to the band.

They left about an hour into the band's second set, Michelle giving her a small wave as they slipped from their table. When the group had finished playing, Caitlin packed up quickly.

'Are you staying on?' Andy asked.

'No, I'm pretty tired and I've an early start – editing.'

'Okay, do you want a lift?'

'I'm driving. Didn't fancy hanging around.' She pulled her jacket on, picked up her scarf and wrapped it round her neck, trying to ignore his wounded look.

'I'll walk you out,' he said.

'Bye guys,' she called over her shoulder. The singer smiled and said goodnight. Brian continued dismantling the keyboard without looking up. Bloody weirdo. She wished they'd never let him join.

The cold hit them as soon as they walked out the door. The quays were quiet, and Caitlin walked straight to the car.

'How is everything?' Andy asked. 'We haven't spoken in days. I was thinking about you, wondering if anything else had happened.'

'No, nothing,' she told him.

He looked surprised. 'Well, that's good.' She thought of the photo of the park, the one that appeared on Twitter, but she said nothing. She appreciated his looking out for her, but it was this overprotectiveness that was making her feel smothered. She needed space. And besides, maybe nothing else would happen. Maybe whoever it was doing these random acts would tire when they didn't get the reaction they wanted. Even as she thought this, she knew that it was herself she was trying to convince.

'I'm sorry about what I said, Caitlin. I know you're still pissed off with me.'

'No, I'm not.'

'Come on. You've been ignoring me. Don't say you haven't.'

She pulled her coat round herself. 'I've been busy. Michelle and Nick had a barbecue, and I've started Zumba classes …'

'How do you know those two?' He was looking at her, curious.

She shrugged. 'Michelle wrote an article for the magazine. She's a volunteer with the Simon Community.'

'Okay. And you don't think it's a bit of a coincidence, him

turning up at the gig, and her submitting the article. Did she send it straight to you?'

'No,' she lied. 'It was just addressed to the magazine.'

'Did you tell her anything about David?'

'Just what everyone else knows: that he disappeared.'

Andy shook his head. 'You don't know who these people are, Caitlin. You're too trusting. Right now, there's nothing to say that this guy isn't the one who's behind that call, the Twitter account, everything.'

'So, what I am supposed to do? Go around suspecting everyone I meet? For all I know, it could be you.' She went around to the back of the car, opened it and carefully placed her violin case inside.

'Don't be ridiculous,' he said. 'Why would I do that? All I want is to protect you.'

'Andy, I don't want to argue. And I appreciate you looking out for me, I really do, but I've been feeling smothered. I'm not pushing you away. You've been a great friend; I just need to breathe on my own. Do you know what I'm saying?'

'And what about the psycho, the one masquerading as David. How are you going to deal with that?'

'The guards …'

'The guards will do nothing, we both know that. They haven't exactly been effective in finding out what happened to David, have they?'

She shrugged. 'Maybe they'll get bored. If I don't respond, they might just find someone else to play their sick games on.'

'And if they don't? If they come after you?'

'Then I'll deal with it. Look, I'll call you – if anything happens – okay?'

She went around to the driver's side, got in and drove away. In the rear-view mirror, she saw Andy turn and walk back into the wine bar. Maybe now he'd let her be.

Chapter Thirty-Six

Michelle

When Michelle arrived at the Capuchin Centre on Bow Street a queue was snaking its way from the arched wooden doors and along the perimeter of the building. The priest in the friary had told her they closed for an hour to prepare lunch, so she'd come at the busiest time. Many types littered the queue, from those constantly on the move to families hoping to get enough groceries to keep them going for a day or two. Some of the homeless had already availed of the morning services; they were clean-shaven, wearing fresh clothes. The only giveaway was a sleeping bag rolled beneath an arm, or a shopping bag stuffed with their few possessions. One man, with a Jack Russell terrier on a lead, was a familiar face on the streets of Dublin.

At 12 p.m., a lock was turned and the assembly streamed through the arched doors and into the dining hall. As Michelle followed the cortège, she felt rather than saw curious eyes upon her. She hung back and waited until the rush began to thin before approaching one of the volunteers, a woman who was busy stacking plates at the head of the queue.

She looked up with a friendly expression. 'What can I do for you, love?'

Explaining that she was from the Simon Community, Michelle took the picture of David from her bag and asked if it would be possible to speak to a few of the volunteers to see if they recognized him. The woman nodded and looked at the photo, but didn't react. 'If you can wait until they're all served up,' she said.

Michelle nodded. People were too busy now to pay her any attention, and she stood back and surveyed the room. Numerous volunteers filled and handed out plates piled with food. They smiled at and seemed to know by name a lot of the people who came. The Capuchins were doing an impressive job. Not only did they provide meals and a warm, safe environment, they gave clothes to those who needed them too. If she had more time, it was something she'd like to get involved in, but she had enough on her plate for now.

The woman she'd spoken to signalled to her when the queues had died down. 'Go ahead, love,' she said, nodding towards her colleagues.

Michelle approached a young man and a girl who were standing chatting and showed them the picture of David. The man looked closely at it. 'I don't know,' he said. 'I couldn't be sure, he looks familiar but …'

The girl leaned in, taking the photo from his hand. She nodded. 'Appearances can change so radically. He does look familiar. There's a guy who used to come in. I haven't seen him for a couple of months though. He had a beard, but … it might have been him.'

She had no more luck with the rest of the Capuchin volunteers. A few of them agreed he looked familiar, but none of them could be sure. Michelle gave them her number and left a copy of the photo with them. 'If you could give me a ring if you do see him,' she said.

She left feeling despondent. The people she'd talked to in the street had got her hopes up, but who knew, she thought, maybe her enquiries would bear fruit yet. It certainly did no harm to get the picture out there.

When she called Nick to tell him, he had news of his own.

Gary had called to inform him that Daniel's death certificate had read "death by misadventure," which could mean anything.

'I have to find out what happened to that child,' he said. 'And then Caitlin … why would she have said she didn't have any siblings? Why wouldn't she have mentioned him? It's odd, no?'

'I don't know, Nick. Maybe because he died so young. I mean why would she tell me – a virtual stranger – about a little brother who died? Maybe she doesn't even remember him. She'd have been what, five, at the time?'

It was logical, wasn't it? Who knew what a five-year-old kid could block out – what they'd choose not to remember. Besides, Michelle needed Nick to drop this. In the state he was in, this wild chase into the past could do him no good. He needed to take care of himself – despite his protests that he was okay, she could see the effects that his sickness was having. This kind of stress was the type of thing that could lead him to drinking again and that would be the end of him getting on any transplant list.

'I don't know,' Nick said. 'Look, is there any way you could bring it up the next time you meet her? Not directly, obviously, but you could find a way, couldn't you? I know you think I should drop this, and I will, but you know me. I won't rest easy until I know what happened. I have to know if I was responsible, if Johnny Davis …'

'Okay. I'll try, Nick. I'll give her a call, see if she wants to meet. Anyway, I was calling to tell you I've just been to the Capuchin.'

'And?'

'A few of the volunteers looked at the photo of David and said he looked familiar, but there was nothing concrete. Someone said they may have seen him a few months ago, but not recently. To be honest it was a bit of a let-down, but I left my number with them just in case.'

She hung up, downhearted, wishing now that she'd never succeeded in finding Caitlin Davis. It was enough having to deal with Nick's illness without him trying to resolve the tragic events of his past life too. Would it do any good, she wondered, if she were to talk to Tessa? Try to persuade her that all this was likely to do Nick more harm than good? But no, she had no right to interfere in his life. And besides, surely the hypnotist would know that anyway. Surely she wouldn't allow the sessions to take them down this route if she thought it would disrupt what they'd set out to achieve.

She texted Caitlin, best to follow Nick's wishes for the moment. She had no idea what she'd say or how to raise the subject when they met. It was only 1 p.m. – maybe she'd catch her before her lunch.

I'm in the city this afternoon. Don't suppose you're free for lunch?

Ten minutes later the phone pinged.

Love to. Ideally somewhere near here? I could meet you at the gateway to Stephen's Green in fifteen mins?

There was nothing like getting everything done in one day, so she texted Nick and told him she had a date.

It was one of those bright November days. Michelle stood at the entrance to the Green and waited for Caitlin. A busker played at the top of Grafton Street. She was early so she wandered over to listen. She wasn't familiar with the song he was playing and wondered if it was an original piece of music. She'd always envied those who could play – she'd attempted guitar once, but her hands were too small, wouldn't stretch to reach those tricky chords. Well they were basic chords she supposed really, but still too difficult for her. Instead she resigned herself to the role of appreciator like she'd always been. Standing in the sun, her back against a store wall, she thought about David, wondered whether he had composed his own pieces for violin, or if he'd played in an orchestra. She'd ask Caitlin if she didn't find it too upsetting to talk about. She still hadn't thought of a way to bring up the dead child and any other topic was preferable to the task Nick had assigned her.

At 1.15 exactly she saw Caitlin stride up North King Street. Her hands were in the pockets of her red trench coat, her dark hair bounced as she walked. She was wearing heels, but even without them she was tall. Michelle searched in her bag and threw some coins into the busker's case before crossing the street to meet her.

At once Caitlin smiled. 'It's such a nice day, I thought we might get sandwiches or something and have them in the park?' She shielded her eyes from the glare of the late autumn sun and looked around, presumably for somewhere they might buy lunch.

'Yeah, that's fine by me. It's nice to be outdoors while we've got the chance.'

In a small convenience store they got what they wanted and strolled back into the Green.

'How have you been?' Caitlin asked. 'And Nick?'

The trees had begun to lose their leaves; by the edges of the path there were clusters of bronze. They walked until they reached a bench near the duck pond and sat down. Michelle was wondering how she might raise the topic of siblings. It made her think of her own sister. Sarah rarely got in touch since their mother had died. It didn't surprise her, she'd always had a tendency to be selfish; too wrapped up in her husband and her children to care about anyone else. When their mother was sick, Sarah visited only every fortnight. She didn't care that Michelle was under a huge amount of pressure trying to work and get her mother to her hospital visits four times a week. When Michelle had come down with a bad flu and was terrified of passing it on to her mother whose immune system was weakened, she'd called Sarah and asked if she could take time off work to take her to her appointments. Sarah had refused point-blank, asked what was wrong with the taxi service the hospital provided, couldn't their mother use that? It wouldn't kill her, would it? Sometimes Michelle wondered if her sister even registered the seriousness of their mother's condition. Instead, she made jibes, told Michelle that she could be a martyr if she wanted to, but she wouldn't. And in that she was true to her word.

Caitlin was rummaging in her bag. She pulled out an early copy of *New Woman* and handed it to Michelle. Michelle she eagerly opened it on the contents page, then skipped forward as Caitlin told her that her article was on page fifteen. Readers had really related to her last article, Caitlin told her. They'd already received emails from people who had, or had almost, been homeless at some point. They verified the stories of the people who Michelle had interviewed. 'Hopefully, it will help in some way,' she said. 'In raising awareness at least.'

Michelle nodded as she scanned through her own words. 'I'll send it to the minister for Housing, as well as local TDs,' she said. 'At least it will feel like I'm doing something.'

Caitlin took her sandwich from its wrapper. Michelle glanced at her. 'I don't suppose you'd be interested in running one on healthcare?' she asked. 'Along the same lines. I told you that my mum died ... I used to go to the hospital with her four days a week for her treatments, so I know the problems first-hand.'

'Okay. What do you have in mind? When you say problems, what exactly do you mean?'

Michelle exhaled. 'The staff shortages. The lack of money. The failure by the government to invest in long-term solutions. Things like that. In my mother's case, late prescriptions so that she couldn't start her chemo on time. Hours spent sitting waiting for an infusion before someone even came to put a needle in her arm, doctors unavailable to see her, test results never returned. She should still be here as far as I'm concerned. She'd been in remission for two years, and they brought her in once a month to do bloods. The cancer was back, had obviously been back for some time for it to have escalated the way it had, and we weren't even told.'

Caitlin stopped eating, put a hand on her arm. 'That's awful. Did you question them about it? Ask them why they hadn't told you?'

'Yeah. But I got nowhere as you can imagine. The consultant

185

agreed with me about the department, said that all the things I'd pointed out were correct. She said she didn't know if it would have made any difference if mum had gone on treatment, or if she had done, what quality of life she'd have had. You know how it is when you talk to these people, they try to convince you and it's hard when you're grieving to see things objectively. Two years have passed now and there are times when I still consider making a complaint, make them pull out the files to see all those results that we never saw. But it wouldn't bring her back.' She paused. 'I'm sorry, I shouldn't talk like this ... it was unthinking ...'

Caitlin brushed the crumbs from her skirt. 'It's a good idea. The Irish health system's a mess, everybody knows that, so to have someone with first-hand experience of it would really ring home.' She stood up, screwed the paper from her sandwich into a ball and made for a nearby litter bin.

Michelle rose too, and they began to walk. 'I was listening to a magistrate on the radio recently. He was talking about what should happen with siblings in an adoptive situation. If someone wants to adopt one child, usually the younger one, but not their brother or sister, is it right to separate the siblings? It was interesting, and I thought of you ... I couldn't remember if you'd said if you had any brothers or sisters?'

She glanced at Caitlin who shook her head. 'No, just me,' she said. 'And I was lucky, I suppose, I didn't spend too much time in the orphanage. I couldn't have been there any more than six months, though to me then, it felt like years. All I wanted was to go home.'

No brothers or sisters. That was that then. Either Caitlin had blocked the memory of her brother or she didn't want to talk about it. The only other way she could find out what had happened to the boy was to pay another visit to Lydia Davis. The idea of Lydia prompted her next question. 'And you didn't have any other family?' she asked. 'Aunts, uncles?'

Caitlin shook her head. 'Just me,' she said. 'Alone in the world until I met David. Gillian's the only family I've got now.'

Michelle glanced at Caitlin, but she was looking out at the duck pond. Could it be that she didn't know about Lydia Davis, that she'd blocked out everything that had happened before the incident, that the only people she remembered were her parents? She'd heard about people blocking bad experiences, knew that the mind was capable of going into shut-down mode. Whatever the truth, there was nothing she was going to glean here that might help Nick uncover the truth. The only alternative was to try Caitlin's aunt again, and hope that she could persuade her to talk this time.

Chapter Thirty-Seven

Nick

Nick was disappointed that Caitlin hadn't admitted to having had a brother, but what had he expected? Either she genuinely didn't remember Daniel, or she didn't like to think about her past, in which case she was hardly going to talk about it with someone she'd only just met, was she? He'd have to wait and see if he discovered anything else through his sessions with Tessa.

The important thing for now was to find out more about David, Caitlin's husband. When he'd spoken to Andy Quinn at the wine bar he'd established that the two men had been friends. If it happened that Caitlin was reluctant to talk to him about her husband, then this was another avenue. It might even prove a better way; after all there were things that men sometimes knew about each other that never reached their wives.

With this in mind, he had arranged to meet Andy. He hadn't told Michelle; she was at her Zumba class and he hadn't expected Andy to agree so readily even though the musician had given him his card in the wine bar and said they must meet for a beer. Now he sat there and thought about the scant information he had about Caitlin's husband. He knew his place of work, the fact that he was a music teacher and that he'd been married to Caitlin. Another search on the Internet had failed to throw anything else up. It seemed that David didn't use social media much and the only information to come up when he put the name into Google were the archived newspaper articles on the case.

He sipped a glass of water, would have given anything to order a pint. What would Andy Quinn make of him? Maybe he would be the type of man who didn't trust other men who didn't drink. He watched the door and raised a hand when he saw Andy enter. He saw him eye the glass before Nick doubtfully.

'Can I get you something?' he asked.

'No, thanks.'

'What's with the water?' Andy asked him when he came back, sipping his own pint of ale and putting it down before him.

'Liver's shot. I was told to stop,' he said.

'Jesus, that bad?'

He nodded. 'I'm on medication – I get sick as a pig if I touch the stuff.' He didn't mention the transplant; that would be a step too far. He didn't want this guy to see him as a dead man walking, which, if he didn't get on that list, was what he was.

They talked about music for a bit. Nick told him about his days with the band, how it had come to an end about six years before. He didn't mention Caitlin. He figured Andy Quinn was as interested in her as he was, but for different reasons, and he didn't have to wait long before he brought her up.

'How did you hear about the sessions in the wine bar?'

Nick sipped his water. 'Social media. Twitter, I think.'

Andy nodded. 'Don't know what we did before it. And your girlfriend – Michelle, is it? Is she a journalist?'

'No, a fitness instructor.'

Andy looked confused. 'Ah, I thought Caitlin said she'd written an article …'

'Yeah, about homelessness. She's a volunteer with the Simon Community; it's the first time she's published something though, she's big into getting the word out. She and Caitlin really seem to have hit it off.' He waited a beat. 'And you and Caitlin, how do you know each other?'

189

Andy looked up from his beer, eyeing him silently before answering. 'We go way back. Myself and David were in university together.'

Nick nodded. 'Caitlin told us about her husband. It doesn't bear imagining. I don't know how she's coped. I suppose you just have to somehow.'

'She's resilient, and she's got support. I've been there, made sure she's okay. David would expect it.'

'She said there were no leads. What do you think happened?'

Andy looked into his glass. 'If I knew that I wouldn't be here,' he said. 'I'd be after the one responsible, making them pay ...'

'You think he's dead?'

'David wasn't the sort to just up and leave. And he certainly wouldn't have done it without telling me ... we were like brothers.'

Nick could hear the hurt in his voice. He hadn't ever formed relationships like that with other men, not even when he was a boy. He'd kept mostly to himself. Sure, there was banter, but he was always on the perimeter. He liked it that way. He thought he'd better try now, though, to form at least some kind of trust with Andy Quinn.

'Look, I know someone who might be able to help,' he said.

'How do you mean? A detective?'

'Not officially, more a freelancer, but he's good. He won't stop until he's got something.'

Andy nodded. 'Okay, set it up. Can't do any harm, can it? I'm happy to help with anything he needs.'

Nick thought for a minute. 'He doesn't quite work like that. He prefers to stay in the shadows; anything you think might be useful for him, it has to go through me.'

Andy Quinn looked at him incredulously, making some sound between a guffaw and a genuine laugh. 'What? What kind of dodgy character is this?' He paused. 'Or is it you, Nick? That's it, isn't it? You're the one playing detective.'

Nick didn't laugh. 'I know people,' he said. 'I'll do whatever I can to help.'

Andy's eyes slid over him – he knew he was trying to decide if he could trust him or not, but given the circumstances, there weren't too many options.

'Okay,' Andy said. 'What do you want to know?'

Over the next twenty minutes, Andy sketched a picture of David – who he'd been, the friendship between the two men. 'Is there anything else?' Nick asked. 'Anything that could be connected with his disappearance?'

Andy shook his head. 'Nothing that I can think of.'

'What about his relationship with Caitlin, any cracks there? Would you say they were as close as they'd always been when he disappeared?'

A pause. 'David loved Caitlin. He'd never have left without saying anything.'

He hadn't answered the question directly. 'Were there any problems though? Anything he may not have told her?'

Andy shrugged. 'No.'

'What about friends … apart from you and Caitlin, who was he friendly with?'

'A couple of the teachers in the school where he worked, this girl, Louise, in particular …'

'Okay. Does she still work at the school?'

'I don't know. Maybe.'

'And did Caitlin know this girl? Were they close?'

Andy shook his head. 'David and Louise were work friends. They spent a lot of time together though. I told David it wasn't a good idea, but he insisted there was nothing going on.'

'Did you believe him?'

'I don't know. Like I say, he loved Caitlin, but that's not to say that nothing happened with Louise. You know how it is.'

Nick picked up his phone and typed the name 'Louise' into the notes app. He'd need to talk to this girl, see if she knew anything.

'There's no chance they went away together? That he just hadn't the guts to tell Caitlin?'

'No, I've seen the girl since. She was with a guy ...'

'Would the police have spoken to her during the initial investigation, do you think?'

'I'd say they spoke to all his colleagues. Anyone who knew him, especially since he went missing after leaving the school.'

Louise. At least he had one avenue to explore and an interesting one, it seemed, given that David's best friend suspected there may have been something between them. Still, it could be nothing. And even if it was something, the girl was still around, so there was nothing to suggest that their friendship had anything to do with David's sudden disappearance.

'Is there anything else you can think of? Any money worries, any way in which he might have landed himself in trouble?'

'No. I don't think so. David was straight up. Caitlin and I ... we went over everything I don't know how many times. His disappearance just doesn't add up.'

Nick nodded. It wasn't much to go on, but it was a start. He'd look Louise up. It shouldn't be hard to find out if she was still working in the school. And if she had truly been a friend of David's, surely she'd be willing to talk to him.

Andy Quinn took another gulp of his beer, eyeing Nick over the glass. 'Why are you doing this?' he asked.

Nick shrugged. 'I want to help. Simple as ... that. A man doesn't simply vanish.'

But even as he said the words, he knew they weren't true, and the way that Andy Quinn was looking at him, it seemed he knew it too. Thousands of people went missing each year, and there was no way for him to explain why he was so keen to help with this one.

Chapter Thirty-Eight

Caitlin

It was the third photo that went up on David A's Twitter feed that made up Caitlin's mind. She'd got home from the wine bar and logged on to see that the photo had been uploaded at nine o'clock that evening. This time it was a picture of her, just her, sitting with the violin in her lap. Nine o'clock: that would have been just after the break. She tried to think of the room. Had she seen anyone suspicious? Had any of the other musicians been absent when she'd taken her seat? Andy had left the table just before her. She couldn't recall whether he'd gone directly to the stage area; she simply assumed he had. As for the others, she really didn't know. But she was determined to find out who it was who had set up that account.

She didn't mention the photo to Andy. He'd blame Nick again, and maybe he was right; Caitlin and Nick had appeared in her life from nowhere. She didn't know a lot about them – particularly Nick. What if he was the one who'd taken the picture?

When she saw the photo, she typed Nick's name into the Twitter search bar, but nothing came up. He didn't appear to have an account, or if he had, the profile picture was of something else – something that wouldn't identify him. Michelle had an account, but she wasn't a frequent tweeter. The last thing she'd shared was the article she'd written for *New Woman*, but prior to that, she hadn't tweeted in two months.

She clicked on her own feed and scrolled through recent tweets; Dar Bryan, it seemed, was online and had retweeted only minutes before – some joke about a dog doing housework. Caitlin clicked on his profile. His picture hadn't changed; it showed him and his girlfriend, Lisa, his arm around her, both smiling and squinting into the sun.

She clicked on new messages and began to type:

@CaitlinDavis: Hey – how are you doing?

@darbryan1: Oh, you know, same old … you?

@CaitlinDavis: Same. I was thinking, maybe we could meet for coffee, talk in real time?

Nothing for a few minutes. Then:

@darbryan1: What, now?

@CaitlinDavis: Lol. No, tomorrow maybe … if you're free.

@darbryan1: Okay. I'm free after six. Where do you want to meet?

@CaitlinDavis: The Bailey? 6.30?

@darbryan1: Cool beans, Caitlin. See you then.

She waited for a few minutes to see if he would tweet anything else, but he didn't, and she presumed that he'd logged off. 'Cool beans!' It was a funny expression – it sounded kind of hipster-ish – and she wondered what Dar Bryan was like. It seemed she wouldn't have too long to find out.

She checked David A's page again, but nothing else had appeared. She went to bed, lay there and thought about who it was that was messing with her and why. What did they know? And how had they found out?

The Bailey wasn't busy. She'd arrived early and sat on one of the leather couches where she had a clear view of the door. She wanted to see him come in, wanted to gauge his every reaction. She was good at reading people and if Dar Bryan had something to hide, she was sure that she'd detect it before he'd even sat down.

The lighting was subdued. The waiter came and asked if she'd like something, and she ordered an Irish coffee even though she hadn't intended to drink. A drink was different from a coffee, a drink was too much like a date, but it looked like a café latte for all the world – he wouldn't know the difference. Then she chided herself, what did she care what this man thought? She was only here on a case of elimination. If Dar Bryan really was who and what he said, then she'd have to admit that the most likely culprit was Nick Drake and she really didn't want Andy to be right on this one.

He didn't see her when he came in. Not exactly the sign of a would-be stalker. In the end, she raised a hand and he nodded and made his way over to the table.

'Sorry, the lighting in here … you look different from your picture.'

'Is that a bad thing?' Caitlin said. And immediately regretted it. The last thing she wanted was to sound as if she were flirting.

'No … of course not, it was hard to recognize you, that's all.' He was awkward, had turned a shade of pink that was unmistakable even in the dull light. She'd been right about the hipster thing. He wore a grey tweed jacket, boot-cut jeans and chequered runners. On his head he wore a fedora which he took off, and then ran a hand, self-consciously, through the flattened curls beneath.

He sat and took out his wallet. 'Can I get you anything?'

'No, thanks. I just ordered a coffee. She left out the word Irish, hoping it wasn't written on the glass. The waiter appeared again, and Dar Bryan ordered a Guinness. No apologies from him for drinking. Why would he?

'Where are you from?' she asked.

'Sligo. What was the giveaway?'

She smiled. 'You don't sound like a Dub.'

'And you, are you a native?'

'Yep – born and bred. Can't you tell? I grew up in Rathfarnham, near the Dublin mountains.'

'Your accent is neutral – like Lisa's.'

'No news since we last spoke, I suppose?'

He shook his head. 'It'll be six years at the end of this month. You stop expecting to hear anything.'

'But you never give up.'

'No.'

She thought of Gillian, David's mother, and felt a pang for all that she'd been through. No mother should ever bury their child, she'd said. But she hadn't buried David. Without a body there was always hope, and Caitlin did everything she could to keep that hope alive.

'You were young when Lisa disappeared,' she said.

'Just gone twenty-five. We met at college, had been hanging out for a couple of years before we started going out officially.'

'What took you so long?'

'Us country lads aren't the fastest in the race. In the end, it was her that made the move, said she was sick of waiting. Truth be told, I never thought she'd be interested in me, not like that.'

The waiter came with a tray and set it down; Dar Bryan insisted on paying.

'Funny,' he said. 'They were both teachers.'

Caitlin had forgotten that. She nodded now, remembering that Dar's girlfriend had been a special needs assistant. 'And what is it you do?' she asked.

'Journalism.'

'Really, who do you work for?'

'I'm a freelancer. Didn't want to associate myself with any specific tabloid. I did for a few years; it was dreadful the things they wanted me to cover. You know they had me go undercover to this girl's house they'd been tipped off was a prostitute. I was to take pictures … get the fix. And you couldn't say no once they'd assigned you a story.'

'So, what did you do?'

'I did it – I went to the house, took the pictures. Of course she went mental when she saw the camera, the poor girl. I felt horrible. I know it's not right what she was doing but … I quit the next day – told him there'd been a mistake. I sent the girl an apology, told her I'd got rid of everything. At least I'd given her warning – she was wise to the fact that she was being watched. Maybe she managed to sort herself out … Anyway, after that I went solo. I don't exactly earn a living from it, but I teach a few classes on the side to help pay the bills.' He took a sip of his pint and licked the froth from his top lip. 'What about you?'

Caitlin smoothed her dress. 'I edit a magazine, set it up a few years ago. I did a degree in publishing and got tired of doing one internship after the next. It's hard to get a job in a publishing house – the ones here can't afford to pay full-time staff. I spent a few years in the UK, but I wasn't happy there, and so I came back all fired up with the idea of the magazine. Then I met David just as things were getting off the ground and settled here.'

Caitlin sipped her drink. She didn't know why she'd told Dar Bryan all that, reliving those years made her sad, so incredibly sad. Except wasn't that the idea of meeting, at least as far as he was concerned, so that they might talk face-to-face? Besides, from the minute he'd walked in she was certain that he wasn't the one who'd set up David A's Twitter account. This young man had nothing to hide. She liked how he coloured when he spoke, and his quiet way of talking. When she was finished she'd order another drink, and hope that he had nowhere to rush off to.

Chapter Thirty-Nine

Michelle

Michelle had continued to puzzle over Caitlin's claim not to have any other family. Surely you wouldn't deny the existence of an aunt, no matter what type of lifestyle she led. Could it be that Caitlin just didn't remember? Searching for answers, Michelle made her way to Thornton's field once more.

As soon as she reached the door of the mobile home, she got the smell. Gas. She knocked at the door, waiting for the barrage of abuse as soon as Lydia saw her, but no answer came. Growing more worried by the strong odour, she pounded at the door and looked at the windows, all of which were closed tight. Damn it, was the woman in there? Michelle went to one of the windows, stood on tiptoe and cupped her hands to the glass, but all she could see was a wellordered kitchen. She ran to the next window – this time she saw Lydia Davis lying prone on the floor of the mobile home.

Caitlin pounded at the window, calling the woman's name, but she got no response. She glanced across the field to the white house, but it was too far. Lydia could be dead from carbon monoxide poisoning, if she wasn't already, by the time she returned with Bill Thornton in tow. Prepared to do whatever she had to, Michelle ran back to the door and pushed down on the handle. Surprisingly, it opened, and the smell of gas intensified. Covering her mouth, she ran inside and shook the woman on the floor who groaned slightly. At least she was alive. As Michelle pulled Lydia from the mobile home, her eye lit on the cause of the gas leak: a hiss was coming from a Superser heater, and as soon as she'd dragged her outside and laid her on the grass, she went back inside and flicked the lever on the gas cylinder to stop the noxious fumes.

'Lydia … Lydia wake up. Can you hear me?'

The woman moaned, trying to open her eyes.

'I'm going to call an ambulance, Lydia. Hang tight, you're going to be fine.'

As Michelle dialled emergency services, she saw movement up at the white house. She stood up and waved but the man who was presumably Bill Thornton didn't see her and vanished again from view.

By the time the emergency services arrived, and two firemen climbed down from an engine saying that there was an ambulance on the way, Lydia Davis had woken up. Michelle had wrapped her in a blanket and kept her outside, opening all the windows in the mobile home to let out the stench of the gas.

'What are you doing round here?' Lydia asked Michelle.

'I just wanted to talk to you … but let's make sure you're okay first. It was the Superser, you must have forgotten to turn it off at the bottle, or maybe the flame went out.'

Lydia Davis nodded. Michelle was sure she could smell alcohol on the woman's breath, and she wasn't sure whether her words were slurry from the poison in her lungs or from something else – maybe from the bottle she'd seen on the small side table next to the woman's armchair.

In the fresh air, Lydia began to come round. By the time the ambulance arrived, she was telling them that she didn't need any help, that she was fine, a bit groggy, that was all. And she certainly wasn't going near any hospital. The paramedics asked Michelle if she could stay and keep an eye on her for the next couple of hours, and grudgingly Lydia relented to the company if it meant not having to go to the hospital.

'I thought I told you I had nothing to say to you,' Lydia said, as soon as the paramedics had left. She settled herself into her armchair, took the bottle from the table and swore silently when she saw that it was empty. 'It's freezing in here,' she said, pulling a blanket round her. 'Light that thing, will you, if you know how?'

'I don't think that would be safe, not yet. There could still be fumes …' Michelle didn't like messing about with gas; her mother had had a fear of it. She remembered how her grandmother had insisted on using a leaky oven right the way through to her death, and how terrified they all were that she would blow herself up. Lydia gave her a look. 'A person would freeze to death,' she said.

'I've just the thing …' Michelle said.

The woman stole a glance at her, curious, and her eyes lit up when she saw Michelle return with a bottle of brandy in her hand.

'For the shock,' she said. She unscrewed the top, and Lydia took it greedily with both hands and raised it to her lips. She closed her eyes, clearly savouring the burn as it went down. Michelle thought of Nick and wondered if his cravings were just as strong. She just hoped the bottle was enough to lubricate the woman's throat and get her talking.

'I wanted to speak to you about your niece, Caitlin.'

Lydia looked up sharply. 'What about her?'

'When did you last see her?' Michelle asked, gently.

Lydia shook her head. 'Not since the accident,' she said.

'You didn't see her after Johnny … died?'

'He and I weren't on speaking terms, not after what happened. He blamed me. He had a right to, of course … he was right, I should have been there, should have prevented it … I went to the funeral and they looked right through me as if I wasn't there.'

Michelle was confused. 'You mean Rachel's death? But how could you …?'

'No, I don't mean Rachel. I'm talking about the child, that little boy …'

'Caitlin's brother?'

Lydia ignored the question, seeming to talk almost to herself. 'I was minding them you see ... supposed to be watching them. If I'd known, I'd never ... I wouldn't have taken my eyes off them.'

'What happened?'

The woman unscrewed the cap again and took another swig of the brandy. 'A salesman came to the door. The kids were out the back playing; I figured they were fine. It was bed linen he was selling. I must have looked through them all. And when I went back in ...'

Lydia trailed off. Michelle leaned forward. 'What happened?'

'They'd climbed up into the old treehouse. I don't know how so small a child made it up there in the first place. There was no time to do anything, no time to stop it. By the time I got through the door, he was already on the ground ...'

'My God, I'm so sorry. But it wasn't your fault ... I mean how could you know that they'd do that? And Caitlin ... she saw her brother fall; she must have been hysterical. I can't begin to imagine ...'

'Did she ... did she send you here?' the old woman asked.

Michelle shook her head. 'No, it's like I said, I'm writing a piece on domestic crimes. I'm not a journalist, not really, it's a piece for a magazine. I read about what happened with Johnny and his wife. People tend to focus on the crime, the atrocity, but I want to look at the reason why people do such things, to find out what Johnny was like before it happened. I promise you I won't write anything without your say-so ...'

The woman picked up the brandy bottle again. 'Have you any more of these?' she asked.

'Sure. I can come out again, get some shopping for you if you like.'

'Johnny was complex, overemotional, but he'd never ... he wasn't violent, if that's what you want to know. After the accident,

202

he was a mess, they both were. He blamed me, like I said he had every right to, but Rachel didn't. Rachel said she knew that it was an accident – she grieved as she was; she didn't turn her hate on me. But it destroyed them.'

'Did she keep in touch then – Rachel – after the rift between you and your brother?'

'She did. And I tried getting in touch with Johnny a few times. I called the house, but if he answered he'd just hang up the phone. If it was Rachel we'd only talk if he wasn't home. She used to come out to see me some mornings when he was at work. She told me the state their marriage was in – that he'd withdrawn, that she couldn't say anything about me without the two of them getting into a fight.'

'So, she turned to someone else?'

Lydia nodded. 'Yes, she turned to a friend, Brendan. And I couldn't blame her. Truth be told there was always a spark between them, but I don't think they'd ever have acted on it if Johnny hadn't acted how he did. He pushed her away – he couldn't get over Daniel's death. I think he blamed himself for the accident too, even though it was my fault, and I knew how he felt … I knew just how rotten he felt, like life couldn't go on.'

'And what about Caitlin? How did she deal with Daniel's death?'

Lydia took another mouthful of brandy. 'She acted as though nothing happened.'

'Do you think she blocked it? Children can do that, can't they, when something is too traumatic?'

'I'd rather not talk about Caitlin. What's done is done, and if it was her who sent you, I'd rather you told her you hadn't found me. Better still, you could tell her I'm dead. If it wasn't for you, I would have been. God knows, there's no one would miss me.'

Lydia stood, shakily. 'So you'll bring me another one of these?' she said, waving the brandy bottle.

Michelle nodded and stood up too. She'd heard all she needed to, at least enough to convince Nick that Johnny Davis was innocent when it came to the death of his son. 'Be careful with that gas,' she told Lydia. She had an urge to put her arms around her, to give her a hug, but she didn't think such a gesture would be welcome. And so, she put a hand out and squeezed the woman's frail one with her own.

'Go on now,' Lydia said brusquely. She stood, hands grasping the door frame, watching, as Michelle drove away.

Chapter Forty

Nick

Nick parked in the car park marked 'Staff Only' and waited for Louise, the young teacher David had been close to, to emerge. It was 3.40 p.m., in ten minutes' time the peace of the deserted grounds would be shattered by the gaggle of students who would burst forth, freed from the last lesson of the day.

He lowered the car window, breathed in the damp autumnal air and tried to ignore the dull pain in his abdomen which had started the night before. He had found Louise Hayes on LinkedIn. With shoulder-length blonde hair and green eyes, he'd put her in her late twenties, thirty at a push, more than a decade younger than Caitlin. She wasn't conventionally attractive, but that meant nothing. There was no knowing what it was that attracted people to one another.

Inside the building a bell sounded, not the typical buzz that he associated with the end of lessons in his own school days, but a series of three notes that rose in pitch. Minutes later, a side door opened, and students began to spill out and diverge in two directions: one set making towards the gates through which he'd entered the car park; the other set drifting round the side of the building where another exit must lie. The main glass doors were obviously reserved for staff members only.

Nick sat in his car and watched the main entrance. The first person to emerge was a man in his twenties. He was dressed conservatively and carried a leather satchel. Teachers were getting younger, he thought, as the man approached and got into a black Volkswagen nearby. Two women were next to emerge, both dark-haired, laughing as they exited the car park on foot in the wake of their yelling students. Still there was no sign of Louise Hayes.

Twenty minutes passed, and the grounds fell silent again. He didn't know what the protocol was for teachers – he knew they often had free periods between classes, but he didn't know if that permitted them to leave early if their teaching duties had finished. He was considering giving up when the doors opened again, and he saw her come out. She was struggling with a large box. The handbag on her shoulder kept slipping to her elbow and she'd stop and balance the box on one knee as she tried to raise the strap of the bag again. Nick waited until he saw the indicator lights flash on a small red car parked opposite before getting out of his car.

'Do you need some help there?'

She'd stopped again to juggle both box and bag. She turned to him, surprised. 'No, I'm okay thanks.'

'Are you Louise, Louise Hayes?'

She bent to put the box on the ground without taking her eyes from him. He saw her throw a quick glance at the main entrance, but there wasn't anyone else around. He supposed she was startled, a strange man approaching her in the school car park, but she stood her ground. 'Do I know you?' she asked.

'No. I'm a private investigator,' he said. 'I believe you were friends with David Casey?'

'We were colleagues, yes. Why?' She opened the passenger door of her car, stooped and juggled the heavy box onto the seat.

He figured she did it so she wouldn't have to meet his eyes.

'I was informed that you and David were close. Good friends. We've received some information that might shed some new light on the case and it's important that we talk to everyone who knew him. I know you've probably gone through all this before, but if

I could just go over a few things with you, it might really help.'

'Who's "we"?' she asked.

'I'm liaising with the police,' he said.

She slammed the car door shut. 'Does it have to be now?' she said. 'I have to be somewhere.'

Nick nodded. 'I'm sorry, I'd have called you if I'd had a number. It won't take long. If we could maybe go somewhere to talk?'

'Where did you get my name?' she asked.

'A friend of David's – Andy Quinn – he said that David had told him about you.' He let the words hang, saw her glance towards the building again.

'We could use one of the classrooms,' she said. 'But I can't stay long.'

'I won't keep you, just a few minutes.'

She locked the car, and he fell into step beside her as they crossed the car park to the brightly lit foyer.

'What did you say your name was?'

'Nick. Nick Drake,' he said.

'Like the singer,' she said.

'Ha, yeah, I get that a lot. Thought you'd be too young to know.'

He followed her down the corridor and was disappointed to see that school buildings were just as depressing as ever – so cold with their brick walls and tiled floors. A cabinet in the corridor displayed trophies won by the school sports teams down through the years. Framed photos captured images of past students as far back as what he imagined was the 1980s – long before Louise would have started teaching. She might even have been one of those awkward teens caught in the lens.

She led him through a set of double doors then swung right into a classroom. She hit a switch on the wall and several fluorescent lights flickered to dispel the gloom. She closed the door, pulled out a chair at the teacher's desk and indicated for him to sit opposite. He felt, momentarily, like a schoolboy again.

'Who do you work for?' she asked.

He gave her the name of an agency he'd found, figuring she'd never check, and told her that David's wife had hired him. She nodded, seemingly satisfied. She didn't even ask to see an ID. It's the first thing he would have done, but again, what would it really prove? IDs could be faked too.

'What's this information then?' she asked.

'What?'

'You said you had new information, a breakthrough?' She was sitting forward in her seat, eager now to hear what he had to say.

'I'm sorry, I can't say,' he told her. 'It may be nothing.'

She nodded. He wondered if the police had spoken to her before, and whether Andy Quinn had told them what he'd told Nick. Or if he'd kept silent for Caitlin's sake. If he spilled something like that to the police, surely Caitlin would know about Louise.

'Have you ever met Andy Quinn?' he asked.

The young teacher shook her head.

'He said that you and David spent a lot of time together ...'

'We hung out some – we were good friends.'

'According to David you were more than friends.'

'That's not true. David wouldn't have said that.' She stood up, agitated, and cast a glance at the closed classroom door. He wondered for a moment if she was going to bolt. He'd definitely touched a nerve.

'Why not? Because he was married? Because he wouldn't want people to find out? His wife, for instance?'

'It wasn't like that,' she said.

'Really? Then why would David have told his friend about you?'

'I don't know. I suppose he mentioned me, like people do. It's not unusual, is it? Nothing happened between us. Like you say, he was married.'

'And what about you, Louise? Were you in a relationship at

208

the time? Or were you simply waiting, hoping that David would leave his wife for you?'

'I don't have to listen to this. What has this got to do with finding David? This is just bullshit.'

Nick kept his voice even. 'Louise, I'm not here to judge anyone – and frankly, I don't care what you did or didn't do with David Casey. My job is to find out what happened to him, and I imagine that, as his friend, that's what you want too.'

She paced before him, hands in the pockets of her smock dress. 'I don't know what I can tell you that would be of any help.'

'Do you know Caitlin Davis? David's wife.'

She stopped pacing. 'No. Why?'

'You never met her … at a work do, anything like that?'

She thought for a moment. 'I saw her once, yeah, but I didn't talk to her.'

'And did David ever talk about his marriage? Would you have known if there were any difficulties there?'

'Why don't you ask Andy whatever-his-name-is? He seems to have plenty to say about David's private life.'

'Maybe, but he got it wrong, didn't he?'

She didn't answer, just stared defiantly past him, then made a thing of looking at her watch despite the clock on the wall in front of her. 'Look, Mr Drake, I told you I didn't have long. Is there anything you want to ask me that's going to be of any use here?'

Nick sighed. 'Louise, you haven't been straight with me. To tell you the truth, I haven't exactly been straight with you either.'

She fiddled with the strap of her bag, wary. 'What do you mean?' she said.

'We know that you and David were involved. What I need to know is who else might have known about the two of you. Is there anyone, apart from Caitlin obviously, who might have found out – a boyfriend, for example? Someone who might have done something …?'

She seemed to pale before him. 'You're wrong,' she said. 'David and I were just friends.'

'Your text messages would suggest otherwise,' he said.

'You found his phone?' She continued to play with the bag, refusing to meet his eye. He didn't confirm or deny it. 'Nothing happened between us,' she said. 'He was married; I had a boyfriend. It was just banter ... flirtation, nothing more.'

'And your boyfriend, did he know about this banter?'

She shook her head. 'That was already falling apart. We're not together anymore. But it had nothing to do with David. It just fizzled out. You know how it is.'

'How did he take it?'

She shrugged. 'He couldn't understand. Kept asking me why.'

'Do you think someone might have told him about David? Maybe someone who'd seen the two of you together? Even if you weren't doing anything, a jealous boyfriend mightn't see it that way. Someone who's just been dumped may go to great lengths to find the reason.'

Louise shook her head. 'It didn't happen like that. David was already gone. I kept ringing and not getting any answer. He didn't show up at work, and then the police came ... said David's car had been found, that he'd been reported missing. I couldn't handle it. Aaron kept asking what was wrong ... he kept hounding me – it got too much.'

'So, you finished it?'

'Yeah, it was going to end one way or the other. But none of this, nothing I've told you, has made any difference, has it? You're no closer to finding David. He's not going to be found – he's dead, isn't he?'

'I'm afraid I can't say. We're following some leads, but we can't release any information to the public, not yet.'

'But his phone, where did his phone turn up?' she asked.

'I'm sorry, Louise. I've said more than I should have. You've been very helpful. I know it isn't easy. I'd best let you get on. Oh, just one thing, if you wouldn't mind giving me your number, I'll call you if we have any news.'

She called out her number, and Nick punched it into his phone. Then he stood up, moved towards the door and gestured for her to do the same.

He watched Louise get into the red car, pretending to search for something on the passenger seat, and waited until she'd reversed out of the parking space and exited the school gates before starting his own car. He'd done well to guess about the text messages – it was a gamble, but he knew that if they had been seeing each other they'd have left a trail. It didn't matter that they hadn't acted on their feelings for each other; the intention had been there. He wondered how much, if anything, Caitlin Davis knew about her husband's indiscretion.

Chapter Forty-One

Caitlin

Caitlin wasn't at all pleased to hear Andy's news. He'd phoned her at lunchtime, and she still hadn't shaken the headache that she'd woken with that morning. She and Dar Bryan had not left the Bailey until close to eleven o'clock, and in that time she'd managed to finish four, or had it been five, glasses of red wine on top of the Irish coffee. She wasn't used to it; she hadn't drunk so much in a long time. The last time she had – she'd felt it loosen her tongue when she was out with Andy one night, and she'd had to leave abruptly before she said something that she'd undoubtedly regret.

Dar Bryan could really put them away. He'd ordered pint after pint of Guinness and had become surprisingly talkative as the alcohol lubricated his tongue. He'd talked a lot about his girlfriend; the false sightings, the lost hope as time elapsed and no new developments occurred. When she'd asked him, gently, if he thought she was still alive, he hadn't answered. His silence was enough to say. She'd put her hand on his arm and told him that she was sorry, that she knew what he was going through, that she of all people understood his conflicted emotions.

He'd ordered another pint then, and when it arrived he'd asked her about herself – not about David, but about her, and that felt good. He was funny when he wasn't talking about the bad stuff. He regaled her with more tales about his days working for a tabloid that he refused to name. He told her that he'd really wanted to become a foreign correspondent, but he hadn't because Lisa thought it was too dangerous. 'The irony,' he'd said, and she'd moved in quickly to change the topic before he regressed again to the past.

After they'd finished their drinks, they'd stood awkwardly in the street. When she told him it would be nice to meet again, he didn't answer, instead raising his hand in half salute and walking away in the direction of Dawson Street. He didn't turn his head, and she'd turned away after a moment and lost herself in the crowds of Thursday night revellers in Grafton Street bound for who-knew-where.

Dar Bryan was not her man, she thought, as she waited for the Luas. He wasn't the one who was playing with her. There was nothing to suggest that he wanted anything from her, nothing to suggest he'd been aware of her existence before she'd tweeted that request. She was too tired by the time she sat on the tram to even consider the other options. Her head was swimming, but she'd enjoyed the night despite everything. And she'd gone to bed and slept until she woke, head throbbing, to the alarm at seven o'clock.

Since then she'd been hiding at her desk, doing as little work as she could get away with all morning. That was the beauty of being her own boss, and on Fridays she didn't have too much to do anyway; the magazine was signed off on a Thursday, so she had plenty of time to work on the next issue. There was nothing that urgently required her attention.

At twelve o'clock she grabbed her coat and bag and headed out for an early lunch. She was walking down Grafton Street when her phone began to ring. She didn't feel like talking to Andy, but given the way she'd been treating him recently, she decided she'd better answer it.

'I went out for a pint with your friend Nick last night,' he told her.

'Oh? How did that come about?' she said, trying to keep the

irritation out of her voice. The idea that Andy was moving in on her new friends bothered her. Why couldn't he just give her the space she needed?

'We exchanged numbers that night in the wine bar. I thought I'd suss him out, see if he was the one behind all this nonsense with the Twitter account – figure out what his agenda could be.'

'And? Do you think it's him?' she asked. Once she'd ruled Dar Bryan out of the equation she couldn't get this thought out of her head. If it wasn't Nick, she couldn't think who else it might be. The idea that it might be someone unknown was even more alarming; there was no way of knowing their motives then. Not that she had any clue why Nick might be doing it either. She waited, anxious for Andy's reply.

'I'm not sure. He said he might be able to help, that he knows people.'

'What do you mean? What people?' She'd stopped, stepping into the doorway of a closed-down store so she could hear what Andy was saying. She pressed the phone close to her ear to block out the voices of passers-by, as well as the music of a nearby busker.

'He wants to help to find David.'

'And you think that means he's not our man? What did he ask you, Andy? What did you tell him?'

'Nothing much. I said he should talk to you.'

Bullshit. They must have talked about something. Had Andy told him about *her*? About that little bitch, Louise? She'd never discussed it with him, but she figured he knew. Men talked, didn't they? They liked to pretend they didn't, but she knew better. And so, she'd played dumb, turned a blind eye as it were. All in the name of self-preservation.

'He has no right poking around in my business,' she said. 'I don't know why you've become so pally with him all of a sudden. You're the one who warned me about him – you're the one who thought he was too eager to get talking. Maybe you were right,

Andy. And I'm going to figure out exactly what it is he's up to.'

'Don't go jumping the gun, Caitie. He seems a decent guy. And the girl, Michelle, you're friendly with her, aren't you? Maybe they genuinely want to help.'

'Yeah, well, I'm not convinced.'

She moved out of the doorway and continued walking. Andy didn't say anything and for a moment she thought they'd been disconnected.

'Okay. Do you want me to have a word with Nick, tell him you'd prefer if he didn't do anything? All I can say is if it were me I'd let him fire away. Anything that might help can't be a bad thing, surely.'

'Hmm. Don't say anything for the moment. I'll talk to Michelle, see what she has to say about it.'

As soon as she ended the call she phoned Michelle, but there was no answer and she hung up without leaving a message. She wasn't sure, after all, what it was she wanted to say. And would they not be better off discussing it face-to-face? She went back to the office, deciding that she would call by Nick and Michelle's place that evening. She wanted to see their reactions when she talked to them – wanted them to convince her that their intentions were benevolent.

Once she was home she logged on to Twitter. She'd resisted looking at it all day. She hoped that maybe Dar Bryan had sent a message saying that he'd enjoyed the evening, but he hadn't tweeted anything that day. Maybe he felt just as hungover as she did. She was only just beginning to feel normal.

Upstairs she got undressed, pulled on her jogging clothes and headed for the park. She wasn't in the mood for a run, but she knew she'd feel better. The evenings were fast closing in as winter approached; the trees had turned bronze and red and ochre. Soon she'd have to forfeit her runs in the park and stick to road running until the days turned lighter again.

When she returned home she made a quick pasta dish, showered and carefully applied her make-up again. She wanted to look good when she confronted her new friends, wanted to look like someone in control.

Before going out she checked her email and was paralyzed when she saw she had a notification in her junk mail telling her she'd received a direct message on Twitter from David A. An invisible vice gripped her insides as she opened her account and saw the white flag highlighting the new message.

@DavidA: Bet you didn't expect to hear from me, Caitlin.

She stared at the screen. What should she answer? Or should she answer at all? Maybe she should wait until she'd spoken to Nick Drake, see if he would say something to hang himself. She felt so creeped out by the message she considered phoning Andy. There was no way this was her husband. It couldn't be. She clicked on the profile again, examining it in detail, trying to figure out if there was any way of tracing it back to the person who had set it up, but there was nothing. Anyone could set up an account on social media; all you needed was an email address.

She thought about blocking or reporting the user, but no – better to leave it be for now. Maybe she could find someone techie who knew a way to trace it back somehow.

She shut down her computer and grabbed her bag, making sure to leave both the kitchen and landing lights on. She didn't want to return to the house in darkness. As a precaution, she texted Nick Drake's address to Andy, saying that she was going over to find out what he was up to.

The response came before she'd even reversed out of the driveway.

Want me to come with you?
No, I'm sure it'll be fine.

She already regretted how dramatic she'd sounded, but it was only sensible to let someone know where she was going. She wasn't about to become another statistic posted on a missing persons site.

Chapter Forty-Two

Michelle

Michelle hadn't been seeking Tessa's number. She'd found the hypnotist's card by accident in the back pocket of Nick's jeans when she was preparing to do a wash. She'd taken the card and put it in her own wallet. Nick had told her of Tessa's reluctance to continue with the regression after it had happened. She was a sceptic, not someone who specialized in these things. She'd done her research; there was a woman up the Dublin mountains who specialized in it. She'd looked at the website, seen that the process took three hours and cost 280 euros. She didn't think that was excessive – 60 euros an hour was a general therapist's fee. But what if the woman was a charlatan? The occult was full of them.

Tessa had regressed Nick by mistake; she'd never set out to do it. But there was a reason why it had happened. Michelle believed there was a reason for everything, including a reason why she'd met Nick. Nothing was random.

Since it had happened, she'd begun re-reading the books she'd read before – books about past lives. She'd always been fascinated by the idea, and now that she had proof that it was true, she was unable to rid herself of a desire to find out about her own past.

Now, Michelle took the card from her wallet. Nick had said that he was going to try to talk to that girl Louise, the one that Andy Quinn had told him about, so he wouldn't get back until late. Michelle had asked him if it wouldn't be better to talk to

218

Caitlin first, but he'd told her it wouldn't make much difference given that the two women didn't know about each other. He'd also told her he planned on calling Caitlin too, to see if he could arrange to meet up with her. He imagined that Andy Quinn would soon relay their conversation if he hadn't done so already, and it would be best coming from him, this offer to trace her missing husband.

Michelle looked at the card, at the hypnotist's name embossed in gold ink, the credentials and number beneath. She couldn't make an appointment for tomorrow as she had the soup run, and the following night she was giving a Zumba class in the community centre. So it was either today if Tessa could fit her in, or she'd have to wait until Thursday. In that case she might have to lie to Nick about where she was going, and she didn't like lying.

She knew that she'd have to lie to the therapist though. Otherwise, the woman would never agree to see her. Michelle picked up the phone and dialled the number. As luck, or maybe fate, would have it, the woman had had a cancellation for an appointment at three thirty that afternoon. When Tessa asked what the problem was, Michelle told her that she'd been having panic attacks and that she'd like to try to get to the root of the problem. Tessa had sounded understanding. Michelle liked the soft, slow way that she spoke, and immediately she felt guilty for lying. At two o'clock though she left the house, bound for Valleymount, a tiny village near the Blessington Lakes in County Wicklow.

She enjoyed the drive out; it was nice to leave the suburbs behind. She took the route, which she'd checked on Google Maps, that took her around the lake until the road branched off and narrowed until it was little more than a boreen. She hoped she wouldn't meet another car coming from the opposite direction. All the time, she was thinking about Nick, seeing the landscape through his eyes. She slowed as she drove past the row of neat houses just off the narrow road until she reached the long white bungalow, which had a sign that said The Arches. She rumbled over the cattle grid, pulled up behind a silver BMW and parked in the driveway. When she got out of the car, she could hear children playing somewhere round the back. She took her time walking up to the door, pausing to look round her. The lawn was littered with leaves, and through the bare trees the people who lived here must have a view of the lake – a silver disk under the white sky.

Unable to delay any longer, she pressed the doorbell. She heard a door open inside, and the sound of heels on a tiled floor. The door opened and a woman in her fifties stood before her. The woman looked at her, curious, and for a moment Michelle thought she'd come to the wrong house.

'I've got an appointment,' she said. 'Michelle Carlin.'

'Of course.' Tessa smiled briefly and stood back to admit her. 'If you'd like to come this way,' she said, and Michelle followed her down the hallway. On a table stood family photos: the woman with a man Michelle imagined was her husband. She wondered what it would be like to work from this beautiful home.

Tessa gestured to a chair and walked round to sit at the other side of the desk. She picked up a pen and smiled reassuringly at Michelle. 'So – you say you've been suffering from anxiety. When did this start?'

Michelle swallowed. 'To be honest, that's not really why I'm here.'

The woman looked up, eyebrows raised. 'Oh?'

'My partner, Nick Drake, is one of your regular clients.'

Tessa sat back, putting down her pen. 'I see. You must know I'm not at liberty to discuss a client with anyone? That what happens here is completely confidential?'

Michelle nodded. 'Nick tells me everything though. I know about the regression, about his past life. I haven't come to ask you anything.'

'Okay, so what can I do for you?'

'I'd like to be hypnotized myself – not just hypnotized but regressed. I want to find out who I was before.'

Tessa sighed, she looked for a moment as if she were about to stand and show Michelle out of the room, but she stayed sitting.

'I'm afraid you've come to the wrong place,' she said. 'I don't work in that area. What happened with Nick was an accident. It wasn't something I set out to do.'

'Yes, but it happened. That's why I'm here. I know what you're saying and I know there are people out there who specialize in this type of thing, but many of them are charlatans and I don't want to take that risk. I need to know who I was … if maybe I knew Nick in the past … Maybe it can help.'

Tessa eyed her over her glasses. 'And what if you don't like what you discover?'

'It doesn't matter. I'll deal with it. I'm with Nick for the long haul. Nothing you tell me can change that.'

'You say that now, but you clearly know how complicated Nick's past is. I don't think you've thought this through. What possible good could come from it?'

Michelle didn't say anything for a moment. 'I'd like to know. I've read that we meet the same people again life after life … soul mates …'

Tessa shook her head. 'You might never have met Nick before; they say that people don't necessarily meet in every life. And even if you were both from the same circle, you could be anything to Nick – a family member, a teacher, a friend.'

Michelle looked at Tessa. 'I thought you didn't believe in all this.'

'I didn't use to, but I've done a lot of research since meeting Nick. I'm not prepared to say that I believe in it, let's just say I'm more open to the possibility.'

'Will you do it? Will you regress me? Whatever happens, I'll deal with it – and if it's not helpful, I won't even mention to Nick

221

that it happened. My priority is to help him. I'm not after anything else … you don't have to worry about that.'

Tessa shook her head. 'I'm sorry, Michelle. I understand that you're curious, but Nick is my patient, and I must consider what's best for him. There are plenty of hypnotists out there, people who would be happy to do what you want. But if you truly want to help Nick, I suggest that you put your own curiosity aside, and focus on helping him in the here and now.'

Tessa stood, leaving Michelle no choice but to do likewise. 'You won't tell Nick I came?' Michelle said.

'No. Like I said, anything said in this room is not for me to divulge …'

Michelle stepped outside and shaded her eyes against the sunlight that bounced off the lake. Maybe Tessa was right – what good would it do them if she discovered something she didn't like? She got in the car, a part of her relieved that Tessa had refused her, and drove out past the lake, in the direction of home.

Chapter Forty-Three

Nick

Nick wasn't expecting to find Caitlin Davis camped out on his doorstep. He wondered for a minute if the girl, Louise, had lied and knew her after all. Maybe she'd called her as soon as she'd driven out of the school. But no – there was no way any woman would have struck up a friendship with a newcomer who had moved in on her husband. Clearly Andy Quinn had spoken to her. Well, maybe this was a good thing, she'd saved him a journey, and she was obviously keen to talk if she'd made her way straight over to his place.

She stood on the front porch and turned, watching as he swung into the driveway. He lifted his fingers from the wheel in greeting, but she didn't smile, she just stood there, hands in the pockets of her long blue coat. When he stepped from the car she barely returned his greeting.

'Is Michelle here?' she asked.

'Doesn't look like it,' he answered, noting the absence of her car. 'I don't imagine she'll be long though. Do you want to come in?'

She nodded and stood silently by as he unlocked the door and ushered her inside. He offered to take her coat, but she refused and stood stiffly before him in the living room.

'I can ring her if you like?' he said, taking his phone from his pocket in an attempt to dispel the awkwardness.

'I've spoken to Andy,' she said. 'He told me you were very interested in David.'

Nick nodded. 'I mentioned that I might know somebody who could help.'

Her eyes narrowed. 'And who is this somebody?'

'A friend,' he said. 'He works in the line of investigation.'

'The police have been working on this case for a year now and turned up nothing. What makes you think your friend could do any better? And more to the point, why are you so keen to help? You hardly know me.'

He caught the anger in her voice, though he could see that she was trying hard to control it. It caught him off guard. If he were in her situation, he'd have been grateful for all the help he could get. Something about her reaction just didn't add up.

He shrugged, trying to ignore a sudden twinge in his insides. 'He knows people, people who might be willing to talk off the record. People rarely just vanish, Caitlin, we know that. All those people out there who are missing, someone knows something, they're just afraid to come forward. As to your question about why I want to help, what happened to your husband is a terrible thing, I'd want to help anyone in that situation. Especially a friend of Michelle's.'

Caitlin took a few steps towards the window and glanced out through the blind. 'But you don't know me,' she said. 'And more to the point, I don't know you. How do I know I can trust you?'

'I see your point, Caitlin, but …'

'But what?' she fired back. 'How do I know, Nick? How do I know you aren't the person who's set up a Twitter account in my husband's name, the person who's been watching me, posting pictures of me online?'

'What? What are you talking about?' He searched her face for some clue but saw none.

'You heard me,' she said. 'It only started since I met you and Michelle. A bit of a coincidence, isn't it?'

224

The door clicked as she said this, and Nick heard Michelle come into the hallway. Relieved, he figured maybe she could defuse the tension, or at least calm Caitlin down so they could get to the bottom of whatever it was she was claiming had happened.

'I'm sorry, Caitlin, I don't know what you're talking about. All we want is to help. You can ask Michelle if you don't believe me.'

'Ask me what?' Michelle asked, appearing in the doorway.

'Caitlin's upset,' he said. 'She thinks we've been interfering in her business.'

Michelle looked at Caitlin. 'I'm sorry you feel that way, Caitlin. We only want to help. What happened to David is terrible.'

'What do you know about David?' she snapped.

Michelle looked surprised. 'Nothing. Only what you told me. What else could I possibly know?'

Nick turned to Caitlin. 'And what's this about a Twitter account? You say that someone set it up in your husband's name? That someone is impersonating him?'

'Come on, Nick. I know it was you. Why don't you just admit it and tell me what the hell you're playing at.'

Her anger, subdued when they were alone, now threatened to boil over. What exactly had Andy Quinn said to her?

'Look, I swear to you, I have no idea what you're talking about. I don't know what else I can say to make you believe me.'

Caitlin didn't answer for a minute. 'Okay, show me your phone – both of you.'

Michelle took a step forward. 'What? I don't understand. Why would you want to see our phones?'

'Because someone's been taking pictures of me in the wine bar. Nick was there both nights that it happened. And whoever this maniac is, they've been tweeting under my husband's name.'

Michelle looked at Nick and handed Caitlin her phone. 'Here,' she said. 'But whatever's going on, it's got nothing to do with us,

Caitlin. We just want to help … Scroll through whatever you want, I've got nothing to hide.'

Caitlin thumbed the screen as Nick and Michelle watched, and, seemingly satisfied, she passed the phone back to Michelle.

'Okay, now yours,' she said to Nick.

Both women looked at Nick, and he felt the blood surge up his neck. 'This is ridiculous,' he said. 'If you can't just take our word …'

'What? Are you afraid I'm going to see something I shouldn't? Or maybe you're afraid Michelle will, is that it, Nick?'

'Right. Whatever,' he said. He took the phone from his pocket, pretending to open the icon for her in the hope that he could delete the picture that kept flashing through his mind before handing it over, but she snatched it from him before he had the chance.

Christ, let her miss it, let her somehow not see it.

He watched as she scrolled through his picture gallery, photos of houses, of potential building sites, then there was something akin to a gasp as she saw it. He closed his eyes. 'I can explain,' he said.

She looked at Michelle. 'Did you know about this?'

'It's not the same picture,' he said. 'I'll bet if you look at the Twitter feed, whoever owns it, it's not the same picture.'

'And what difference does that make? This picture or another one, what does that prove?'

He looked at Michelle, appealing to her to help him. 'Tell her,' he said. 'Tell her it's not what she thinks.'

Michelle looked at him silently. 'I think this needs to come from you. I think you'd better explain the whole thing.'

'What the hell are you two talking about? Why are you spying on me?'

'Caitlin, look, I know how this seems, and in your shoes, I'd think the same thing, but if you'll only let Nick explain. We want to help you, that's all. Nick didn't post those pictures; he barely even knows how to use Twitter. Will you sit down, give him a chance to tell you the truth?'

Caitlin handed the phone back to him. 'All I want to know is who the hell you are and what makes you think you've got any right to stick your nose into my business.' Her voice shook with anger.

'Can we sit?' Nick gestured at the sofa. 'I'll explain everything, but I swear to you what Michelle is saying is true, I know nothing about any Twitter account, or any other social media for that matter. I'll explain the picture, my meeting you in the wine bar, the whole thing, but first I need to give you the background. I need you to listen and not think I'm crazy.'

Caitlin glanced at Michelle who nodded, and reluctantly she sat down. 'Okay, but if you've been spying on me, if you know anything about my husband, you can be sure I'm going straight to the guards. Andy knows I'm here by the way, I sent him your address.'

Nick took a breath before starting. 'Six weeks ago, I went to see a doctor; I was diagnosed with liver failure. He told me that if I didn't stop drinking I'd be dead in a year. So, I decided to go to a hypnotist to help me to stop drinking – the only way I might be saved is if I can get on the transplant list and I've got to be six months clean to do that.'

Caitlin didn't react. In other circumstances he imagined she might have said she was sorry, but she was clearly too angry to do that.

'Anyway, here's the weird bit, and I don't know how I can expect you to believe this, but please hear me out. During hypnosis, something happened, I saw myself in a different place, a different time. I didn't know what it was, a dream maybe, some kind of hallucination – until I checked the facts and they turned out to be true.'

He stopped talking, glancing at Michelle.

Caitlin was getting impatient. 'I'm sorry, sorry about your illness, but what does any of this have to do with me or with David or anything?'

'Caitlin, under hypnosis, I was regressed. I was accidentally brought back to a previous life. I know you're not going to believe me, but before you walk out that door, let me prove it.'

Caitlin looked confused. 'Prove what? What are you talking about?' she said.

'In my past life, my name was John Davis.'

She got up from her seat, shaking. She looked from him to Michelle. 'You people are insane,' she said. 'What kind of sick game is this?'

Nick spread his hands. 'It's true. I wish it wasn't, but in 1980, I did something terrible, then, not able to bear it, I took my own life. Ask me anything, Caitie, anything, and I can prove it to you.'

'Right, when is my birthday?'

'The 6th of January. You were born in 1975.'

'That doesn't prove anything. You could have found that out online with all your snooping.'

Panicked, he tried to remember what he'd seen in his flashbacks. 'Your mother, Rachel, and I used to take you camping. We'd take a tent, go up the mountains. She loved to sing, 'Kisses Sweeter than Wine', do you remember that?' You had a teddy bear, you brought it everywhere with you – Noel, you called it, because you got it at Christmas. You had a whole stack of them, but Noel was your favourite.'

Caitlin was staring at him now, disbelieving. 'How do you know all this? Who are you?'

'I told you, I'm … I was Johnny Davis. I'm sorry, Caitie, so sorry. When I found out, I had to look you up, had to know if you were okay, and then you told Michelle about David. I figured it was the one thing I could do for you … to help you in some way. If you still don't believe me, you can talk to Tessa, the hypnotist, she'll verify everything.'

Caitlin was standing staring at him. 'What did you buy me for my fifth birthday?' she asked.

'A blue bicycle with a basket on the front. You tried to carry the dog in it.'

She put her hand over her mouth.

Michelle sat next to Caitlin and took her hand. 'How did your parents die, Caitlin?'

Caitlin shook her head. 'An accident …' she said. 'The car went off the pier, but I was rescued.'

Nick stared at her. 'Before that, do you know what happened before?'

Caitlin looked up, stared at him for a moment. 'You killed her. You killed my mother.'

Chapter Forty-Four

Caitlin

They sat in the low light of the room for a long time. Every now and then Caitlin stole glances at Nick, the man who claimed to be her father. There was no denying he knew things only her father could know, but how was this all possible?

Michelle had left them alone. Her job was done, Caitlin supposed, in bringing the two of them together. She must really love Nick to have believed in everything he'd told her; another woman would have thought he was insane. She certainly would have. If David had spun her a story like that, there was no way she'd have believed it.

'She was sleeping with him, wasn't she?'

'What?'

'My mother. And the man you killed. That's the reason you did it, isn't it, because they were together?'

Nick nodded.

'Why did she do that?'

'I don't think I was a very good husband. I don't know. I had these flashbacks under hypnosis, the things I told you about: the three of us in the mountains, building a campfire, you on my shoulders walking through the woods, singing – you must have been what? Three years old. And the man, he was someone I knew … a friend.'

'Uncle Brendan.'

'What?' Nick looked at her, waiting for an explanation.

'He wasn't really an uncle,' she said. 'But he was always in the house, always with you and mam, so I called him Uncle Brendan.'

Caitlin thought of Andy then – of herself, David and Andy – always together, a triad. It had been a similar situation with Brendan, hadn't it? Only he often came over when her father was out. Sometimes when that happened, they'd send her to play outside if her mother couldn't arrange for her to be at a friend's house. That's where she'd been the day when her father came home unexpectedly. She hadn't heard his car, she was playing among the trees at the end of the garden, but she'd heard the shouts: Uncle Brendan's yells and then her mother's terrified screams. She'd left her teddy bears, gone inside and stood at the bottom of the stairs. There was no more screaming, but she heard a man sobbing. She'd crept up the stairs, holding tight onto the banister like her mother always warned her to, and when her eyes were level with the landing, she'd seen her father leaning over the bed, crying. There was blood on the sheets. She could see one of Uncle Brendan's blue-clad legs, but the rest of him was hidden behind the bedroom door. Her father had seen her then, he'd jumped to his feet and rushed into the landing. She'd asked him where they were going when he'd buckled her into the car, but he hadn't answered.

She looked at Nick now as she tried to piece it all together, the bits of the jigsaw that had continued to elude her despite having stumbled upon those newspaper articles.

She still didn't remember anyone telling her her parents were dead, but somebody must have. There were two boxes in the church – one for her father and one for her mother. Nobody mentioned Uncle Brendan. She'd stayed with their neighbours, the Barrys, for almost a month, and then a woman had come and taken her away.

'You drove us off the pier,' she said.

Nick nodded. 'I can't remember. I read about it … the articles … there are so many blanks, Caitie. I wish I could tell you what was going through Johnny's mind, wish I could explain it.' He looked up then. 'It's what I used to call you, isn't it? Caitie?'

She looked at Nick. He didn't look like her father, not physically. And yet she still felt that pull towards him, that familiarity she'd felt the first time they'd met at the wine bar and she was sure she'd met him somewhere before.

'There's something I have to ask you … something I have seen under hypnosis … you had a brother, didn't you? Daniel.'

Caitlin stiffened. Of course, he would know about the boy – if he knew about her, he'd know about the boy too. She'd told Michelle that she didn't have any siblings, but that wasn't technically a lie, was it? 'He died,' she said.

Nick looked at her, hard. 'How?' he asked.

'There was an accident. He fell from the treehouse.'

'Jesus.' Nick looked stricken. 'How old was he?'

'Two and a half …'

She didn't tell him the rest. Didn't mention how she'd been glad Daniel was gone, that it was just the three of them again. Well, the three of them and Uncle Brendan. If it hadn't been for him, everything would have been fine. She'd thought about that many times over the years. She sometimes thought that if her father hadn't killed him, she'd have vowed to do it herself. He deserved it after all. He was the one who'd ruined everything.

'What happened to you afterwards? Michelle told me you were adopted, but that the couple split up?'

She nodded. 'They lost a little girl, and they thought taking me in would be a way to replace her. The man didn't like me, but the woman, Violet, she did what she could – she had her own problems.'

Nick took her hand, awkwardly, and she let him. 'I'm so sorry, Caitie. So sorry for doing that to you. I had no right, it doesn't matter what they did, nothing can justify leaving you alone. What I did … there's no way back from that. That's why I want to help you now, to help you to find David.'

232

'I don't think you can, Nick. The guards tried everything. All they found were dead ends. There's nothing you can do that they haven't tried already.'

'But what was it you told us before? That somebody had set up a profile in your husband's name? That was the reason you came here tonight, because you thought that we were the ones.'

Christ, with everything he'd told her, she'd stopped thinking about that. There was too much to take in, too much about the past. But if Nick had nothing to do with the Twitter profile, then who was it?

'A few weeks ago, I went on Twitter and saw that I had a new follower: David A – my husband's name was David Anthony Casey. He was a musician and whoever set up the account uploaded a photo of a violin as his profile picture. They even put his place of work as St Gabriel's, the school where he taught.'

'And obviously you suspected Michelle and me because we'd come on the scene out of nowhere.'

'I didn't, not at the start, but then Andy reckoned it might have been you. And I began to see his point. Before that I'd had a phone call, about a month ago, on the evening of the anniversary of David's disappearance. The phone rang, and a man told me that David was alive, but that I wasn't to try to find him. He said it would be dangerous for me and for David if I did.'

'What did you do? I assume you told the guards.'

'They said it was probably a crank call, someone who'd seen David mentioned in the papers. It turned out they were right, at least I thought so, because a few days before there'd been a supplement in the paper about missing people and David had been featured in it.'

'So you still have no idea who might be doing this? Or why?'

Caitlin shook her head. 'Not the slightest. Whoever it is, they're trying to freak me out. Scare me.'

'And the pictures, you said there were photos of you posted on this site?'

'On David A's Twitter feed.'

She took out her phone, logged in to Twitter and clicked onto David A's profile. She showed Nick the photo – the latest one of her in the wine bar. He looked at it and nodded. 'So, he was there that night. No wonder you thought it was me.'

She nodded. 'I didn't know what to think.'

Nick was silent as he thumbed the screen and scrolled back through David A's last few tweets.

'How long have you known Andy Quinn?'

'Andy? Oh, years. He and David were at college together. I met them both at the same time; they were rarely apart. It didn't bother me, in fact the three of us hung out together all the time. Andy was constantly in our place when David and I moved in together. In fact, he's still there a lot. He's the only friend who's stood by me since the whole thing happened. He adored David.'

'And he adores you too by the sounds of things.'

'It makes me feel guilty to be honest. I've been a bit of a bitch to him lately. I know he means well but he's been getting under my skin. He worries about me, you know? But sometimes it's too much. He's overprotective.'

'What does he think about the call, the Twitter thing, all of it? Apart from thinking it was me, that is?'

'I suppose that's what's made him so full on. I mean, he's been great. He stayed over one night when I was feeling a bit freaked out by it all. And then I thanked him by taking the head off him the next morning.'

'You don't think he could be the one behind it?'

'What, Andy? No, he was David's best friend – and mine. What would he have to gain?'

'Maybe it's a way of getting closer to you. You said he's the one who's come to the rescue. If something happens, if you're scared, he's the first person you call, isn't he?'

Her mind was a maelstrom. Could there be any substance to

Nick's suggestion? Maybe that was the reason Andy had tried to make her believe it was Nick, to take the heat off himself. But was he capable of something so underhand, so despicable, just to get close to her? Or did he have another agenda? She would have to be careful.

'Jesus, I don't know, Nick. I don't know what to think. I need time to absorb everything … my head is beginning to ache with it all.'

Nick nodded. 'Of course, I can imagine. Why don't I drive you home? Give you an opportunity to think about all that we've talked about. We can talk tomorrow … or whenever you want. I'm here for you, Caitlin. I want you to know that.'

When Nick drove her home, she noticed Andy's white van following at a discreet distance. Of course, she'd sent him Nick's address, and he wanted to make sure she was safe. But was that all? She ignored the van and sat in the passenger seat of Nick's car, relieved to buy some time to decide how she was going to handle Andy.

They were both quiet on the drive to her house.

Nick turned to her when he'd stopped the car outside. 'Are you okay?' he asked. 'I can imagine how this must be; your head must be spinning with it all.'

She gave a short laugh. 'You could say that. I'll call you when I've had a chance to think about what you've told me. I'll need time …' Nick nodded as she trailed off.

She got out of the car, waved to Nick as he pulled away from the kerb. The night was eerily calm as Andy's white van drew up in front of her. She'd have to play it normal, not lose her head like she had done when she'd gone to Nick's. She didn't know what it was that Andy wanted or what he knew. One thing she did know was that she wouldn't be confiding in him about what Nick had just told her – she needed to get her head around it, and she needed to do that alone.

'Hey, is everything okay?' he asked, slamming the van door shut and coming towards her.

'Yeah.' She forced a smile. 'You coming in?'

He followed her into the house. She threw her bag down on the table and took off her coat.

'Thanks for looking out for me, Andy.'

'It's what David would want me to do.'

David. Is this what it was all about? Did it have nothing to do with her at all? She thought of Nick's suggestion. It made sense. Andy knew that if she was scared, she would turn to him; the person who had stood by her through everything. But now she worried his agenda was different from what she'd thought.

'So, what happened? Did you talk to him? I'm assuming he had nothing to do with the phone call or the Twitter profile seeing as you let him drive you home?'

She shook her head, cautious. 'He didn't know anything about it,' she said. 'Like you said, all he wants to do is help.'

'And do you think he can?'

She shrugged. 'I don't know. I don't want to get my hopes up … not after everything. There's nothing new for him to go on, nothing that the police don't already know.'

She didn't like the way Andy was looking at her. 'Caitie, there might be something …' he said.

'What do you mean? What could there possibly be? We've been over this, I don't think I can do it again.'

'There's something I haven't told you. I didn't want to hurt you …'

She stood up, moving away from him, suddenly sure she knew what he was about to say. 'I don't want to hear it, Andy.'

He continued as if she'd said nothing. 'There's this girl who worked …'

'I said I don't want to know.' She shouted it, trying to kill his words.

'There may have been something …'

236

She rushed out of the room, expecting Andy to follow her, but he didn't. He knew, he damn well knew. She'd often wondered. What had David told him about her, about that slut, Louise? She couldn't let Andy see she'd already known about it. He'd insist on telling her, she knew that. And she couldn't stop him. She'd have to feign shock, horror at what he was saying. She'd deny it the way she'd denied it before she'd seen those text messages on David's phone, the way David had failed to deny it when she'd accused him.

'He was seeing someone else, Caitie.'

His voice behind her, there was no blocking it out now. She felt the tears rising in her throat. No harm to let him see that. She turned towards him. 'That's a lie,' she said.

Andy shook his head. He was standing in the doorway, blocking her exit. 'I'm really sorry, I couldn't tell you before …'

'It's a damn lie! Where would he have met someone? When he wasn't at school, he was at home or practising …'

'She's a teacher,' he told her. 'At Gabe's.'

She didn't answer. Should she accept it, act the scorned wife and allow him to comfort her, go along with his plan? She sat on the edge of the bed, trying to work out what he knew.

'You didn't suspect anything?' he asked.

She shook her head. It was true. Until she'd borrowed David's phone to make a call, she hadn't suspected a thing. The message had pinged as she was dialling the number, popped up on the screen, unbidden. *Louise.* Who the hell was Louise? She'd read the message, hands shaking as she'd scrolled back and read through the chain. It had started over a month before … flirtatious double-meaning messages to which he'd answered in kind. He'd hung his head when she'd demanded an explanation – too pathetic to even defend himself.

'Did he tell you?' she asked.

'Not in so many words.'

'So … how do you know for sure? How do I know that what you're saying is even true, Andy?'

She stood up and moved away from him towards the window. Anger, he'd expect anger. She wasn't the type of woman to fall apart.

'Why would I invent something like this, Caitie? The reason I didn't tell you in the first place was because I couldn't stand to hurt you. You were so cut up; how could I add to that?'

'Well, what if it was important?' she said. 'A lead for the guards? Have you talked to this … this person … found out what she knows?'

Andy looked away. 'I told Nick about her.'

'Nick?'

'Yeah, when he said he wanted to help – I told him about the girl. That's why I'm telling you now, Caitie, I figured he might tell you and I didn't want you to hear something like that from a virtual stranger. It's the only reason …'

'Who is she?'

'Just some girl – a stupid ego-boost.'

'But they were seeing each other, you know this for a fact, do you?' She didn't have to pretend to be annoyed; she was. The fact that Andy had known all along and hadn't told her made her feel betrayed. Some friend. But whatever happened she couldn't let him know that she already knew about the girl. Feigned ignorance was the only thing that could save her.

'I saw them together.'

'Where?'

'In a park near the school.'

'And what does that prove exactly?'

'I saw her kiss him. And he didn't push her away.'

'Jesus. Near the school, anyone could have seen.'

She knew David had lied to her when he'd said that nothing had happened. He hadn't slept with her, he'd said. Even if that was true, the texts had already sent her over the edge; she didn't need to hear the details.

Andy was staring at her, assessing her reaction. 'You really didn't know?' he said.

She shook her head. 'How would I? It's not like I had a friend who thought to set me straight.'

'Caitie …'

'What did you tell Nick?' she asked.

He shrugged. 'There wasn't a whole lot I *could* tell him. I mentioned the girl, said she and Nick were close. I didn't tell him I'd seen them together.' He paused. 'Is there anything else you can tell him? Something I'm not aware of, maybe?'

Her skin went hot, then cold. 'No,' she said. 'I've already told you everything I know.'

She didn't like how he was looking at her. She thought of the crank phone call again, the Twitter account, and the message she'd received. Could that really have been Andy? Was he doing it because he wanted her, wanted to be the hero? Or because he thought she had killed David and by freaking her out he would drive her over the edge to tell the truth? Whatever the reason, she needed to keep her head, had to get him on side. Otherwise, who knew where he'd take this?

'I'm sorry I snapped. It's just … what you're telling me … I feel like a fool. David's made a complete fool out of me.'

'I'm sure he never meant to,' he said, quietly.

She stood up and put her hand on his arm. 'I understand why you didn't tell me, you wanted to save me from this, from feeling so stupid.' She reached up to kiss his cheek. 'You've only ever looked out for me.'

When she pulled away he looked awkward, her warmth had clearly blindsided him. Just what she'd intended. She thought of Nick Drake, he was smart – of course he was, he'd been her father. He knew what it was like to be backed into a corner and to lash out. And what's more, he believed he owed her. Suddenly a plan started forming in her head. If she could just keep Andy off the scent, maybe, just maybe, Nick could help her.

Chapter Forty-Five

Michelle

Michelle had waited until she knew everything was okay before she left the room. She thought Caitlin had been about to get angry again when she'd said that Johnny Davis had killed her mother, but she hadn't. It didn't make sense. In Caitlin's shoes, she'd have lost it. If anyone had done anything to hurt her mother, she'd have made sure they paid the price, no matter what the circumstances.

After getting up and slipping from the room as discreetly as she could, she had gone out to the utility room, taken Rowdy's lead, clipped it on and slipped out the back door with the dog gambolling round her feet. She expected it would be some time before Caitlin and Nick finished talking.

The temperature had dropped, and she zipped her fleece up to the neck. Instinctively, she thought of the people sleeping in the street that night. Then she thought of the volunteers doing the rounds. She hadn't heard anything back from the workers in the Capuchin Centre. Clearly no one had any information to add about the man who looked like Caitlin's husband.

She walked on, trying to still her thoughts, to slow them down and think clearly about everything that had happened since Nick told her about his illness. He hadn't been feeling well for a while, she knew that. She used to hear him get up in the middle of the night – was sure she'd heard him vomit in the toilet, but he never said anything. She'd gone and stood outside the bathroom door one night and asked if he was okay. He'd assured her that he was fine, but he didn't look fine. He'd used mouthwash to disguise the fact that he'd been sick, which had only made it more obvious.

When she reached the end of the street she turned left to round the block. The house was in sight again now, the light burning in the front window. She wondered if Caitlin was still there or if she'd left by now – what would she have told Nick about his past? As she drew nearer, she noticed a white van parked on the other side of the road. It was dark, but she could make out the outline of a man sitting in the driver's seat. He wasn't parked outside one house in particular, but along the kerb where a small green square separated two blocks of houses.

Michelle quickened her step, but Rowdy stopped to smell at something in the grass, forcing her to a halt. She glanced at the van again; she could still make nothing out but a silhouette in the darkness. She pulled Rowdy's lead, clucking her tongue to call him to her. She wasn't usually nervous walking at night, particularly in the estate, but tonight she felt jumpy. She stooped and unclipped the lead from the dog's collar and watched as he raced ahead and in through the garden gate. She walked round to the side entrance, where she might slip again, unseen, into the house.

She eased open the back door. Rowdy ran straight for his water bowl, and she tiptoed out to the hall. There were voices in the front room, Caitlin hadn't left yet. Not wanting to interrupt, she climbed the stairs, went into the bedroom and crossed to the window to pull the blind down. The white van was still parked across the street. She couldn't say why, but something about it made her uneasy. She sat on the edge of the bed, turned on the light and picked up a book. She read distractedly, her mind on what was happening downstairs.

A short time later she heard the living room door opening, and she put her book down and made her way into the landing. She heard Nick call her name.

'Up here,' she said, making her way downstairs.

'I'm just going to run Caitlin home,' he told her.

'I'll be back soon okay?' Nick took his keys, kissed Michelle's cheek and the two of them left.

She sat on the sofa, which was still warm from Nick's body, and turned the television on in time for the news. It would take him at least half an hour to drop Caitlin home and return. A reporter was standing on the shore of a lake. She turned up the volume and realized he was talking about a French tourist whose remains had been found the month before. Apparently, the shattered pieces of a small boat had surfaced. A woman whose house overlooked the lake had come forward to say that she'd seen a couple out in the boat, and now the Garda were preparing a diving team to see if they could locate a second body. Michelle changed the channel. She'd had enough scares, all she wanted now was to watch something mindless – at least until Nick came back.

About half an hour later, she heard Nick's key in the door. He looked exhausted when he came in. He flopped down on the sofa next to her and put his hand on her leg. 'I can't believe I told her,' he said. 'But I had no choice. She came over ready to attack us over that Twitter thing …'

'It went okay though. She believed it at least.'

He nodded. 'Just as well I was able to tell her the things I could. I don't know how I did … that thing about the bike for her fifth birthday, I didn't see that in the sessions, I just knew.'

'What do you think is going on with that Twitter account?'

'I'm not sure. She thinks someone's set it up to freak her out, but she doesn't know why. She showed me the profile, and she was right about the pictures that had been posted, they were definitely taken in the wine bar. Jesus, when she asked to check my phone, I figured no matter what I told her, she wouldn't believe me. I had visions of her going to the guards and telling them I was some weirdo who was stalking her. I do have my own theory on it though …'

'Oh?'

'Her friend, Andy Quinn. I reckon he's the one behind it, not in a malicious way, though it is a pretty sick way of going about things. I told you the first time I saw them, he seemed really possessive of her … I reckon he thinks it's been a year since David disappeared, a decent period before moving in on her. Only she doesn't seem interested. She's been pushing him away. But he knows that if she's scared, he's the one she'll turn to.'

'And what about that girl, Louise? Did you talk to her?'

Nick nodded. 'I went around to the school and caught her as she was leaving for the day.'

'And what did she say?'

'At first she denied that anything had gone on between them. She was bristly though and I figured she was hiding something, so I took a risk. I told her that we knew they'd been having an affair, that we'd read the text messages between them. She still said nothing had happened, that it had just been a flirtation, a bit of banter.'

'Do you believe her?'

'It's possible. The thing is, there was a boyfriend. She broke up with him just after David disappeared. She said she couldn't take the pressure anymore and that the relationship had fizzled out, probably because of David. I'd say there's no doubt she and David would have crossed the line if he hadn't vanished.'

Michelle's mind was working fast. Caitlin's husband had been on the cusp of an affair. Was there any way she could have found out? She didn't seem the type of wife who would turn a blind eye, and if she *had* found out, what would she have done? Confronted him?

'Lots of people who've been dumped without reason will go to great lengths to find out why it happened. I'm thinking there's every possibility that this ex asked around and discovered Louise had been spending a lot of time with David. He may have gone to the school, confronted him about it ...'

'You think it could have something to do with David's disappearance?'

'I don't know, but it could have got nasty, couldn't it? I'm not saying this boyfriend would have done anything intentionally, but you never know how these things are going to turn out, especially if it got physical.'

'Do you reckon Caitlin knows ... about this Louise I mean?'

'Doubt it. Unless she turned a blind eye, but ...'

'And if she knew?' Michelle paused.

Nick shrugged. 'Then they'd probably have had one mighty bust-up, but it would hardly account for him vanishing.'

Michelle looked at Nick but said nothing. She felt uneasy. Couldn't his theory hold true the other way round? How would Caitlin have reacted if she'd discovered her husband was having an affair? 'I guess,' she said.

'Anyway, I think we should meet Andy Quinn again, try to figure out if he's the one behind the social media stuff. Despite what he claims, he must have his own theory about what happened to David, and I'd like to hear it.'

Michelle nodded, but her mind was back at Thornton's field, thinking of Lydia Davis and her reluctance to talk about her niece.

Chapter Forty-Six

Nick

Nick was delayed to the meeting he and Michelle had arranged with Andy Quinn because of his appointment with the consultant. He'd got a phone call that morning telling him that Professor Ennis wanted to see him as a matter of urgency. He'd known it couldn't be good news. Now, as he arrived at the café on South William Street, he saw Michelle sitting by the window and tried to put it from his head. As he pushed open the door, a sharp pain forced him to pause and the doctor's words played in his mind again: *significantly scarred tissue … worse than we'd initially thought …*

Inside the café, Andy Quinn was turning from the counter, a cup and saucer in each hand. Nick was about to call his name when his phone vibrated in his pocket. He took it out and clicked on the text:

Andy's behind the Twitter account. Just saw the app on his phone.

He glanced over at the table where Andy Quinn was now setting a coffee down before Michelle. He didn't know if she'd seen him come in. If she had, she hadn't let on. Good work, however she'd managed it. At least now he had something to hold over Andy.

After getting a cup of coffee for himself, Nick headed over to the table. 'Thanks for agreeing to meet us, Andy.' He shook the other man's hand before sitting in the chair next to Michelle who passed him her extra sugar without being asked.

'Did you speak with that girl, Louise?' Andy asked.

'Yeah, she claims that nothing happened between her and David. A flirtation, but that was all. Of course, that could be enough.'

Andy leaned forward, eyes on Nick. 'Enough to what?' he said.

Nick shrugged. 'To end a relationship in some cases.' He stirred his coffee slowly. Michelle said nothing. Andy Quinn sipped his cappuccino and looked like he was about to speak, then changed his mind.

'Andy, does Caitlin have any idea about this? Could she have found out?'

Andy sighed. 'I talked to her about it last night. She said she had no clue.'

'Do you believe her?'

'I don't know.'

'And why did you never tell her about it before? You've known this for quite some time, why bring it up now?'

'I didn't want to upset her. I thought it was best to leave it … she was going through enough.'

'But you kept potentially important information from the guards. You care a lot about Caitlin, don't you?'

'Of course. She's David's wife. The three of us spent a lot of time together.'

'Andy, why did you set up that Twitter account?' Nick looked up from his cup, casually.

Andy shook his head. 'I don't know anything about that.'

'Yes, you do. I had a friend trace the account. Don't worry, I haven't told anyone. Look, I need you to be honest with me, Andy. You say that you were friends with David since college – that's what – close on twenty years, I imagine? A long time to know someone. What do you think happened? You must have

246

some theory? Let's hear it, doesn't matter if you have no evidence, nothing to prove it, doesn't matter if you were trying to scare Caitlin into sleeping with you … I just want to know what it is you think happened to your friend?'

'I wasn't trying to scare Caitie, I …'

'No? You know that you're the first person she'd turn to. You're the one who's been there for her since David disappeared, haven't you? Isn't that what it was about, the call, the profile? You knew she'd never think it was real, that wasn't it, you wanted her to turn to you … to become indispensable to her … Maybe before all this you even wanted your friend out of the way to get to her.'

Andy Quinn slammed his cup down. 'That's preposterous. Why would I be sitting here talking to you about David, why would I have told you anything about it to begin with, if I had even the slightest involvement in David's disappearance?'

A couple at a table nearby turned at the sound of raised voices. Michelle kicked Nick under the table, but he paid no attention.

'So you know nothing about it then? You didn't have an argument with David about it, a fight that may have ended badly?'

'No, I didn't. You're on completely the wrong track here, Nick. David and I were …'

'Like brothers, you said.'

Andy Quinn nodded, clearly agitated, as much as he was trying to keep his anger in check. 'I'll be straight with you, Nick. You're right about the account. But you're not right about the phone call, that was some crank who must have seen the article about David in the paper. I know how it must look, setting up a profile in David's name, but I only did it because I want to find out what happened, and yeah, I do have a theory. At least I had until last night. Now I don't know what I think.'

'Well, why don't you tell me what you thought until last night, and we'll go from there?'

'I thought Caitlin knew about the girl, Louise, but when I told her, she reacted like it was the first time she'd heard about it.'

'Okay. So, let's imagine she did know … what do you think might have happened?'

Andy took a deep breath. 'If I'm wrong about this …'

'If you're wrong, you're wrong. No one else need ever know about it except us. Just tell us.'

'Caitie has always been jealous. She and David used to have lots of petty arguments about it at the start of their relationship. If he was talking to some girl, she'd want to know who she was, if there'd been anything between them … David wasn't bothered by it. He thought it was sweet and I suppose as time went on she settled in and he didn't give her anything to be jealous about. But if she'd found out about Louise, I hate to imagine how she'd have reacted.'

Nick was quiet for a moment, and Michelle took the opportunity to get involved.

'But if you'd known about Louise, and about this possibility, why didn't this occur to you sooner?'

Andy looked at Michelle. 'It did,' he said. 'But she was that cut up, we both were … she totally fell apart … the way she behaved made me sure I was wrong. But then …'

Nick leaned forward. 'Go on.'

'I don't know if you heard about this, but a month or two ago remains were found washed up on the shores of Blessington Lake. Now naturally, that's cause for alarm for anyone whose loved one is missing, but I couldn't figure why Caitlin got so … I don't know … obsessive about the details. She wanted to know how they'd identify a decomposed body, you know, not having a database here or anything. Anyway, a couple of weeks passed and the whole time she was irritable, nervy. Finally, the body was identified – it was a French tourist who it was assumed had gone swimming in the reservoir six months before, ignoring all the signs saying it was prohibited. There have been a lot of drownings there over the years, something to do with currents, and sink holes from the village underneath.'

Nick nodded. He was only too familiar with the lake. His grandmother had had to move from the village back in the forties when the ESB decided to flood the valley to make the reservoir, but he didn't mention that now to Andy Quinn. He wanted to keep him on track.

'Anyway, I started thinking again about that evening, the day David went missing. I'd gone around to Caitlin and David's house at about seven. He was expecting me, but when I rang the bell no one answered. I was sure at the time that I heard someone inside moving around and so I rang a second time, but nothing. It was strange – like I said, he knew I was coming ...' Andy shook his head.

'What are you saying, Andy?' Nick asked.

'I think something happened, that maybe they argued and Caitlin lost it ... And now it's like she wants to move on. She's been pushing me away, and when I told her you wanted to help, she got really pissed.'

He felt Michelle glance at him, but he didn't take his eyes from Andy's face. 'Did you mention it to Caitlin – about going to the house that evening?'

'Of course. She phoned and left a message in the early hours of the morning. She was in a state, said David hadn't come home, did I know where he was. I went around straight away when I got it. When I told her I'd been over to the house, she said she'd been out running. I thought it was strange at the time: I'd definitely heard something ... but then I started to doubt it, thought maybe the noise had come from the neighbours. Now, I don't know.'

Nick sat back in his chair. 'Okay. Look, don't say anything to Caitlin about what you've told me. I'll talk to her tomorrow, see if I can figure out if there's any substance to your suspicions.'

Andy raised an eyebrow. 'But why would she talk to you? I mean, no offence, but she hardly knows you.'

'You're right,' Nick said. 'But sometimes it's easier to talk to someone removed from the situation. She's not about to confess to you if she did something, is she? You were David's best friend.'

'Okay, it's worth a shot I suppose. And I'll see if I can find out anything else in the meantime. She's invited me round for dinner tonight … But Nick, when you talk to her, don't say that I said anything, will you? If I'm wrong on this …'

Nick drained his cup. 'Don't worry, your name won't come into it.'

Chapter Forty-Seven

Caitlin

Caitlin swirled the wine in her glass, took a sip and studied it. She'd left an almost empty glass next to her when she was cooking so that Andy would think she'd started early, that she was tipsy, when in fact she was totally sober. She lifted the bottle and topped up Andy's glass.

'You know when I met you and David, it was you I fancied in the beginning.'

'That's not true,' he said, the colour rising to his cheeks.

'Ah, but you were too slow to notice, it was David who made the move.'

He smiled. 'David was always the one to make the move,' he said.

'So it seems.'

She got the injured tone to perfection. He reached a hand across the table, tipped her fingers with his, then withdrew awkwardly. 'Ah, that's not what I meant. It's just he always had more confidence than I did. He wasn't afraid of making a fool of himself, not that he ever did. If I didn't love David, I think I'd have hated him – all that talent …'

The words hung between them.

'Was there anyone else, Andy?'

'What?'

'Besides that teacher, was there anyone else over the years?'

251

He shook his head. 'Don't torment yourself.'

'It's hard not to. I feel so stupid.'

'What would you have done if you'd found out?'

'I don't know. Screamed, shouted. After that …' She shrugged. 'I'd probably have told him to get out, which is ironic, isn't it?' She laughed, took a large mouthful of wine and lifted the bottle though she had no intention of drinking any more than the glass she'd already poured.

'Why is it you've never met anyone, Andy?'

'What do you mean? I have. There was Alba …'

'That only lasted a few months. I mean something longer, something that might last …'

'She went back to Spain.'

She smirked at him. 'Exactly. I think you pick these foreign girls just because you know they're going home.'

Andy laughed. 'I suppose there could be something in that.'

'For a while I used to even wonder about you and David.'

'What? Oh, come on, you don't really believe that.'

She smiled. 'No, I don't. I'm just teasing. You both wanted me.'

'Caitlin …'

'What? It's true, isn't it? At least it was. I never thought David would start chasing young girls. She was, wasn't she? Younger than me?'

'Yeah, but that's … look men are stupid, okay?'

'Yeah, maybe. Or maybe I'm the stupid one. Maybe we should all take our pleasure where we can get it. God knows it's been a long time. Even before David disappeared, I should have known there was something going on. He didn't want sex those last few months. Since you told me, I've been thinking, why not go out and do it with some stranger, no strings attached? Except maybe I'd feel worse than before …'

Andy shook his head. 'Don't do that.' He stood, starting to clear the dishes away.

She stood too and put a hand on his arm. 'You're right. It'd

252

be better with a friend, with someone who cares.' She put her arms around his neck, but he untangled them, keeping a hold of her hands.

'No, Caitie, look, you're just reacting …'

She moved closer. 'Yeah, reacting to something we should have done a long time ago. Now we can, no guilt, no more pushing you away.'

The next morning, Caitlin had to admit that if she was honest, it was easy. What she'd said wasn't a total lie. She'd been craving sex for months and she was pleased to discover that Andy was a generous lover. She took far more than she gave, but she didn't care. The idea was to get him so far on side that he'd never act against her, no matter what suspicions he had. And now, if he did he'd be implicated. The social media account, the photos, the fact that he was sleeping with his best friend's wife would all point to the fact that it was him who wanted David out of the way.

He was still sleeping as she got up, careful not to disturb him. It was one thing using him for her own agenda, her own needs, but she didn't want to risk morning sex or, worse still, an embrace from someone who wasn't David.

Cautiously, she pulled out some clothes from the wardrobe, slipped to the bathroom and got dressed. Thankfully she had to be in work today; so did he. She didn't shower. She'd wait till he'd gone, pretend to be leaving for work herself and then take her time about getting to the office. It was a Friday, a slow day, winding down after this week's edition had made its way onto the newsagent and supermarket shelves.

'Morning.' Andy appeared in the doorway as she was making coffee. 'Smells like manna,' he said. 'Think I might have gone a bit heavy on that wine last night.'

She smiled and took two mugs from the press. 'Yeah, I feel a bit fragile myself. There's porridge if you fancy?' She kept her tone light.

Andy was tentative as he took the mug of coffee from her. 'We good?' he asked.

'Yeah, we're good. There's no need to tiptoe around each other. And no pressure either, okay? It's just a bit of fun, consenting adults and all that.'

Andy hovered as she ate breakfast, but he made no attempt to touch her and she was glad. She wasn't ready for that.

When she came outside to see him to his van, he kissed her on the forehead. 'I'll give you a call a later,' he said.

Caitlin went back inside before he'd driven away, relieved to be alone. She showered, washing the smell of sex from her skin. She'd enjoyed it, she couldn't deny that. Andy had been a leisurely lover. And she'd let him do what he wanted. When he'd parted her legs and buried his face there, licking and kissing, she'd clamped her thighs and thrust her body towards him, unconcerned about anything but her own satisfaction. As she'd climaxed she'd ridden a wave that made her want to giggle, as she'd always done with David, but she'd bitten her lip and turned over, drawing him into her from behind. Not looking at him she could pretend he was a stranger – it made the experience that bit more erotic. She'd placed his hands on her breasts, clenched and unclenched, and felt a real satisfaction in hearing him moan when he came and fell against her. Then she did laugh, and they'd lain back, sweat-soaked, and slept.

In the office, Caitlin switched on her computer and logged into her Twitter account. There were no new messages, no updates on David A's account. Was it any wonder, when the likely culprit had been in her bed? She logged out, clicked onto MSN and was about to check her email when she saw the news story:

Divers prepare to search lake for missing person.

Guts clenched, she clicked on the link and read how the remains of a small boat had washed up on shore and how a local woman had recognized the boat and remembered seeing two people in it. One was likely to be the French tourist who had been found a month or two before, but now a team of divers were being sent down to search for more remains. Caitlin felt ill. She checked the date of the article and saw that the news had broken two days ago.

She hadn't watched the news, so intent was she on seducing Andy. Had it been for nothing? If the divers found that sleeping bag, that was it, wasn't it? It wouldn't make any difference whether David's friend announced his suspicions or not. She needed to think of another plan – and then she thought again of Nick Drake and all that he felt he owed her.

Chapter Forty-Eight

Michelle

Michelle had been uneasy ever since she and Nick had spoken to Andy. Now, on her way out to the Ashbourne Road, she replayed things in her head. She had to know why Lydia Davis was so reluctant to talk about Caitlin. Why it was that she'd had no contact with her niece after the accident, that she wanted no contact with her now even though she was a grown woman and probably the only relative she had?

When she neared the mobile home, she saw a lamp was burning. The soft yellow light was a beacon in the darkness of Thornton's field. Michelle pulled up outside the gate and reached into the back of the car for the bag she'd brought with a bottle of brandy and a few groceries. It had been a while since her last visit and she hoped Lydia would be just as pliable as last time once she saw the gifts Michelle bore. She heard the television playing as she tapped softly on the door.

'Who's there?' Lydia asked through the closed door.

'It's Michelle. I've brought you a few things.'

The door opened a crack and the woman peered out suspiciously. 'Oh, it's you,' she said. She eyed the bag and then stood back for Michelle to enter. As she closed the door behind her, Michelle noticed that she had a small wooden bat in her hand. 'Can't be too careful out here,' Lydia told her when she saw

Michelle looking. She hung the bat on a hook inside the door.

'Tea?' Lydia asked.

'Sure, that'd be lovely.'

'Kettle's over there. You might make me one while you're at it. Unless you've something stronger in that bag?'

Michelle went to the counter, turned on the kettle and began emptying out the bag of groceries. She handed the brandy to Lydia who took it and immediately screwed the top off.

'It's been a while since I last saw you.'

'Yeah, my boyfriend is sick.' She thought about telling Lydia about the transplant, but changed her mind when she saw her guzzle the brandy. What was the point in scaring her? She didn't need to know about that anyway. She still hadn't decided how much of the story she would tell her. She needed to keep the focus on Caitlin and see how she reacted.

They sat for a while. Michelle sipped her tea, waited for the brandy to loosen Lydia's tongue. She didn't want to mention Caitlin too soon lest the woman clam up and tell her nothing.

'Did you write that article in the end?' Lydia asked her suddenly.

Michelle shook her head. 'No. I decided not to. What you told me, it seemed too private, and I told you I wouldn't, not without your go-ahead. Your family suffered so much it didn't seem right for me to exploit that.'

Lydia made some sound, a grunt of appreciation maybe.

'How did you end up living out here?' Michelle asked her.

The woman shrugged. 'Didn't feel like living among people. The neighbours were keen enough that I move on too. The way they looked at me … I stopped going out, was housebound for years, the neighbourhood pariah. Not that I'd ever belonged among them anyway. I've always been a private person, didn't like to mix, if you did they'd be on the doorstep day and night. I made that mistake when I moved back. Is that how you found me, someone on the estate told you?'

Michelle nodded. 'A woman two doors down from your old

house said a man called Thornton let you live on his land.'

Lydia took another mouthful of brandy. She was drinking it too fast, the liquor making her words come easy.

'Bill's an old friend of mine.' It was the smile that pulled at the corners of her mouth that suggested that Bill Thornton may have been more than an old friend, at least at one time.

'Does he know?'

'About the past? Sure, Bill knows everything. I've been close to Bill since we were kids, used to run in the fields together, wild we were. He was the only one I could turn to after it happened, the only one who wouldn't judge. It seemed like our family was cursed, first Daniel, then Johnny and what he did to Rachel.'

'If it's a curse, it hasn't been lifted,' Michelle ventured.

Lydia Davis lowered the bottle to look at her. 'What do you mean?'

'A year ago Caitlin's husband went missing. There are no leads – he seems to have just vanished off the face of the earth.'

'How do you know Caitlin?'

'She owns a women's weekly. I work with the Simon Community and she ran an article I did about homelessness.'

'Was it her who sent you up here? She wants the details about what happened to her mother. If it wasn't for that child …' Her anger, sudden like the flare of a match, surprised Michelle.

'No, she doesn't know anything about my being here.' Michelle paused. 'Look, I'm going to level with you, Lydia. The reason I'm here is because some people suspect that Caitlin's husband didn't simply go missing, that maybe something … sinister happened. This is nothing journalistic, I'm not snooping for a story here, it's personal. My boyfriend, Nick, he owes Caitlin, there was something … between them in the past and I'm worried he may be getting involved in something he shouldn't.' She paused, looking down at her hands steepled in her lap. 'Last time I was out here, you told me about the accident – when Caitlin and her brother were little. Did Daniel really fall from the treehouse? Did Caitlin do something …?'

Lydia stared at Michelle, then shook her head and looked away. 'It's the reason I didn't adopt her … people wondered, thought I was a heartless bitch allowing them to take her like that.' She stopped and swigged from the bottle, leaving the top off. 'I saw them through the kitchen window. Somehow, she'd got him up there, he was too small to climb that ladder on his own. He was teetering at the edge and I saw her reach out … next thing he was on the ground, and I was running, but it was no good …'

'Are you saying she pushed him?'

Lydia was crying now, her mouth jagged as she tried to suppress the tears that ran freely down her lined face. 'I could never be sure, but yes I think she might have. I told Johnny, but of course he didn't believe it. He thought I was saying it to take the blame off myself. That it was my fault, no one else's.' She took a moment to compose herself, swiping at the tears with the sleeve of her sweater. 'Of course, they spoiled her – they were totally wrapped up in her and she in them until Daniel came along. Then they had someone else to consider and she didn't like that – she used to pretend to be sick just to get their attention. For a whole month she refused to go to school until finally Rachel made her. She became clingy and difficult. She didn't like anyone else being near her parents, me included. I don't know where it came from, such a possessive streak. It wasn't from Johnny, you might think so, given what happened, but no … he'd never been jealous before the accident. If anything, he'd probably been too laid back when it came to Rachel and Brendan's friendship, but the way he looked at it, they'd known each other for years. If something was going to happen, it would have done so before he came along.'

Clingy. Difficult. If Caitlin's jealousy had driven her to shove her little brother from a treehouse, there was no telling how it might have manifested itself in adulthood, was there? Michelle looked directly at Lydia. 'Caitlin's husband was having an affair,' she said.

Lydia didn't answer but gave her a sharp, knowing look and raised the bottle to her lips again. 'That girl,' she said, 'is capable of anything.'

Chapter Forty-Nine

Nick

When she opened the door, Caitlin seemed agitated, but she stood back and ushered Nick into the living room. He was surprised to see a fire in the grate, a real one. The curtains were pulled closed and the room was cosy.

'I was hoping you'd call by,' she said. 'There's something I want to show you, something I'd like you to hear.' She crossed to the mantelpiece, took something and then held it up for him to see. It was a cassette. 'Before I was taken to the orphanage, they took me over to the house. They told me I could take just two toys from my room – the rest would be given away – but I also managed to take this.'

'What is it?'

'Listen,' she said, inserting the tape into a hi-fi system – he didn't even know they still sold ones that played cassettes. 'It might bring something back to you.'

He sat down with no idea what to expect. Caitlin stood by the system and pressed play. There was some crackling on the tape, the noise of someone recording. Then a woman began to sing. She began to laugh as she neared the end of a verse and a man joined in, the two voices fusing and rising in perfect harmony. He remembered the flashback he'd had under hypnosis – him and Rachel singing as they'd crossed the fields, Caitlin on his shoulders as they'd traipsed through the long grass. He closed his eyes. The voices were familiar, as familiar as any that he'd known in this life. The song finished, and he heard the man talking, coaxing, and then a child's voice reciting a nursery rhyme. He opened his eyes. 'It's you?' Caitlin nodded.

'Sounds like a cliché but we were such a happy family. You know, when it happened, they told me my parents had been killed in a car accident. I only found out the truth when I was twelve years old. Violet, the woman who adopted me, she had this stack of papers she kept in a shoebox in her room, and I went there looking for my birth certificate. Inside the box there was this newspaper clipping with a picture of my parents. When I read it, I couldn't believe it … but I didn't blame my father … I'd seen how my mother was with Uncle Brendan. Even at the time I knew it wasn't right, but I didn't fully understand.'

He listened to Caitlin trying to justify Johnny's actions, *his* actions, and dreaded the reasons that compelled her to come to this conclusion. But there was no point in putting off the reason he'd come any longer.

'Caitie, I talked to Andy. He told me about David, and about the girl, Louise.'

She nodded. 'He only just told me about it too. Can you believe it? He'd known all along and didn't have the guts to tell me.'

'He didn't want to hurt you. He cares for you a lot, Caitlin.'

'Yeah, so did David. And look what he did.'

'Did you know that something was going on? I mean, before Andy told you?'

'No, how could I?' Her tone was sharp.

'You might have sensed something, people often do. Strange behaviour, unexplained text messages …'

'Yeah, well I didn't have a clue. You have no idea how stupid that makes me feel.'

'All I'm saying is, it can happen. A confrontation, things get heated. I know that better than anyone.'

'What? You think I did something to David?'

'Did you?'

She stared at him, defiantly. 'And what if I did, Nick? How would you help me? Anyway, I thought you suspected Andy?'

'Andy thinks it was you, Caitlin. He said he heard someone in the house the evening David disappeared, but when he rang the bell there was no answer.'

She shrugged. 'I don't know what he heard, but I wasn't here when he came by. I was out running.'

Nick paused. 'Caitlin, I'm sick. Sicker than they first suspected. Yesterday, I got a call, and I had to go in to see the consultant. I haven't even told Michelle this yet, but he says I'm running out of time, that my liver is severely scarred. I might only have six weeks left. I've thought this through, and if you've got yourself into trouble, if something happened and you're afraid to tell anyone ...'

She looked at him in disbelief. 'Jesus, are you suggesting you would take the rap for me?'

He nodded. 'I'm dying, and if it weren't for me, for Johnny Davis, you would have had a normal life. This is the only way I can think of to make things right.'

Her eyes narrowed. 'How do I know this isn't a trick? Something that Andy's put you up to, or Michelle. Surely, you'd have talked to her first about all this?'

'It's not a trick. I swear to you, at this point I've got nothing to lose. I'll sign a confession if you want, right now, before you tell me anything. But you, you've still got so much of your life ahead of you, Caitie. Whatever you've done, whatever mistakes you made, it's down to me. To what happened in the past.'

Caitlin stood up and moved away from him. He wondered what she was doing and for a moment thought that he'd got it wrong after all and that she was about to call the guards. But then she opened a drawer and returned to him with a notepad and pen.

'Okay, do it,' she said.

He took the pen and – his hand shaking – wrote a short confession and signed his name to it. 'Now tell me what happened,' he said. 'When the guards question me, I need to know. I need to know everything.'

Chapter Fifty

Caitlin

Caitlin looked at the notebook in her hand. 'Are you serious about this?'

'It's the only thing I can do.'

She stared at it, at the scrawl of Nick's signature on the paper before her. 'Give me your phone,' she said.

'What?'

'Take out your phone and unlock it.'

He took his phone from his pocket, punched in the code and passed it to her. She looked at the screen, checking to make sure he wasn't recording their conversation. Then she turned it off and laid it on the table. The way she saw it she had two choices. She could tell Nick what had happened and let him take the blame, or she could take her chances that the divers wouldn't find David's body.

'Okay, you asked so I'll tell you, but you can't go changing your mind afterwards.'

'I won't, I swear it.'

She nodded, satisfied that, crazy though it seemed, Nick was willing to do this to make it up for the past.

'I'd borrowed David's phone to make a call. A message popped up on the screen before I had a chance to start dialling. He was in the bathroom, shaving. After reading the text that had just come in I checked his phone for other messages. I couldn't believe what I read there. He was too stupid to even delete them. Or maybe he wanted to keep them. When he came out of the bathroom I held the phone out to him and told him he'd just got a message from his girlfriend. He tried to laugh it off, took the phone from me, but I could tell from his expression that he knew he'd been caught out. There was no point in his denying it. He told me he was "sorry", he told me it was nothing. "Just a stupid joke" … I told him to give me the phone. He didn't want to, but I didn't give him much option. I took out my own phone and started to dial her number. He asked me what I was doing, tried to take the phone from me. "I'll ring the little whore, will I? Ask her?" I walked out of the room, but he followed me, still swearing nothing had happened and begging me not to call her. Then he tried to take my phone from me and I lashed out. We were in the landing, he stumbled, fell backwards down the stairs. There was this terrible noise as his head hit the floor.'

She stopped talking and stole a glance at Nick.

'It was an accident?' he said.

She nodded. 'I didn't mean to …'

'But you didn't call anyone, an ambulance?'

'I was scared. What if they thought I'd done it on purpose? And when I checked, he was already dead. He'd cracked his head open in the fall.'

'But what did you do with the body?'

Caitlin stood up, pacing the floor. She stopped by the sink, couldn't look at him as she explained what had happened. 'It was early evening. I waited, sat by him, I kept thinking he'd wake up even though I knew he was dead. I thought if I left him for a minute I'd come back to find him gone. After a while I got a sleeping bag and rolled him inside, zipping it up like a body bag. I thought of all the cases I'd read in the newspapers, of bodies being found in shallow graves in the mountains, and I thought I'd wait until dark. But then I also knew I couldn't risk anyone ever finding him.

'The bell rang when I was in the hall trying to pull the sleeping bag into the kitchen. I managed to get it out of sight, dragged it under the stairs. I stayed quiet, hoping I hadn't been heard. I crept into the sitting room. The bell went again, and I stayed crouched under the window. A few minutes later I heard a van start and, like you said, it was Andy. For a minute, I almost ran out after him, thinking I could ask him to help me, but then he was gone, and I didn't.'

'I still don't understand why you didn't phone someone? It was an accident; it could have happened to anyone.'

'I don't know, I was frightened no one would believe me. If it came out that David was having an affair, if the girl came forward, I'd have been the one in the frame; it's what you thought as soon as you heard, after all.'

'So, what did you do after Andy left?'

'I waited until about one in the morning. It was so quiet, all the neighbours gone to bed. I went outside, unlocked the car and made space in the boot. Then I dragged the sleeping bag with David in it and managed to get him inside. I got in the car and I drove. I didn't know where to go, but I knew I had to get him far from the house. Then I remembered a place he used to go – he'd taken me there once – it was a reservoir out past the N81, a flooded valley. On a clear day, he told me, you could still see what remained of the village beneath. You weren't allowed to swim there, because too many people had drowned. But the day we went together we did it anyway ... found a secluded spot.

'I drove out there, to the lake, down the little laneway between the trees until I came to the spot. It was pitch-black. When I got there I realized I couldn't just roll him in: the water was too shallow at the edges. Somebody would find him. So instead I took a flashlight from the boot and I searched around in the trees until I found some rocks. I gathered them, enough to weigh down the sleeping bag, and I put them inside with David, and drove back up to the bridge. There was nobody around. I hauled the bag from the boot – it was even harder then because of the rocks – but I managed to drag him to the edge and I pushed him over, heard him hit the water below. I was crying so hard I couldn't see anything. I made my way down under the bridge and shone the light out onto the water. The bag was still there, but it didn't take long for it to sink.

'Later that night I phoned Andy. It must have been about three in the morning. I told him David hadn't come home and asked if he was sleeping at Andy's place. The next morning, he called me back. He came over and we went to the Garda station where I reported David missing. I prayed there were enough rocks to keep the sleeping bag down. I watched the news every day in the days that followed, terrified that they'd find his body. But there was nothing. Luckily for me, the guards were totally inept. It didn't even seem like they tried very hard.

'And that's it. That's what I did. It wasn't right, I know that, but I can't undo it now. I can't go telling the guards that I panicked, that I drove out there and dumped David in the lake.'

Nick exhaled. For a moment he seemed lost for words. 'You'll have to show me,' he said. 'I'll need to know exactly where you threw him in.'

'What, now?'

He shrugged. 'Why not? The sooner the better for me to get all the details together. We don't know what your friend Andy might do.'

'And what if someone saw you coming in here? People have seen us together before now, they might still think I was involved. Andy, for instance, why should he believe that you acted alone, that we weren't in this together?'

'Andy Quinn is in love with you. Right now, he's torn between his feelings for you and doing what's right by David. He'll be happy to see you in the clear. As for suspecting that we're in league, I'll just have to convince him that I'm a big enough creep to have wanted your husband out of the picture so I could have you to myself.'

'And what about Michelle, does she know your plan?'

'I don't want Michelle involved in this.'

She didn't believe him; Michelle had to know. She'd been in on everything from the beginning. Nick had trusted her enough to tell her what had happened at his hypnosis sessions, and she'd stuck by him. Michelle was the one who'd made contact with Caitlin first and all because Nick had wanted to meet her. Of course, he must have discussed his suspicions with her too.

'But Michelle *is* involved. You can't help that. What's she going to think if you suddenly hand yourself over to the police for killing my husband? Do you think she's going to be okay with that, Nick, just because she's gone along with everything else up to now? There's no way she will. You might be able to convince Andy, but not your own girlfriend, not when she knows what she does.'

'Michelle doesn't know about the prognosis. When I tell her, she won't go against me, not if I tell her that this is what I want … my dying wish … Trust me, you won't have to worry about that.'

She bit a nail. 'Yeah, well I am worried. I can't have anyone knowing the truth, Nick. What if she goes to the guards before you have a chance to go to them yourself? What if she can't bear to see you go down for something that I did? What then?'

'She won't. I know Michelle. She's stuck by me through everything. She's not stupid, she'll understand why I'm doing it. Look, I admit I'm no saint. If I wasn't dying I probably wouldn't be doing this, but as it is, I've got nothing to lose. Now, there's something I've got to take care of, but how about I meet you back here in a little over an hour? We'll drive out to the lake and you can show me the place …'

Caitlin took a step towards him. 'Where are you going? How do I know you're not going to talk to someone?'

'I am, but not about this – you'll have to trust me on that – right now I've an appointment with my solicitor to get my affairs in order.'

Reluctantly, Caitlin let him leave. He'd already agreed to cover for her; she didn't want to do anything that might make him change his mind.

Chapter Fifty-One

Michelle

As soon as Michelle was in the car she called Nick. He'd told her he was going over to talk to Caitlin; he could still be there now. Who knew what kind of danger he was putting himself in? The phone rang out, clicked to voicemail. 'Nick, it's me. I've just spoken to Lydia Davis. She told me about Daniel's death. It didn't happen how Caitlin said … look, call me as soon as you get this.'

Caitlin's car was in the driveway when she pulled up, but there was no sign of Nick's. Apart from a light that shone from the back room, the house was in darkness. She took out her phone and texted Nick.

At Caitlin's now. Where are you?

She rang the bell and waited, her whole body shaking with nervous adrenalin. Maybe she should have waited, talked to Nick alone first, but she was here now, and just because Nick's car wasn't … Suddenly there was the sound of a door opening somewhere inside, then tentative footsteps in the hall, followed by silence. She pictured Caitlin viewing her through the spyhole.

There was a cough inside, a rattle, and the door opened. 'Michelle, come in.' Caitlin's smile was tight as she stood back and allowed Michelle to pass into the harsh light of the dining room. Michelle looked around. It seemed as though Caitlin had been preparing dinner. A steak lay with the fat half-trimmed on a cutting board, next to a bowl of salad.

'He told you then?' Caitlin said.

Michelle's mind whirled, told her what? She decided to go along with it and nodded.

'And you're here to talk me out of it. I knew you would. I told him. But he said you'd understand. Men. How stupid are they really? I don't blame you, of course, but he owes me and he's dying.'

'What are you talking about?'

'He didn't tell you that? About the consultant? He's got six weeks left, Michelle, it's the only reason he's doing it ...'

Suddenly, it all clicked into place. Caitlin had told Nick she'd done something to David, and he'd agreed to go down for it. But six weeks ... when did he find this out? Why hadn't he told her? Of course, it could all be lies. She couldn't believe anything Caitlin said now, not from the woman who'd killed her baby brother. And from the looks of it her husband too.

'You're willing to let Nick go down for killing your husband?' Michelle's voice shook. She kept her distance, afraid of what she might do if Caitlin were to lay a conciliatory hand on her arm.

'I didn't ask him to,' she said. 'He feels he has to, because of what he did. He left me orphaned, you know; he stabbed my mother to death. I ended up in an orphanage. You have no idea what it was like ... Now he wants to pay the price, it's only fair.'

'And when will you pay the price, Caitlin, for what you did?'

'I've been paying every day. I loved David, you have no idea, what happened was an accident.'

Trembling, Michelle took a step closer. 'And what about Daniel?' she said.

'What do you mean?'

'Your little brother, Caitlin. What? You don't remember how you lured him up to the treehouse? How you pushed him off the edge because you couldn't bear the fact that he was stealing the attention away from you? I talked with Lydia and she told me everything. Nick doesn't know this yet, but he will, I'm going to tell him everything. If you think I'm going to let him pay for what you've done, you …'

Caitlin had turned pale. 'That crazy old bitch! She's a drunk, she doesn't know what she's talking about. My father barred her from the house. He wouldn't have anything to do with her after what she did.'

'She knows the truth; she knows what you did … she hasn't forgotten that. Let's see if you can convince Nick to take the fall for you when he hears about Daniel. You wouldn't get away with it anyway, your friend Andy has as good as said you're guilty.'

Michelle didn't know where it had come from, but suddenly a knife appeared in Caitlin's hand and, baffled, she glanced at the steak on the chopping board. Could Caitlin have hidden the knife up her sleeve before she'd answered the door?

'You think I'm going to let you ruin this for me?' Caitlin said.

She advanced a few steps and Michelle withdrew. She looked round for something to grab, to throw at her. She saw the violin case and she snatched it.

'Don't you touch that. That was David's.'

'Well he doesn't need it now though, thanks to you, does he?' Michelle hurled the case at Caitlin, but Caitlin side-stepped, and it went crashing across the tiled floor. It didn't stop her – now she advanced towards Michelle with the knife outstretched.

Michelle looked round again for something else to defend herself with. She moved quickly, putting the table between them. Caitlin leaned forward, swiping at her with the knife, but Michelle was too quick. Still, she knew this wouldn't end unless she could manage to disarm Caitlin.

The buzzing of the bell provided the distraction she needed. She came out from behind the table and kicked Caitlin hard in the stomach, knocking her backwards. Caitlin knocked over a chair but somehow managed not to lose her balance, and came at Michelle again with the knife. Michelle grabbed another of the kitchen chairs and flung it at her to stop her advancing.

Neither of them were expecting it when the back door was flung open and Nick entered, clearly having heard the commotion from the front door. Michelle saw him take in the knife in Caitlin's hand. He rushed at her, grabbing her wrist until the knife clattered to the floor. But she was too quick. She bit his arm, and before Michelle had a chance to do anything she bent down to grab the knife in her other hand and sank the blade into Nick's chest.

Nick crumpled to the ground. Michelle screamed and slammed into Caitlin, knocking the knife from her hand again so that it skittered across the floor.

'What have you done? Look what you've done, you bitch …'

Nick held his hand to his chest; a dark stain had begun to spread across his shirt. He attempted to sit up, leaning on one elbow, but collapsed again onto his back. Michelle dropped to her knees, grabbed the knife from the floor, and held it out in front of her, shielding Nick from Caitlin with her body.

She didn't know what she might have done if Andy Quinn hadn't appeared in the doorway at that precise moment. She screamed at him to call for help, heard him say Caitlin's name, and then saw Caitlin turn and run from the room.

Michelle cradled Nick in her arms and screamed at Andy again to call for an ambulance.

Chapter Fifty-Two

Nick

It is as he imagined when the blade pierces his flesh. The pain is sharp; he feels the warm blood soak his shirt, and his hand becomes sticky with it. Michelle has wrestled the knife from Caitlin's grip, and before he loses consciousness, he becomes aware of Andy Quinn, who must have arrived at some point during the fracas and is crouching over him.

'Nick, there's an ambulance on the way. Hold on.'

'Caitlin ...' he says.

'She's gone, fled. But don't worry, they'll catch up with her.'

Michelle is crying. Her hands are bloodied and there are stains on her face.

'Are you hurt?' he asks.

She shakes her head, cradling him, as Andy Quinn presses a cloth to the wound on Nick's chest, trying to stop the blood. 'Caitlin killed Daniel, she pushed him from a treehouse, that's what I wanted to tell you. What you did didn't make her become a bad person, she'd already murdered her baby brother before you did anything. You don't owe her anything.'

He tries to lift a hand. 'I'm sorry,' he tells her.

And then it all goes black.

He's aware of the voices in the ambulance, of the paramedics attempting to keep him alive. 'He's lost a lot of blood,' one of them says. 'We'd better radio ahead, he's going to need an urgent transfusion. Do you know his blood type?'

He hears Michelle tell them he's O negative. She tells them about his liver, that he's waiting for a transplant. The paramedics don't say much in response, or maybe he doesn't hear them above the roaring of the siren.

He's bumped onto a stretcher, rushed through the emergency unit. They're talking about a blood transfusion again. He hears Michelle telling him to hold on. She doesn't say that he's going to be okay; she'd never tell a lie like that. He wonders if Caitlin has told her that he's dying and wishes that he'd told her himself.

'I'm sorry, you'll have to wait here,' the paramedics tell her, and he wants to tell them no, that he needs to talk to her, to tell her how sorry he is, but all that comes out is a gasp.

After that the doctors inject him and it becomes a psychedelic nightmare. He drifts between this life and the last one. He hears Caitie's voice, but she's a child. And he still loves her. He dreams of Daniel, two years old, traipsing round his father's muddy garden in wellington boots. He dreams of the car crashing from the pier, and he feels his lungs fill with water. Then he realizes that it's in this life and not the other that he's drowning. There's a loud noise, panicked voices. 'Flatline,' someone says. And then he's at the ceiling.

It's the strangest sensation looking down on the room. He sees himself on the operating table surrounded by surgeons. What seems to be the head surgeon has removed his mask. Suddenly, there's a woman with a defibrillator about to shock his heart. He wants to tell her that he's okay, that he's alive, but he can't communicate with her. Oddly, rather than panicked, he feels calm.

As they shock the body on the table, he leaves the room. Outside, in the waiting area, Michelle sits with Andy Quinn. She's been crying, and he wants to comfort her.

'I'm okay.'

He doesn't know if he's said the words aloud, but Michelle looks up, looks right at him. And for a moment he thinks she sees him, not like the surgeons whose attention is taken up by the body on the table – too preoccupied to hear Nick tell them he was fine. But then Michelle turns away again. Andy puts his arm around her, comforting her. He's glad that there's someone to help her, to tell her it'll be okay.

He doesn't know how it is that he leaves that room, but he finds himself drifting towards a light. He travels through layers, dimensions, aware of a sound that is music and not music. The pain has subsided, and he feels weightless. Time has ceased to have meaning. He drifts onwards, upwards through the vortex, and his memory is cleared once more.

Epilogue

Two years later ...

'What am I doing boy?' Michelle asked Rowdy as the doorbell went and she rose to let Andy in.

'Are you ready?' Andy asked.

'As I'll ever be, I guess.' She took one last glance in the mirror in the hall before following him out to the van.

She'd never been inside a prison before; she had no idea what to expect except for what she'd seen in the movies. She could have asked Andy, but she didn't really want to know.

'She wants to see you, you know,' he said. 'I think she really *has* changed.'

Michelle didn't answer. She thought about Nick and about what he'd want; about how all he'd wished to do was to atone for his past sins. She wondered sometimes if Caitlin's killing him had wiped the slate clean.

David Casey's body had never been found. Andy still had his suspicions that his friend lay at the bottom of the lake, but the guards had dismissed his suggestion and even though he visited Caitlin in the prison every week, she refused to be drawn on it. Michelle suspected that despite everything Andy was still in love with Caitlin, and that he wanted to believe she'd changed.

'I could have told her ... if you didn't want to do this,' Andy said.

Michelle shook her head. 'It's better coming from me.'

She picked up her bag, saw a text from Conor wishing her luck, before she took a deep breath and got out of the van.

'I'll be here when you come out,' Andy told her, and she smiled, grateful that he'd become such a good friend.

She didn't recognize Caitlin at first, but then she was too afraid to look too closely at the room of tough-looking women, and her eyes passed over the thin brunette in the corner of the room. The prison guard pointed her out, and when Michelle followed her line of vision, she saw that Caitlin had already seen her, that she was waiting for Michelle to approach.

'Andy said you'd come, but I didn't believe it.'

Michelle sat, trying to ignore the fleeting images at the back of her mind – the flash of the blade, Nick dying in her arms.

'How are you?' Michelle asked.

Caitlin shrugged. 'How you'd expect. Days are endless, often I just lose count … if it weren't for Gillian and Andy, I'd probably go mad.'

Mad. Caitlin's lawyers had tried to claim insanity when she'd been arrested for Nick's murder, but psychologists had said that there was nothing wrong with her, that she was perfectly sane. Manslaughter was the final charge.

'David's mother comes to see you?' Michelle asked.

'Why wouldn't she?' The words were spat back, a flash of the old vehemence. And Michelle understood – Caitlin's mother-in-law still believed that her son was missing. There was no evidence to the contrary. Who knew what Caitlin had told her in relation to her attack on Nick – she'd have claimed her own innocence, of that much she was sure.

'Lydia's dead,' Michelle told her.

Caitlin shrugged.

'She died intestate, which means that everything goes to you.'

'What could she possibly have? Living out there in that old mobile home?'

'More than you think.' Michelle told her. 'About sixty thousand euros.'

Caitlin looked at her, suspicious. 'How do you know this?'

'She told me. I used to visit her, take her groceries. She'd said she was going to make a will. She was going to donate a large sum to the Simon Community … but she didn't get around to it. She went peacefully in her sleep.'

'Is that all you came to tell me?' Caitlin asked.

'No. I wanted to give you this.' Michelle took the photo from her purse. She handed it to Caitlin and waited for her reaction. Caitlin looked at the picture, then dropped it on the table as though it had burned her fingers. She glanced at Michelle and then looked again.

Michelle had found the photo among several others in a box of Lydia's things when they'd cleaned out the mobile home. Caitlin was a little girl, her dark hair tied in two pigtails. She wore a blue denim pinafore and by her side was a small boy – a toddler, not even two years old. They held hands and smiled at the camera. Michelle could see now from Caitlin's expression that she'd hit a nerve.

'That's him, isn't it? That's Daniel?'

Caitlin nodded. 'Where did you get this?'

'Lydia had it. There are more, lots more. They're all yours now – I've given them to Andy to keep safe.'

Michelle didn't tell her that she'd kept one for herself: a photo of Johnny Davis before his life had gone so terribly wrong. She kept it among her photos of Nick.

She stood up, prepared to leave. 'What happened – it's all in the past now. It's what Nick would want …'

Caitlin stood too, and Michelle noticed just how much weight she'd lost. She may not have been caught for Daniel's death, or David's, but she was paying the price. It would be another six years at least before she got out.

'Will I see you again?' Caitlin asked her, suddenly.

Michelle shook her head. 'It'll all go through probate. I'm sure they'll be in touch.'

As she got back into the van, Michelle ran a protective hand across her belly.

'Well, how was it?' Andy asked.

'Better,' she said. 'We said everything we needed to.' They were quiet as they drove back towards Nick's house – she would always think of it as Nick's house, even though it was now hers.

'Andy … Conor and I went for another scan yesterday …'

'And?'

Michelle smiled. 'It's a boy … we wondered if you'd like to be godfather?'

Andy took one hand off the wheel to squeeze hers and as he did so, she felt a kick. 'Any ideas what you're going to call him?'

'Yes. His name's Nick,' she said. 'We're both agreed on that.'

Acknowledgements

This one is for the inner-circle who have continued to stand by me down the years, and for whose friendship I am truly grateful: Antoinette McGough, Adriana Devine, Keith Burke, David Giltenane and Eamon Keane. Also for my great friends: Dave and Anna O' Keefe, Gary Brady, Orla Coffey, Marcus Maher, Paul Brennan, and Ken Huang. For my old school pals: Liam and Keith Evans and Karl Melvin. Big love and gratitude to you all.

Huge thanks to my editor Kathryn Cheshire for all her hard work on this book, and for all the team at Killer Reads for their continued support. Thanks also to Lucy Dauman whose enthusiasm for *The Girl Behind the Lens* led to me becoming a HarperCollins author – the realisation of a childhood dream.

Thanks to Alan Hayes, my publisher at Arlen House, whose immense dedication to Irish writers and their work is unsurpassed. And to all the amazing writers I've met on this journey – the vast array of talent in this country is not only astounding, but sometimes terrifying. Special thanks for previous endorsements and recognition of my work go to: Alan McMonagle, Donal Ryan, Mary O' Donnell, and Sam Blake. Also to Declan Burke and Declan Hughes – two giants of Irish crime writing.

For my family: the Farrelly, Cleary, Butler and Hussey clans. In particular, to the men in my life: my wondrous husband, David Butler, for his unwavering support and ready involvement in all my mad notions. And to Tom, the glue that sticks us all.

Finally, in memory of the women who came before me: my beloved mother, Patsy Cleary, and my grandmother Jean Cleary – your light burns bright in my heart and mind. X